ALIEN™

RIVER OF PAIN

ALSO AVAILABLE FROM TITAN BOOKS

ALIEN™: OUT OF THE SHADOWS
ALIEN: SEA OF SORROWS

THE OFFICIAL MOVIE NOVELIZATIONS
ALIEN
ALIENS™
ALIEN3
ALIEN RESURRECTION
ALIEN: COVENANT

ALIEN

RIVER OF PAIN

CHRISTOPHER GOLDEN

TITAN BOOKS

ALIEN™: RIVER OF PAIN

Print edition ISBN: 9781783292868
E-book edition ISBN: 9781781162736

Published by Titan Books
A division of Titan Publishing Group Ltd
144 Southwark Street, London SE1 0UP

First edition: November 2014
4 6 8 10 9 7 5 3

A CIP catalogue record for this title is available from the British Library.

Printed and bound in Great Britain by CPI Group (UK) Ltd, Croydon CR0 4YY

1

OUR GUEST

DATE: 4 JUNE, 2122

For a long time Ripley had tried her best to avoid the *Nostromo*'s medical bay. Its white walls and bright lights chased away even the smallest shadows. The air was full of electric buzz and the sounds of machines.

As warrant officer on board the *Nostromo*, she'd spent far more time in the gray gloom of its corridors and compartments, flickering work lights the only intrusion into the darkness. Strange, really, but in her time on board one ship after another, she had grown more accustomed to shadows than light.

All that had changed.

The *Nostromo* had been traveling through the Zeta-2-Reticuli system, carrying twenty million tons of mineral ore bound for Earth, when the ship's on-board computer, designated "Mother," had responded to a distress signal from a planetoid called LV-426. Mother had woken the crew early from hypersleep, with instructions to investigate.

Ripley was uneasy with the order from the start. They weren't planetary explorers or colonists. It wasn't their job.

But orders had been clear. The captain, Dallas, had reminded her that their "job" was whatever the corporation decided it should be. And so they'd gone.

Upon landing, Dallas had taken his executive officer, Kane, and their navigator, Lambert, out onto the surface to investigate the source of the distress signal—a derelict spacecraft that was decidedly not of human origin. At that point, all of Ripley's internal alarm bells had gone off. They had no idea what dangers might await them inside that ship, and the captain, the XO, and their pilot shouldn't have been the ones checking it out.

They walked into a nightmare.

Ripley no longer felt comfortable in the *Nostromo*'s shadows. She sought out the medical bay, not for treatment, but for its light. Ash was there—the ship's science officer. He had an air of superiority that pissed her off. Sometimes he seemed to be looking down on the rest of them, as if they were specimens viewed through his microscope.

It made her skin crawl.

Nevertheless, as the ship's science officer, he might be their best hope of figuring out what the hell had really happened down there in the raging atmospheric storms on the surface of LV-426… what had happened to Kane.

But Ripley wouldn't just blindly follow orders, not anymore. The company's demands had made her uneasy. Mother's focus on whatever xenomorphic life they had encountered down on that ugly moon had troubled her. But when she voiced her concerns, the others had been unwilling to listen.

Well, to hell with that. She wasn't going to give them a choice. She had a daughter back on Earth—she had promised Amanda that she would come home safely, and she refused to break that promise.

So she'd follow her instincts, ask whatever questions demanded answers, and not worry about whose toes she might be stepping on.

Ripley entered the medical bay quietly. It felt like crossing the border into a foreign land without the permission of the king. She surveyed the lab area, all screens and white walls and yellow buttons, the lighting subdued now.

She stepped through into a second compartment and saw Ash off to her right, studying a vid-screen. A small man, his presence nevertheless held a certain weight. His brown hair had just begun to gray, and his eyes were icy blue.

Ash bent to peer through a microscope, diverting his attention enough that she managed to get within a few feet without him taking notice. The image on the computer screen made Ripley shiver with revulsion.

It looked like a scan of the spidery alien creature that had attached itself to the face of the XO, but she couldn't quite make out the details. The thing had some sort of tail that wrapped around Kane's throat, and it tightened any time they attempted to remove it. They'd cut into it, but the hideous thing had bled acid that had burned its way down through three levels of the *Nostromo*. Another deck or two, it would have eaten through the hull, and they'd all be dead now.

Ash was fascinated with it.

Ripley just wanted it dead.

"That's amazing," she said quietly, nodding toward the image on the screen. "What is it?"

Ash glanced up abruptly.

"Oh, this?" he said. "I don't know yet." He clicked off the screen, straightening his back, and attempted an air of courtesy that was unlike him. "Did you want something?"

So polite, she thought. *We're both being so damn polite.*

"Yes, I... to have a little talk," she muttered. To tell the truth, she wasn't quite sure *why* she was there. "How's Kane?"

The air between them had a buzz all its own, not unlike the persistent hum of electricity. From the moment Ash had joined the crew—foisted upon them by the company, right before they'd set off from Thedus with their cargo—she had harbored a dislike for him. Some people had that effect on her. They'd walk into a room and she'd be instantly on guard. If she'd been a cat—like Jones, the ship's mascot—an encounter with Ash would have made her hair stand up.

He avoided direct eye contact, and she could tell he wanted her to leave.

"He's holding. No changes."

Ripley nodded toward the darkened screen.

"And our guest?" That got her a glance.

"Well, as I said, I'm still… collating, actually," Ash replied. He picked up a micro-scanner tablet and studied its display. "But I have confirmed that he's got an outer layer of protein polysaccharides. Has a funny habit of shedding his cells and replacing them with polarized silicon, which gives him prolonged resistance to adverse environmental conditions." He paused, and gave her a little smile. "Is that enough?"

Enough, she thought. *Is that enough?* He might as well have asked her to get the fuck out.

"That's plenty," she replied, but she stood her ground. "What does it mean?" she asked, bending to look into the microscope.

Ash stiffened. "Please don't do that."

Ripley cocked her head, unable to keep from making a face. She knew he was more than a little persnickety about his lab, but why get so uptight about her looking into a microscope? She hadn't even touched it.

"I'm sorry," she said, her tone making it clear that she wasn't.

Ash recovered his composure.

"Well, it's an interesting combination of elements," he said, "making him a tough little son of a bitch."

A chill went through Ripley.

"And you let him in," she said.

Ash lifted his chin, looking offended.

"I was obeying a direct order, remember?" he replied testily.

Ripley studied him closely, and at that moment she knew exactly why she had come to the medical bay.

"Ash, when Dallas and Kane are off the ship, I'm senior officer," she said.

His expression went blank.

"Oh, yes. I forgot."

But he hadn't. She knew that, and so did he. He hadn't even

attempted to sound convincing. What troubled her, however, was the *why* of it all. Was it just another example of Ash being a prick? Did he not respect her place in the command hierarchy? Or did it not have anything to do with her? Did he just feel like he could do whatever the hell he wanted, without facing any repercussions?

That stops now, she decided.

"You also forgot the science division's basic quarantine law," she said.

"No, *that* I didn't forget," he replied calmly.

"Oh, I see," she said. "You just broke it, huh?"

Ash bristled, peering straight at her, his right hand resting on his hip.

"Look, what would you have done with Kane, hmm? You know his only chance for survival was to get him in here."

His irritation pleased her. It was nice to know she could get to him.

"Unfortunately, by breaking quarantine you risk everybody's life," Ripley countered.

"Maybe I should have left him outside," Ash replied. Then he fell back to his usual air of aloof superiority. "Maybe I've jeopardized the rest of us, but it was a risk I was willing to take."

Ripley edged a bit closer, her gaze locked with his.

"That's a pretty big risk for a science officer," she said. "It's not exactly out of the manual, is it?"

"I do take my responsibilities as seriously as you, you know?" Ash replied.

Ripley cast another glance at the screen. She wanted a look at that computer, but she wasn't even sure she would understand what she was seeing.

Ash stared defiantly at her.

"You do your job," he added, "and let me do mine, yes?"

A dozen possible replies raced through her mind, none of them polite or pleasant. Instead, Ripley took a breath, let it out, then turned and strode from the room. All she had wanted all along was for Ash to do his job, but he seemed more interested in the creature attached to Kane's face than he was in saving the XO.

Why?

2

TREMORS

DATE: 11 OCTOBER, 2165

Greg Hansard stood in the raging atmospheric stew on the surface of LV-426, and wished he could scream. Above him, the atmosphere processor gave a shriek of grinding metal and shuddered so powerfully that he could feel the trembling of the machine in the ground underfoot.

"What the hell are you guys doing in there?" Hansard bellowed into his comm link.

His heart slammed in his chest, beating in rhythm with the banging of the processor, and he felt as if he was suffocating inside his breathing mask. The irony wasn't lost on him, but it didn't lessen the urge to tear the mask off. He wouldn't do it, though—he might be going crazy out there in the grit-storm, but not *that* crazy.

"Our best—that's what we're doing," one of the engineers shouted in reply. Over the roar of the wind, Hansard couldn't tell who it was. "There's a crack in the generator housing! If we bring it down to half-speed, we may be able to make repairs without shutting the whole thing down."

"Do it," Hansard shouted back. "Just get it done as fast as you can! We can't afford any more delays."

"Hell, boss, we didn't pick the damn planet," the engineer replied.

Hansard hung his head in exasperation.

"I know, man," he said. "And I'd like to throttle the idiot who did."

"Hansard, you better get over here!" another voice shouted over the comm. This one he recognized.

"What is it, Najit?" he asked as he began to circle around the machine. The atmosphere processor towered sixty-seven feet above his head, juddering and banging and spewing out breathable air.

"You'd better see for yourself," Najit replied.

There were three engineers inside the atmosphere processor, and half a dozen outside. Najit was a structural engineer. For six years the company had been trying to terraform LV-426—now called Acheron—even as they built the foundations for the colony to come. The main structure of the central complex was in place, and a dozen colonists were already living down there with the builders and engineers, all under the management of the colonial administrator, Al Simpson.

Barely a day went by without Simpson tracking him down to bitch at him over the speed of the terraforming efforts. As far as Hansard was concerned, Simpson was an idiot in the employ of people whose idiocy existed on a far grander scale.

The colony—dubbed Hadley's Hope, after one of its designers—was a joint endeavor sponsored by the Earth government and the Weyland-Yutani Corporation, overseen by the colonial administration and *supposedly* adhering to all rules established by the Interstellar Commerce Commission. Acheron itself wasn't really a planet, even though they referred to it that way. It was a rock in the middle of nowhere, one of the moons of a planet called Calpamos.

Its storms were near constant, a blinding torrent of wind and grit and dust. No matter how well Hansard sealed himself inside his mask and hood and exposure suit, the grit still got everywhere.

Everywhere.

Every damn day.

Of all the places Weyland-Yutani could have chosen as the cradle for a new human colony, why this one? Atmospheric conditions had prevented them from properly mapping the topography from space, and yet some asshole had decided it was prime real estate.

It seemed to Hansard as if the place itself didn't want them there. They had managed to place atmosphere processors at various intervals around the surface, and the most important one—the massive, cathedral-like Processor One—was under construction. But they had run into all sorts of problems along the way. Tremors cracked the terrain and swallowed one of the smaller processors whole. Accidents and surveying errors and faulty equipment had caused all kinds of delays.

And now... what?

He marched around the base of the processor, unnerved by the machine's knocking. The ground trembled, and Hansard thought he might have trembled along with it. He tasted dirt in his mouth.

"Najit?" he called, thinking he ought to have found the man already.

"Here!" came the reply.

Hansard peered through the blowing veil of grit and spotted three figures, but they weren't anywhere near the processor. They stood a dozen feet from the hull of the machine, staring down at the ground.

Oh shit, Hansard thought. *Please don't tell me—*

The processor shook. Hansard spun to stare at it, holding his breath. The machine shuddered so violently that he could see the hull shifting. Suddenly he realized that not all of the tremors were coming from the machine itself.

"Son of a bitch!" he shouted.

The grinding of metal inside the structure grew into a squealing thunder.

Turning, Hansard ran to the others. Three men outside, yes. But there were three men inside as well. Inside with that grinding, shrieking metal.

"What the hell—" he began.

"It's another fissure," Najit shouted.

As he drew closer, Hansard could see the crack in the ground beneath their feet, thick layers of atmospheric dust and volcanic ash spilling like sand into the fissure. Najit ran along the crack, following it away from the processor to determine its length, then paused and turned back to face the other two structural engineers.

"Fifteen feet!" Najit called. "And growing!"

Hansard didn't give a shit how far it went *away* from the atmosphere processor. He ran to the outer hull and stared at the fissure where it disappeared underneath the machine.

"No," he whispered. "No no no no."

He gazed up through the curtain of windblown grit. The processor shuddered and the clanking from inside reminded him of an archival clip he'd seen of an ancient locomotive.

"Shut it down!" he roared. "Shut the whole thing down and get out!"

"Boss..." Najit started, caution in his voice.

Hansard rounded on the three structural engineers.

"Get back, you idiots," he said, waving them away. "Don't you remember Processor Three?"

On his comm he could hear the engineers inside the processor, shouting to each other—commands and profanities in a cocktail of panicked words.

"You think it's going to get worse?" Najit called.

The ground continued to tremble. The quake was localized, but there was no way of knowing how long it would last. They'd surveyed this sector for eighteen months before beginning construction, with no sign of localized tremors.

Until it was too late to stop.

"It's already bad enough," Hansard barked.

The processor gasped, and the hum inside it went silent, but its hull continued to tremble. A lull in the storm gave him a clearer view up the side of the machine, where he spotted a crack in the otherwise smooth metal, twenty feet off the ground.

Shit!

"Get out of there, *now*," he shouted. "Nguyen! Mendez! Get—"

Suddenly Hansard stopped, and stared down at his feet. The ground seemed to settle, and the tremor eased. He held his breath for several seconds until he felt sure it had ended. Not that it mattered.

The processor might be repairable, but there was no point. The next tremor—a day or ten years from now—might destroy it altogether. This machine would have to be abandoned, just a metal hulk that they would scavenge for parts as they built one on ground they deemed more stable. On Acheron, however, they would never know for sure if any ground was stable enough.

"Boss?" Najit said, coming to stand beside him.

Hansard stared off into the storm, buffeted by the wind.

Defeated.

Whoever had given LV-426 its new name had recognized the absurdity of it all. In ancient Greek mythology, Acheron had been one of the rivers that wound through the netherworld. The word had a grim translation.

River of Pain.

3

REBECCA

DATE: 15 MARCH, 2173

Russ Jorden stared at the beads of sweat on his wife's forehead and felt a tightening in his heart. She squeezed his hand so hard he felt the bones grind together, and he could see that she was holding her breath, her face scrunched into a mask of fury and pain.

"Breathe, Anne," he pleaded. "Come on, honey, breathe."

Anne gasped and her whole body relaxed a moment before she pursed her lips and began to blow out long drafts of air. Her face had been pale for hours, but now she looked almost gray and the circles beneath her eyes were bruise-blue. She let her head loll to one side and her eyes pleaded with him to do something, though they both knew the best he could do was be at her side and keep loving her.

"Why won't she just *get* here?" Anne asked.

"She's all cozy in there," Russ replied. "It's warm and she can hear your heartbeat. It's a big, scary universe out here."

Anne glanced down at her enormous belly, which had shifted dramatically lower in the past few hours. She frowned, her forehead etched with stern lines.

"Come on out, baby girl. If you're gonna be a part of this family, you've got to be courageous, and a little bit crazy."

Russ laughed softly, but he couldn't give in to the humor of the words the way he normally would have. Anne had been in labor for seventeen hours, and for the past three, her cervix had been stuck at seven centimeters dilated and sixty percent effaced. Dr. Komiskey had given her drugs to jump-start the process, with a warning that forcing the uterus into action might amplify the usual pain of labor.

Anne gave a deep groan, and her breathing quickened.

"Russell…"

"She'll be here soon," he vowed. "I promise." Silently he added, *C'mon, Rebecca. It's time.*

The nurse came into the room as Anne gritted her teeth and arched her back, her entire body going tense. Russ held his breath along with her—seeing Anne in pain made him want to scream. He glanced over in panic and frustration.

"Can't you do anything for her, Joel?"

The nurse, slender and dark, gave a sympathetic shake of his head.

"I've told you, Russ. She wanted to go natural, the way she did with Tim. Now it's too late to give her anything that would offer any significant relief. The painkillers she's already taken are the best we can do without endangering the baby."

Anne swore at him. Joel moved to the bedside and put a hand on her shoulder as she began to breathe again, easing down from another contraction.

"Dr. Komiskey will be here in a second to evaluate you again."

Russ glared at him. "And if she hasn't progressed?"

"I don't want a cesarean!" Anne snapped between gasps.

Joel patted her shoulder.

"You know it's perfectly safe. And if you're worried about scarring—"

"Don't be stupid. C-sections haven't left a scar since my grandmother was born," Anne said breathlessly.

"That's what I'm saying," the nurse replied. "For the sake of the baby—"

Stricken, Anne turned to stare at him.

"Joel, is there something wrong with the baby?"

"Not now," Joel said. "Everything we've seen looks perfectly normal, and all blood and genetic tests show a healthy child. But there can be complications if... Look, this is really something Dr. Komiskey should be talking to you about."

"Damn it, Joel, we've known you two years now," Russ barked. "The colony's not that big. If there's something to worry about—"

"No. Just stop," Joel said, holding up a hand. "If you were on your own, you'd have something to worry about. But you're not alone. You've got the med-staff looking out for you and your baby, and the whole colony waiting for the little girl to show her face."

Anne cried out and squeezed Russ's hand again. He stared at his wife's beautiful face, contorted with pain, and realized that one of the beads of moisture on her cheek wasn't sweat at all, but a tear, and he knew they had let it go on too long.

"Get Komiskey in here," Russ snapped.

"She'll be here any—" Joel began.

"Get her!"

"Okay, okay." Joel rushed from the room, leaving the Jordens alone with their fear and hope and a baby who didn't seem to want to meet them.

Worried silence fell between Russ and Anne. Exhausted, she used the low ebbs between the agonizing crests of her contractions to breathe and rest and pray that when Dr. Komiskey returned, her cervix would be fully dilated so that she could push the baby out.

"I don't understand," she whispered tiredly. "Tim took four hours from first contraction to last. And my back... God, my back didn't hurt like this. What's wrong?"

Russ stared at the white smoothness of the monitors stationed above and beside the bed. If the baby went into distress, alarms would go off, but for the moment the monitors blinked green and blue and made no sound but a soft, almost musical hum. Beyond the monitors, quiet and dark, there stood a much larger machine, a huge unit with a mostly transparent hood.

If Komiskey had to surgically remove the baby, she would move Anne into that unit. It wasn't scarring that frightened Anne, but the idea that she would no longer be treated by human hands. The natal surgery unit would perform the C-section essentially by itself, and the thought terrified both of the Jordens. Humans might make errors, but at least they cared about the outcome. Machines did not understand consequences, or the value of life.

"Did we make a mistake?" Anne rasped.

Russ pressed a cold, damp cloth against her forehead.

"Timmy was so easy," he said. "We couldn't have known it would be like this. Trying to deliver naturally made sense at the time."

"Not that," his wife said, one hand fluttering weakly upward, moving her fingers as if she could erase his reply. "I mean coming to Acheron. To Hadley's Hope."

Russ frowned. "We had no choice. There was no work at home. We were lucky to get the opportunity to work off-planet. You know—"

"I do," she rasped, and then she began to stiffen, hissing breath through her teeth as another contraction came on. "But having children… *here*…"

The monitors flickered red, just for an instant, as Anne went rigid and roared in pain.

"That's it!" Russ snapped. He jumped from his seat, knocking the chair over behind him, and turned toward the door, but Anne would not release her grip on his hand. He turned to plead with her and saw that the monitor lights were all back to green. No alarms had sounded.

He didn't care. That one flicker had been enough.

"Komiskey!"

As he drew a breath to shout the doctor's name again, Dr. Theodora Komiskey came breezing through the door, a squat woman with blue eyes and a mass of brown curls. Joel followed dutifully in her wake.

"Let's see how far we've come," the doctor said, smiling and upbeat as ever.

"Halfway across the fucking universe," Russ growled.

He despised the false cheer so many doctors wore like a mask, and wanted to scream the smile off Dr. Komiskey's face, but that wouldn't have done anything to help Anne or the baby. Instead, he could only stand there while the barrel-shaped woman pulled on a pair of medical gloves, perched on a stool, and reached up between Anne's thighs, feeling around as if searching for something she'd lost.

"I can feel her head," Dr. Komiskey said, concern in her voice. "And now I understand the trouble. The baby's presenting in the posterior position—"

Russ felt his heart clench.

"What does that mean?"

Komiskey ignored him, addressing Anne instead. "She's facing your abdomen, which means the back of her skull is putting pressure on your sacrum—your tailbone. The good news is that you're fully dilated and effaced. Your baby is about to make her big debut as the adorable princess of Hadley's Hope."

Russ hung his head. "Thank God."

"What's..." Anne said, sucking in a breath. "What's the bad news?"

"The bad news is that it's gonna hurt like hell," Komiskey said.

Anne shook with relief.

"I'm ready when you are, Theo. Let's get the little newt out of there."

Russ smiled. They'd been calling the baby that for months, imagining her growing from tiny speck to odd little newt to full-fledged fetus.

"All right, then," Dr. Komiskey said. "When the next contraction hits, you're going to—"

But Anne didn't need to be told. She'd already given birth once. The contraction hit her and she shouted again, but this time her roar sounded less like a scream of pain and more like a battle cry.

Thirteen minutes later, Dr. Komiskey slipped Rebecca Jorden into her mother's arms. Russ smiled so wide that his face hurt, his chest so full of love he thought it might burst. As Anne kissed the baby girl's forehead, Russ touched her tiny hand and his infant daughter gripped his finger tightly, already strong.

"Hello, little newt," Anne whispered to the baby, and kissed her again. "Better be careful or that nickname's gonna stick."

Russ laughed and Anne turned to smile at him.

Newt, he thought. *You're a lucky little girl.*

DATE: 2 APRIL, 2173

When the new recreational center at the Hadley's Hope colony opened, nobody bothered with anything as formal or old-fashioned as a ribbon cutting. Al Simpson, the colony's administrator, unlocked the door and swung it open, and the party began. The Finch brothers brought some of their homemade whiskey, Samantha Monet and her sister had decorated the facility, and Bronagh Flaherty, the cook, put out a selection of cakes and cookies that she had made for the occasion.

The star of the evening, however, was two-and-a-half-week-old Newt Jorden. Al Simpson stood in the corner of the main room and sipped at a mug of hot Irish coffee, watching the rest of the colonists take turns fussing over the baby girl.

Swaddled in a blanket, cradled in her mother's arms, she was a beautiful little thing, no question about that. As a rule, Al had no fondness for babies. More often than not they were crying, crapping machines and looked like shriveled, hairless monkeys. Not little Newt, though. He'd barely heard a peep out of her since the party began, and she had big lovely peepers that made her seem like a curious old soul gazing out from within a ruddy, healthy baby face.

The Jordens' boy, Tim, had been an infant himself when they first arrived on LV-426, but Newt was a reason for the whole colony to celebrate—the first baby actually born on Acheron. Al thought that if all of the colony's future babies turned out like Newt, it wouldn't be so bad having them around. But he had a feeling that Newt would be an exception, and that he wasn't about to change his feelings toward newborns… or children in general, now that he thought about it.

"Cute kid," a voice said beside him.

Al flinched, coffee sloshing out of his mug. He swore as it burned his fingers and quickly switched the mug from his right to left hand.

"Don't sneak up on me like that," he said as he shook the coffee droplets from his fingers, and then blew on them.

"Damn, Al, I'm sorry about that," Greg Hansard said, wincing in sympathy.

Al shook his fingers again, but the pain had started to fade.

"Good thing I put a good dollop of Irish cream in there," he said. "Cooled it down a bit."

Hansard smiled. "Well, now, if you're not badly burned you might just have to show me where you're hiding that bottle."

Al didn't really want to share, but Hansard was the colony's chief engineer, and always good company. He supposed he could spare a few ounces of his private stock.

"I might be persuaded," he said, taking a long sip from his mug. Before he troubled himself to get Hansard a cup, he wanted to drink his own coffee while it was still hot. "You're right, though. The Jorden kid is kind of adorable. I don't know where she gets it, considering the parents."

Hansard uttered a dry laugh.

"They *are* pretty scruffy."

Al grinned, hiding the smile behind his cup as he glanced around. He had always been a man full of opinions, but the colonists were all stuck with each other and it would complicate relationships around Hadley's Hope if the colonial administrator started talking shit about people behind their backs. On the other hand, it wasn't Anne Jorden's wild, unruly curls that irritated him, or the fact that Russ always looked as if he'd had too much to drink the night before.

"Wildcatters are pretty much always scruffy, aren't they?" Al said quietly.

"They're trouble, is what they are," Hansard replied. He nodded toward the cluster of people still cooing and ahhing over the baby. Otto Finch had crouched down to talk to young Tim, the Jordens' son, and had handed him some kind of furry doll. "Nice enough people, the Jordens. But I worry about the boy."

Al frowned, turning to him. He didn't like the sound of that.

"What do you mean?"

Hansard grimaced, brows knitted as if already regretting that he'd spoken.

"Greg, you brought it up," Al said. "I'm the administrator. I can't let it go. If you think there's a problem—"

"Depends what you mean by 'problem.'"

Al glanced over at the Jordens again. Father and mother looked tired, but they both were smiling happily, so proud of their little family. They were surveyors employed by the colony, but like half of the survey team, they moonlighted on the side as wildcatters—prospectors—searching sectors of the planetoid's surface for mineral deposits, meteor crash sites, and other things of interest to the company. The colony's Weyland-Yutani science team used prospectors to retrieve soil and mineral samples, and to map out sections of the planet. The excursions were often very dangerous.

"It's not just that the lifestyle is crazy," Hansard said thoughtfully. "Yeah, colonists are going to have kids. That's the nature of what we're doing here. But wildcatting is risky, and Anne and Russ don't seem to recognize the dangers involved. Bad enough for most of them—who's going to raise their kids if something goes wrong? And the Jordens… well, they take it a step further, don't they? Just today, Russ took Tim out with him in the tractor, prospecting ten kilometers north."

Al stared at him. "You're sure of this?"

Hansard nodded. "I don't want to start something. Not tonight, anyway. But the kid's not safe out there. I've been in more of the damn atmo-storms than anyone, and if the tractor gets stuck…"

Al held up a hand.

"I'm with you, but there's no rule against it. I've mentioned it to several of the prospectors before, but they look at it the same way farmers do—it's a family business, and if they take their kids out into the fields, they're just teaching them for the future, giving them a sense of proprietorship."

"That's idiotic."

"I didn't say I agreed with them." Al scratched the back of his neck, suddenly feeling tired. "I blame Weyland-Yutani, if you want to know the truth."

Hansard arched an eyebrow.

"Dangerous opinion, Al. Talk like that can cost your job."

"We're floating on a desolate rock where they're trying to seed a little civilization. I don't think they're gonna care what I say as long as I do my job. And since when are you so in love with the company?"

"I'm not," Hansard admitted. "But I'm well paid, and when I leave here—when all the work is finally done—I'm hoping to get an easier assignment. Hell, since my first day on Acheron I've been wondering who I pissed off to end up here."

"Maybe they just had faith in you. Obviously not an easy job, trying to make this place livable." Al sipped his mug again, letting the coffee warm him and the alcohol loosen him up. No matter how high they set the heat inside the colony buildings, he still felt cold. *Just too damn far from the sun*, he thought.

He lowered his voice and glanced around to make sure he wasn't overheard.

"My point is that they tend to recruit daredevils and dimwits as colonists, not to mention people who are looking for a new start because they've burned all their bridges back home."

"You like the Jordens, though," Hansard said.

Al shrugged. "I like 'em fine, but they're too cavalier, too desperate to earn bonuses. The science team uses wildcatters because they're willing to take risks. I just worry they're going to put us all at risk one of these days. We've got a lot of years to go before this colony is fully established and populated. A decade or more. With that kind of time, anything could go wrong."

He looked over at Anne Jorden, who cradled her new baby close, kissing her soft cheeks and whispering love into her ears. Russ had knelt down beside young Tim, who pouted with his arms defiantly crossed, apparently upset over something to do with the baby.

"Mark my words," Al said, "if we ever have any serious trouble on this dirtball, it's gonna be because of people like them."

4

ARRIVALS

DATE: 16 MAY, 2179

For the first time in Jernigan's career, it looked like he'd claim salvage on a ship he hadn't even been looking for. He stood in the airlock that led into the retrieval bay and suited up, watching his two companions and wondering what they were thinking.

Not that it was hard to imagine what Landers would be thinking. The greedy bastard would just be eager to see what goodies the drifting vessel might contain. Fleet, though… he was an enigma. Jernigan had spent three years and four expeditions trying to figure him out. Landers laughed and said he should give up, that Fleet was almost an alien species. But Jernigan wasn't a quitter.

"Target ship gathered," a buzzing voice said in his earpiece. Moore, up on the flight deck. He was their eyes and ears right now, and Jernigan was comfortable with that.

"Any indication of its origins?" Jernigan asked.

"Negative. No beacons, no transmission, no signs of life. I've hailed another dozen times since you guys went to suit up. Nothing. No auto-response from on-board computers, no sign that it's even picking up my transmissions. Quiet as the grave."

"So what do you think?" Landers asked. "Some old military shuttle?"

"Not military," Moore said, and Jernigan saw Landers' disappointment in the way he slumped. Anything military wasn't legally salvage, but way out here there was no one to police what they stripped out, packaged up, and sold to the highest bidder. Usually they went for ships or orbiting stations that they knew had been damaged or abandoned. The information was sent by the company who owned the wreck, or sometimes by private contacts who knew who to speak to, and how much a good salvage could net.

There was often dubious information passed on from shady sources, and several times he'd found himself boarding vessels that showed signs of forced abandonment or criminal activity. Once he'd found the remains of a firefight.

Deep-salvage had never been the most respectable of professions, but Jernigan really didn't give a shit what people thought. He had his own moral code, and he was quite proud to do a job that most people wouldn't.

Sometimes they'd reach a target vessel and find survivors on board. That changed everything. They still charged the company the cost of time and transport, but there was never a cut of anything larger. Even Landers had never raised any objection when they pulled back from stripping or towing in a ship that still had a living crew member or passenger.

Not quite respectable, never quite criminal.

"Not military," Jernigan said. "But no indication where it comes from? No ship's signature attached?"

"No, but it *is* old," Moore said. "Don't think I've seen anything like it outside of history holos." He paused, then added, "Right, just docking and pressurizing. Hold onto your nuts."

A soft vibration passed through the ship, and when Jernigan looked through the viewing port he saw moisture condense rapidly on the other side, turning quickly to ice. He made sure his suit's climate control systems were set to a comfortable level, then waited for all of the lights to turn green.

Landers and Fleet were experienced salvage workers, and Jernigan had no hesitation about working with either of them.

They'd boarded at least twenty vessels and stations together, and seen each other through a few hairy moments. This one would go like clockwork.

He was sure of it.

As always, he felt the seed of excitement. One day, he was certain, they'd find something amazing.

When the lights were green, the three men left the airlock and entered the hold. Fleet fired up the remote cutting robot, trundling it across to the ship using a handheld control unit and igniting its cutting laser. He glanced at Landers, who'd taken position at a small panel close to where the salvaged ship had been gripped tight by a network of grappling arms.

Landers did one more quick check across all systems, then nodded.

"Clean as a virgin's pussy," he said. "Nothing in there to cause worry."

"And what would you know about virgins' pussies?" Fleet asked.

"Ask your sister," Landers said. Fleet didn't answer, or give any indication that he'd even heard. He steered the cutting robot toward the ship, used a scanner to measure the door and plan a cut. Then he hit *deploy*.

It took the laser a minute to cut through. Jernigan swayed slightly from foot to foot.

Weird-looking ship, he thought. *Old shuttle, maybe. Not a lifeboat*. There was evidence of damage around the door's exterior—scrapes and scratches, and a blast-scar close to the engines. Like everything they found and salvaged, this vessel had a story to tell.

The door fell inward with a heavy clang. Fleet withdrew the cutter and sent in a scanner. None of them expected that they'd find anything surprising, but they all knew the rules. Better safe than sorry.

The scanner did its work.

"Anything?" Jernigan asked.

"Looks like a hypersleep capsule," Fleet said.

"Oh, man," Landers said. "Anyone alive in there?" Jernigan hated the hint of disappointment in his colleague's voice.

"Can't tell," Fleet said. "Let's check it out."

The scanner withdrew and Jernigan went first, the other two following him in. There was a space suit splayed over the flight chair, and what looked like some sort of grappling gun dropped on the controls. The single hypersleep pod was coated in a layer of frost.

Jernigan brushed his hand across the curved canopy, revealing the striking woman inside. Hunkered down next to her was a cat. *Holy cow.* He hadn't seen a cat since he was a kid.

"Bio readouts are all in the green—looks like she's alive," he said. He slipped off his helmet and sighed. "Well, there goes our salvage, guys."

And that's a face with a story to tell, for sure, he thought.

DATE: 10 JUNE, 2179
TIME: 0945

The hum of the dropship turned into a metallic groan as it hit the atmosphere of LV-426. Captain Demian Brackett kept his boots flat on the floor and held onto the safety rig that kept him locked into his seat. The vessel slewed wickedly from side to side for several seconds before straightening out, and then it bounced like a speedboat skipping across high seas.

Alarms began to sound, red lights blinking all over the cockpit up front.

"What've we hit?" he shouted to the pilot.

The woman didn't turn around, too focused on keeping them on course.

"Just the atmosphere," she replied. "Acheron's never smooth sailing." She slapped a couple of buttons and the alarms died, though the lights continued to blink in distress.

Brackett gritted his teeth as the dropship filled with the noise of atmospheric debris plunking and scraping the hull. There seemed to be a *lot* of it.

"Am I missing something?" he called, raising his voice to be heard over the noise of the debris peppering the ship. "Haven't they been terraforming this planet for fifteen years?"

"More," the pilot shouted. "You should've seen what it was like trying to land here ten years ago, when I first got here."

No, thanks, Brackett thought. He had a stomach like iron, but even he had begun to feel queasy. His jaw hurt from clenching his teeth. *Gonna scramble my brains*, he thought, as the whole dropship shook violently around him.

For a moment the barrage ceased. He started to relax, and then the ship plummeted abruptly, as if their controlled freefall had just become a suicide run. Cursing silently, he braced himself and twisted around to try to see through the cockpit to the outside.

"I'd rather not die on the first day of my command," he called. "Y'know, if it's no trouble for you."

The pilot glanced back at him, a scowl on her face.

"Take a breath, Captain. Seven crashes, and I've never had a passenger die on me."

"Seven *what*?"

They hit another air pocket and the drop threw him forward a second before the atmosphere thickened again, jerking him back so hard he slammed his head against the hull of the ship.

Son of a—

"Here you go, handsome," the pilot announced. The retro-rockets kicked in, lofted them up a dozen feet, and then began to lower them slowly. She guided the dropship gingerly forward and descended until it settled gently to the ground.

A hydraulic hiss came from the ship, as if it were exhaling right along with him, and Brackett released the catch on his restraints. The emergency lights shut down and the cabin brightened into a blue-white glow.

"Safe and sound, just like I promised," the pilot said. She disengaged the door locks and stood up from her seat, a mischievous smile on her face. For the first time, Brackett noticed her curves, and the way she looked at him.

"As good as your word," he said. "Yet I just now realized that I don't even know your name."

"Tressa," she said, holding out her hand. "At your service."

"Demian Brackett," he said as they shook.

She stepped over to the starboard door and entered a code into a control pad. The door hissed open, and a short ramp slid out with a rattle, clunking onto the planetary surface.

"So what crime did you commit to get stuck out here at the ass-end of the universe?" Tressa asked.

Brackett smiled. "I'm a good marine," he said. "I go where I'm told."

The wind began to howl, blowing a scouring dust into the ship. He took a look outside and his smile faded. Acheron was a world of black and gray, save for the growing colony whose buildings were mere silhouettes in the obscuring storm. After several seconds the wind died down again, giving him a better view, but there wasn't much more to see. Box structures, a glassoid greenhouse hemisphere, and in the distance the towering, ominous, hundred-and-fifty-foot high atmosphere processor, belching oxygen into the air.

"Home sweet home."

"Yeah," Tressa said, "you're not gonna get a lot of beach days. How long are you stationed here?"

Brackett picked up the duffel filled with his gear and slung it over his shoulder.

"Until they reassign me."

She tilted her head and cocked her hip and he flattered himself into thinking he saw regret in her eyes.

"Well, I hope we meet again, Captain Brackett. Somewhere far from Acheron."

DATE: 10 JUNE, 2179

There was somebody in the room with Ellen Ripley. She kept her eyes closed. The smell of disinfectant filled the air, and she heard the comforting sound of medical machines. The sensation of sheets against her skin and a mattress beneath her back was luxurious.

None of it prevented her from feeling like shit.

She felt no danger from the presence, no threat, and yet in her memory there was a deep, heavy weight of darkness striving to break through. It was a solid mass somewhere within her, and its gravity was relentless.

I'm so tired, she thought. But as she opened her eyes at last, she knew that she was lucky to be alive. A nurse bustled around her, checking readouts, fine-tuning the equipment, taking notes. As she watched the woman going about her work, Ripley caught sight of a window that had never been open before. It offered a wide, uninterrupted view out into space, the complex arms and habitation pods of a space station she did not recognize… and the surface of the planet below.

A planet she recognized as home.

Something warm flushed through her, spreading from her core and touching her cheeks. Happiness, and hope. She'd made it. She had survived the *Nostromo*, defeated the beast, and made it back home. She'd be seeing Amanda again soon.

Yet something was far from right. She felt sick in the pit of her stomach, and not just as a result of being clumsily pulled out of hypersleep. That darkness in her memory was pregnant with terror, bulging with nightmares waiting to be birthed. It lured her in. She thought of Dallas, Kane and the others, and the terrible fate that had befallen them, and in her mind their faces were old and sad, like faded photographs found at the bottom of an old suitcase.

She thought of the bastard Ash, and he seemed not so distant.

There was something else, too. Something… closer.

"How are we today?" the nurse asked.

Ripley tried to speak, but her tongue felt swollen and dry. She smacked her lips together.

"Terrible," she croaked.

"Well, better than yesterday, at least," the nurse said. She sounded so chirpy and upbeat, but there was something impersonal about her voice, too. As if she wanted to keep one step removed from her patient.

"Where am I?" Ripley asked.

"You're safe. You're at Gateway Station, been here a couple of days." She helped Ripley sit up and rearranged the pillows behind her. "You were pretty groggy at first, but now you're okay."

This is wrong, Ripley thought. Gateway Station? She'd never heard of it. She'd been away for a while, true, but unless this place was top secret, even military, she'd have known about it.

"Looks like you've got a visitor," the nurse said. Ripley turned around, and when the door opened it wasn't the man she saw, but the cat he carried.

"Jonesy!" she said, and her smile felt good. "Hey, come here." She reached out for the cat and the man brought him forward. "Where were you, you stupid cat? How are you? Where have you been?"

The guy sat as she made a fuss. She knew how foolish it looked and sounded, her talking to a cat. But it was Jonesy. Her link to the past, the *Nostromo*, and—

And?

That darkness inside, luring her in with its dreadful gravity. Maybe she just needed to puke.

"Guess you two have met, huh?"

Ripley looked at the man for the first time, and took an instant dislike to him. What he said next did nothing to dilute that.

"I'm Burke, Carter Burke. I work for the Company." He paused, then added, "But don't let that fool you, I'm really an okay guy."

Okay? Ripley thought. *Yeah, right. Smooth, shifty, slick, won't meet my eyes. Dammit, I still feel like shit*. She wanted him to go away, to leave her with Jonesy and her pains, and that thing inside—the memory, that terrible threat—which she had yet to understand.

But he was Company, which meant that he was here for a reason.

"I'm glad to see you're feeling a little better," he smarmed. "They tell me that all the weakness and disorientation should pass soon. It's just natural side effects of an unusually long hypersleep." He shrugged. "Something like that."

And there it is, Ripley thought. *The beginning of the truth. Nothing can turn out fine. I'm not that lucky*.

"What do you mean?" she asked. "How long was I out there?"

Burke's slickness melted away, and he suddenly seemed uncomfortable. She preferred him smarmy.

"Has no one discussed this with you yet?" he asked.

"No," Ripley said. "But, I mean..." She looked from the window again. "I don't recognize this place."

"I know," Burke said. "Ahh... okay. It's just that this might be a shock to you."

How long? Ripley thought, and Amanda stared at her from memory.

"It's longer than—" he began.

"How long?" she demanded. Amanda, in her mind's eye, was crying. "Please."

"Fifty-seven years," he said.

"What?"

No. No, no way, that's not possible, that's not— But in her memory her crew were faded figures, whispers on the tip of her tongue. Ash, though. He was almost still there.

"That's the thing, you were out there for fifty-seven years. What happened was, you had drifted right through the core systems, and it's really just... blind luck that a deep-salvage team found you when they did."

Ripley's heart beat faster.

Fifty-seven years.

Amanda turned away from her, fading, becoming a shadow of a memory just like her old crew.

No! Ripley thought. *Amanda! I came through so much to get back to you and—*

What *had* she gone through? That weight within her pulsed, almost playful with the promise of sickening, shattering revelation.

"It was one in a thousand, really," Burke said, but his voice was becoming more distant, less relevant. "You're damn lucky to be alive, kiddo."

Kiddo. She'd called Amanda "kiddo." She tried now, but her voice would not work, and her little girl was lost to her.

Lost.

"You could have been floating around out there forever..." His words faded to nothing, all meaning stolen by what was happening inside her. That weight she carried, beginning to reveal itself at last.

Ripley tried to catch her breath. Jonesy hissed at her. Cats saw everything.

But when the unbearable weight broke open at last, it wasn't a memory at all.

It was one of *them*.

She felt it inside her, invading, squirming inside her ribcage as it prepared to be born in sick, evil mockery of the daughter she had lost. She flipped back on the bed in agony, thrashing her arms. Burke tried to hold her down, shouting for help. She knocked a glass from his hand and heard it shattering on the floor. Her drip stand fell, ripping a needle from her arm.

Others rushed into the room. They didn't know what was wrong and there was no way she could tell them, no way to explain, other than to plead with them to help.

"Please!" she said. "Kill me!"

It pushed and bulged, cracking ribs, stretching skin, and through the white-hot blaze of agony she rolled up her gown and saw—

Ripley snapped awake in her bed, hand clutched to her chest. She felt rapid, fluttering movement, but it was only the beating of her heart.

Reality crashed in, and it was awful. She looked from the window and saw the beautiful curve of the Earth. So near and yet so far—but that no longer mattered. To Ripley it no longer felt like home.

The small screen on the med-monitor unit beside her bed flickered into life, and her nurse's face appeared.

"Bad dreams again?" she asked. "You want something to help you sleep?"

"No!" Ripley snapped. "I've slept enough." The nurse nodded and the screen went blank.

Jonesy had been sleeping on the bed with her. The medics didn't like it, but Burke had persuaded them that it would do her good. *After the shock she's had*, she had heard him telling them. She supposed she should have been grateful to him, but her first opinion stuck.

She didn't like the little fuck.

"Jonesy," she said, picking up the cat and cuddling him to her. "It's all right, it's all right. It's over."

But that dark, heavy weight remained within her, something very much a part of her and yet unknown. And in saying those calming words to the cat, she was only trying to persuade herself.

5

ROUGH TERRAIN

DATE: 10 JUNE, 2179
TIME: 1022

Two marines awaited Brackett on the surface. They saluted as he came down the ramp and he returned the gesture, striding hurriedly toward them.

"Welcome to Acheron, Captain," the first said. She was a tall woman with skin nearly as dark brown as Brackett's, and the pale line of an old scar across her left cheek. She gestured to the short, barrel-chested marine beside her, a pale man with bright orange hair and thick goggles covering his eyes. "I'm Lieutenant Julisa Paris. This is Sergeant Coughlin—"

"Nice to meet you both," Brackett replied. "And thanks for coming out into the storm to greet me, but let's continue this inside."

Sgt. Coughlin took his duffel with one hand, lugging it with an ease that bespoke notable strength, and the three of them hurried toward the nearest door, which led into a two-story gray building whose windows were long horizontal slits, some covered by heavy metal weather shielding.

"Hate to break it to you, Cap," Lt. Paris said, gesturing around them, "but this crap? This is a typical day out here." She led the way inside, stopped at the entrance to let them pass, and then slammed the door behind them. The sound of the scouring wind died instantly and the door sealed with a hiss.

White lights flickered and grew brighter. Brackett looked around at the clean, wide corridor that went deep into the building. Music played quietly from overhead speakers—early 22nd century jazz—and the captain decided he could have done worse. There were a lot of command posts where it would be almost impossible not to develop at least low-level claustrophobia. There'd be room to move here, and people to get to know—civilians and marines alike.

"Okay, let's do this right," he said, shaking hands with Paris and Coughlin. "Demian Brackett. Your new CO. And I figure since you two came out to greet me, that gives me three options. You're either good marines, suck-ups, or you drew the short straw. Which is it?"

Coughlin let out a barking laugh, his face reddening. "Oh, I'm definitely a suck-up," he said, hefting his burden. "I'm carrying your damn bag."

"And you, Lieutenant?" Brackett said, arching an eyebrow as he glanced at Paris.

A smile flickered across her features, but only one side of her mouth lifted. On the left side, beneath the scar, the muscles did not seem to respond.

"Give it time, Captain," Paris said. "I'm sure you'll figure me out."

"Fair enough. Lead the way."

As Lt. Paris guided him deeper into the building, Coughlin began to rattle off what he apparently considered the amenities of Hadley's Hope, including fresh greenhouse vegetables, a game room, vast, incomplete subterranean levels with plenty of room for running, and a cook who was—the sergeant claimed—a virtuoso when it came to Italian pastries.

The colony was only in its nascent stages. Someday it would be a sprawling hub, as Weyland-Yutani continued to promote expansion into this quadrant. Both the company and the government supported the scientific research that was already going on here, but eventually the real value of Hadley's Hope would be as a way station or port.

"I've gotta say," Coughlin went on, "it doesn't hurt that there are some lovely women among the colonists."

He seemed to catch himself, hitched Brackett's duffel higher on his shoulder, and shot a quick worried glance toward Paris.

"Say, Cap... our last CO was kind of a hardass when it came to, uhm, fraternizing with the colonists. That gonna be a problem with you?"

Brackett had given it some thought when he'd first received the assignment. While he didn't want the drama of romantic and sexual entanglements between his marines and the colonists, he didn't see how he could effectively prevent them. Better to have things out in the open than deal with the foolishness of people trying to maintain covert relationships.

"I'm not in favor," he said, "but I'd rather have you sleeping with the colonists than with other marines. There are regulations for a reason. I don't want you mooning over Lt. Paris in the midst of an op, and stumbling off a cliff."

Coughlin blinked, mouth gaping.

"Me an' the Loot? Nah, Captain, there's nothing like... I mean I wouldn't... well not that I wouldn't, but..."

Paris started to laugh and shook her head. Brackett had maintained a straight face, but Coughlin saw Paris's expression and blushed furiously.

"You're screwing with me."

"Yes, Sergeant," Brackett admitted. "I'm screwing with you."

Coughlin sighed. "Nice one, Cap. I see how it's gonna be."

"So, I'm not going to have any trouble with you, Sergeant Coughlin?"

"Not with him," Lt. Paris said. "But we've got our share of meatheads."

"Care to give me a heads-up?" Brackett said. "Let me know who to look out for?"

Paris didn't reply. Any trace of a smile vanished from her face. As she reached a door and keyed it open, she wore an expression that said she regretted having spoken.

* * *

As the three of them moved deeper inside the colony, they passed several civilians. Brackett heard laughter down a side corridor, and glanced over to see a pair of children doing cartwheels along the floor. That would take some getting used to—having kids around.

"What about you, Cap?" Coughlin said.

Brackett furrowed his brow. "What about what, Sarge?"

"You got someone in your life? Someone you left behind?"

Ahead, a row of high windows looked in on the spacious command block, where security and operations personnel sat at workstations and studied display screens. In the middle of the room, a heavyset white man appeared to be dressing down a scraggly, bearded young guy who held a blueprint scroll in his hand.

"Administration," Lt. Paris said. "That's Al Simpson. You're catching him on one of his better days."

Simpson's face turned red as he yelled at the young fellow. Paris didn't seem to be joking about this being one of the colonial administrator's better days, though. Brackett hoped the man wasn't going to be a problem. He didn't do well with civilian interference.

Paris caught Simpson's attention, and the man gestured to indicate that he'd be out in a moment.

"Seems like quite the charmer," Brackett said.

"He's not so bad," Lt. Paris mused. "But I wouldn't want to have to answer to him."

A companionable silence fell among the three marines as they waited in the corridor. Curious civilians smiled or nodded at the newly arrived CO as they passed. Coughlin slid the duffel to the ground and leaned against the wall.

Brackett turned to the Sergeant.

"The answer's no, by the way."

"What's that?"

"There isn't anyone I left behind."

Which wasn't a lie, but it wasn't the truth, either.

He'd had mixed feelings about this command from the very beginning. He'd been stationed on colonies before—each one maintained a small marine detachment assigned by the United States government, the same way the Colonial Marines offered protective services to all signatories of the United Americas pact.

In recent years, Weyland-Yutani—who owned or exerted influence over what seemed like half the universe—had gotten into the colonization business. The rumors about their business practices were utterly appalling, yet the realities were bad enough. Could you call it corruption, he had often wondered, if the malice and greed were purely intentional—part of the foundation of the business? Hadley's Hope was a joint endeavor between the government and the company, and he didn't like the idea of taking orders from corporate stooges.

There was another reason why being assigned to LV-426 had unsettled him.

Sgt. Coughlin had asked if he had left anyone behind, and Brackett hadn't been lying when he'd said no. He hadn't left anyone behind on Earth, but years ago, when he had joined the Colonial Marines, he'd been forced to break off a relationship with a woman he loved. She'd gone on to find a new life with another man. By the time he'd returned home for a furlough—hoping at least to say hello, to see her smile—she and her new husband had left the planet entirely.

Now, somehow, their paths were slated to cross again. His old girlfriend and her husband had been among the first colonists to arrive on Acheron more than a dozen years before. Brackett wondered if she still had the same smile, and whether or not she'd be happy to see him.

Her name had been Anne Ridley in those days.

DATE: 10 JUNE, 2179
TIME: 1105

Curtis Finch felt like strangling his brother. He might've considered actually doing it, except that if he took his hands off of the land crawler's steering wheel, they'd have been blown into a ditch.

"I want off, man," Otto said, bracing himself on the dashboard with both hands as the storm pummeled the six-wheeled vehicle with gusts of wind like the fists of a giant.

A burst of derisive laughter came from the back seat. The two Colonial Marines had been silent for long minutes while Curtis navigated them down out of the rugged hills, but now Sgt. Marvin Draper bent forward, icy eyes glaring at the elder Finch.

"You wanna get out here, be my guest," Draper sneered. "Nut job."

Otto flushed red as he whipped around to glare at both Draper and the gravely quiet, dark-eyed Pvt. Ankita Yousseff.

"Shut yer trap, Draper. I said off, not out. Off, off, off. Off this godforsaken rock! I want to go home."

Draper let his restraints pull him back against the rear seat. He smiled, then spoke out of the corner of his mouth, addressing Pvt. Yousseff.

"Otto wants his mommy."

"Our mother's dead," Otto snapped, crying out as a gust lifted the left side of the crawler off the ground for a second before it crashed back down and the vehicle kept rolling. "But I'd dig my way down into the grave with her if it meant I didn't have to live here any—"

"Shut it!" Curtis barked. He'd had enough.

Otto stared at him. He had the blue eyes and dark red hair of their mother, while Curtis's brown eyes and hair favored their father, but no one could have looked at them and not known they were brothers.

Curtis peered straight ahead, lips dry, heart smashing in his chest as he tried desperately to maneuver the vehicle through the storm. He'd driven out this way a dozen times, but with the dust and debris, visibility had dropped to maybe ten percent in the past fifteen minutes. Continuing on like this—nearly blind—was foolhardy at best, but if he'd gauged their progress correctly, they only had a short distance to cover before they reached shelter.

It would be safer than trying to weather the storm inside the land crawler. They were still twenty miles out from Hadley's Hope, with no chance of getting back to the colony until the grit-storm had blown over.

"Curt—"

"I'm not joking, Otto," he told his brother, raising his voice to be heard over the screaming wind and the shushing roar of the dirt scouring the vehicle. "I'll put you out right here."

"Are you telling me you don't regret the day we set foot on Acheron?"

Curtis twisted toward him.

"Are you shitting me?" he said. "We wouldn't even be here if not for you."

"Here we go again!" Draper groaned in the back seat. "Yousseff, please put a bullet in my head so I don't have to listen to these two anymore."

Draper outranked her, but Yousseff didn't seem to take this as an order. Curtis almost wished she had. The hugely muscled Draper had a long scar on the right side of his face, going up from the corner of his mouth as if someone had tried to extend his smile. On his throat he bore a tattoo of a scorpion, and somehow the combination of scar and tattoo made Curtis very nervous. Like a scorpion, Draper seemed as if he might strike at any moment, his humor a cover for inner volatility.

Yet the same seemed true of Yousseff, who had no scars or tattoos. Her eyes were calm, and yet full of the promise of violence. Otto had once said that was just the mark of a soldier, but Curtis disagreed. He had known many other marines, and most of them hadn't been the type to take imminent violence as a given.

"Curtis…" Otto began warily.

"No." He didn't want to hear it. Curtis and Otto—the older brother by two years—had been on Acheron for forty-seven months as surveyors and wildcat prospectors. Their time with the colony might be nothing compared to people like Meznick and Generazio, and Russ and Anne Jorden, but some people were just cut out for this kind of work, while others were not. Otto had been the one who talked Curtis into joining the colony, but within the past few months, he had been falling apart.

Curtis understood, of course. All these years of terraforming had only partially tamed Acheron's violent atmosphere. Always turbulent, the weather patterns kicked up massive storms strong enough to overturn vehicles, kicking up so much soil that it became impossible to see, and for instruments to navigate. The environment could be deadly, and the substandard equipment seemed constantly on the verge of lethal malfunction.

As much as they liked the other colonists, the competition among the wildcatters—to find and stake claim on anything that would be valuable to the company—made it difficult to develop any real camaraderie.

Otto had been defeated by the oppressive nature of the place. Trouble was, they couldn't go home without earning enough money to pay for the journey, and for at least six months' rent back on Earth.

Curtis gripped the wheel even tighter and bent forward, slowing the vehicle. The gale raged around them, and for a few long seconds he could see nothing beyond the windshield. The lights from the crawler's control panel cast the interior in a green glow, turning their faces ghostly pale, but outside all was black.

He held his breath.

The crawler shook.

It rumbled through several dips in the landscape. He braked nearly to a stop, unwilling to risk the unknown. Then the wind lessened and he saw a familiar dark block silhouette in the storm ahead. Hitting the accelerator, he picked up speed.

"I can't do this," Otto whined. "I can't be here, Curt. It's like the whole planet is trying to kill us!"

Curtis took one hand off the wheel, turned, and punched his brother hard on the shoulder, as if they were small children again. Otto cried out, and clapped a hand to his arm.

"What the hell?" he shouted.

"Damn it, Finch!" Draper roared.

Yousseff spoke the only two words she'd offered that day.

"Stupid bastard."

Curtis looked forward again, grabbed the wheel tightly, and tried to turn—but too late to avoid the ditch. His heart sank as the left side of the crawler dipped and then dropped, and they scraped to a grinding halt, the right-hand tires spinning up dirt while the tires on the left spun at nothing but air.

"Gun it!" Draper said angrily.

"Won't do any good," Curtis told him, gunning it anyway. The crawler slewed a bit, the rear of the vehicle edging further over into the ditch.

"Stop!" Otto said, staring at him. "The undercarriage is caught on a ridge. We slide any more, and we'll roll right over."

Curtis took a slow breath, still clutching the wheel. The bedrock in the area consisted of stone flats and ridges buried in thick soil, with a top layer of dust and ash that shifted with the storms, so the visual details of the terrain changed considerably from day to day. Some of the ditches were as deep as twenty or thirty feet. If they rolled now, and managed to land right side up, he thought the crawler would be all right. They could make their way along the bottom of the ditch until they found a place where the grade wasn't too steep to let them out.

But if they landed upside down…

"We're bailing out," he said, and he killed the engine.

Yousseff swore.

As Curtis unlatched his restraints, Draper grabbed his shoulder from behind.

"What are you doing, Finch?"

"Don't be brainless!" his brother said. "You'll die out there."

Otto snatched up the handheld radio, stretching the cord. Wireless didn't work out in these storms.

"Admin, come in, this is Otto Finch," he barked into the radio. "Come in!"

They all froze, listening to the static that sputtered in response. For just a sliver of a moment the line cleared and they heard a burble of language—just a few unintelligible words. Until the atmosphere calmed down, communications would be nigh impossible. They might be able to get their message through, but admin would have trouble tracking them. With all of the mineral dust and volcanic ash whipping around, external instrument readings were always tricky.

"I'm not suicidal," Curtis said. He pointed through the windshield. "Look out there."

"What am I looking at?" Draper growled.

The storm had kicked up again. The crawler rocked on the ridge, then slid a bit further. The tower Curtis had seen before had been blotted out by the blowing grit.

"There's a processor tower about a hundred yards ahead," he said. "Processor Six. We hunker down there until the wind quits. Once we get through to admin, they'll send someone out to help. Even if we can't get through, they'll find us by tracking our personal data transmitters. We'll be fine."

He turned to his brother, saw the fear in his eyes, and actually felt sorry for him.

"Otto," he said. "We'll be all right."

6

THE LADDER

As they ran through the storm, scoured by grit and brutalized by the wind, Otto kept his head down. Goggles protected his eyes, but he felt safer looking at the ground.

A dreadful fear had been building in him for months, a kind of chasm opening up in his gut. In his nightmares, fissures split the surface of Acheron and dark things stirred down inside the planet's guts. Any time they left the colony, he felt as if he were standing on the edge of a roof a thousand feet up, looking at the ground far below. The urge to just fling himself over the edge, to plummet to his death, tugged at him. Every logical part of him fought that urge, but still it teased him forward, seductive as the voice of the serpent.

Thanatos, it was called. He'd read it somewhere. *The death urge.*

A tiny voice inside Otto Finch had grown steadily more convinced that Acheron meant to do him harm, and tempted him to surrender to its malicious purpose.

"I don't want to die here," he whispered, his words stolen by the storm.

He glanced up, saw Curtis's back, and kept trudging ahead. Draper and Yousseff were behind him, but he couldn't be sure they would pick him up if he fell. His brother, though—he had to believe that if he cried out, if he stumbled, Curtis would save him. They were brothers, after all.

Please, God, he thought. *Please, God. Don't let me die here.*

Yet it felt like a hollow prayer. He hadn't always believed in God, but if such a deity existed, he couldn't escape the feeling that He lived far, far away from here.

A loud scrape of metal made Otto look up.

Ahead, Curtis had reached the processor and as Otto staggered toward him, nearly blown off his feet by a gust, the heavy door rose up into its housing. It occurred to him that without Curtis they wouldn't have been able to enter—all surveyors knew the override code for these things, but Otto had forgotten it.

Thank you, my brother, he thought.

But then he staggered inside, out of the storm, and suddenly he felt a lot less grateful. He tore off his goggles and spun around, staring at the cylindrical ductwork that ran up the walls and overhead. The outlying atmosphere processors scattered around Acheron were tiny in comparison to the huge, arena-sized Processor One back at the colony, but the building was still impressive. The interior of Processor Six was fifty feet in diameter. In the corner was a small control room full of levers and gauges, a communications array, and a pair of computers that did most of the work. Pipes and ducts and ladders went up into a vast sphere—the core processor—and then into the darkness fifty or sixty feet overhead.

Otto didn't need to climb or use the control room to see that there was a problem. Steam hissed from the joints, and as he approached the nearest of the two-foot-wide ducts, he could see that the metal surface was vibrating. A clamorous buzz filled the interior of the station, the micro-rattle of thousands of feet of ductwork shaking against the brackets and rings that held it in place.

"Jeezus," Draper said, stripping off his coat. "Why's it so hot in here?"

Normally the innocent curiosity on his face—after what they'd just been through—would have made Otto want to laugh. But he wasn't capable of finding anything funny just then.

"Curtis," Otto called, loud enough to be heard over the hiss and rattle inside, and the roar of the storm outside.

Back toward the door, Curtis had removed his own heavy protective jacket. He stood with his goggles on his forehead, grimed with dust and sweat, and spoke quietly to Yousseff. The Colonial Marine sergeant seemed to ignore his flirtations half the time, and the other half she spent indulging him with the arch of an eyebrow or a slanted smile at some idiocy he'd spouted.

Otto hated her for that. He understood that his brother found the woman beautiful—with her dusky skin and those big, hypnotic brown eyes, anyone would have been captivated by her at first. But Yousseff had never seemed like anything but a cold bitch to Otto. Her half-smiles mocked Curtis for his lonely but hopeful heart.

"Curtis, damn it!" he shouted. "You'll have time to make a fool of yourself later!" He hated the crack in his voice, the edge of panic that lurked there.

Only when his brother glared at him, hostile to cover the sting of truth, did Otto realize what he'd said.

"You know what—" Curtis began, moving toward him.

"Stop!" Otto snapped, shaking his head and holding out a hand. "Just… stop. Be mad at me later, okay? We've got a problem."

Draper had dropped down to sit on the floor, knees drawn to his chest and his back against the wall. Now he laughed.

"Shit, just *one*?"

Otto felt like he couldn't breathe. When he and Curtis had been small boys, their father had punished them for misbehavior by locking them in the closet. The darkness had frightened him, but the closeness had been worse. Sometimes he had imagined that the thick air had a presence, that it did not like intruders—especially naughty little boys—and that it wanted to suffocate him. There in the dark, lying on a pile of his parents' shoes, with his mother's long coats brushing the back of his neck, he could feel it sliding over him in a heavy, dusty embrace. It would get warm very quickly and sweat beaded on his skin. He never dared pound on the door—his father had warned him many times about that—but he would cry and beg to be set free, and when at last he lay quietly on top of those shoes, he could smell the oil from the factory where the old man worked.

The inside of the processor had the same oil smell. Dark and hot, the air close. He stared at his brother as Curtis moved toward him, searching his eyes and wondering why Curtis didn't understand.

"Can't you hear it?" Otto asked, running a hand through his tangle of red hair. "Can't you *feel* it?"

Curtis froze, listening.

Draper glanced at Yousseff.

"What? D'you hear something?"

Then they all heard it. A chugging, grinding noise coming from overhead. Curtis pushed past Otto and put his hand on the same duct, felt the vibration, and then tried to see up into the darkness.

"It's machines," Draper said. "Just friggin' machines."

"Of course it's machines," Curtis said, shooting him a withering look. "Machines that are breaking down."

Yousseff perked up at that. No arched eyebrow or flirty half-smile now.

"What do you mean 'breaking down?'"

"Clogged," Otto said, his hands fluttering nervously. He pulled at the small curls on the back of his neck, a painful habit he'd picked up recently. "The unit's clogged. Too many storms lately, too long since the last maintenance. Draper said it's hot. Well, he's right, but it's more than that—it's overheating. From the sound of it, the unit's choking up there, all the filters need flushing and venting…"

Otto put his hand on the duct. It had grown hotter.

"…and it needs to be done in the next few hours, I'd say. Probably less, though." He tugged at his red curls. "I'm an optimist."

"Or what?" Draper demanded. "So the unit breaks down—that's not our problem. Soon as this grit-storm's over, we'll be able to get a signal through, and they'll send someone out from the colony."

Otto glanced at his brother and then lowered his gaze.

"Curtis?" Yousseff said, worry in her voice.

"Best case, Draper's right," Curtis replied. "The core's supposed to shut down if the filters clog enough—if the sphere is hot enough. But it's pretty hot in here already, and that hasn't happened."

"Do I want to ask what happens if the core doesn't do its automatic shutdown?" Draper asked.

Otto put his hands together and sprang them apart.

"Boom."

Yousseff cursed, turned to the door and unlatched it. She peered outside for just a second before shutting it tightly again.

"No sign of the storm letting up, I suppose," Curtis said. The look on her face was the only reply they needed. The four of them studied each other for several long moments. Otto saw beads of sweat on Draper's forehead, felt it on his own back, and knew the temperature had gone up just in the few minutes they'd been inside.

"Curtis!" Otto shouted.

His brother stared at him.

"I know, okay?" Cursing under his breath, Curtis hurried over to a ladder that was clamped to the wall just beside the door to the control room.

"Wait, what are you doing?" Draper demanded, wiping the sweat from his brow.

Curtis shot him a look. "You know how to flush the filters, vent the clog and send it outside?"

Draper threw his arms out, drawing attention to his uniform attire and his heavily muscled form.

"Do I *look* like a maintenance man?"

Curtis nodded upward. "That's why I'm climbing. I'm the only one here who knows how to do this. If I can clear the filters, this place doesn't blow up. If I can't, we take our chances with the storm."

"Well, hell, then… climb away," Draper said, gesturing toward the ladder.

Otto could see the way the rungs vibrated in his brother's hands as Curtis climbed the first few feet. *Must be rattling his bones*, he thought.

Yousseff came and stood at the base of the ladder.

"Be careful."

Curtis shot a grin down at Otto as if to say, *I told you so*.

The grinding and chugging grew louder above them. Otto could feel the place shaking under his feet, right up through his body. He clenched his jaw, watching his brother climb, and his teeth chattered from the tremor in the floor. His heart raced, and another bead of sweat ran down his neck.

"Hate this planet," he said quietly, convinced he spoke only to himself. "I hate this godforsaken—"

"It's a moon," Yousseff said.

Otto spun on her, practically snarling. "Hate this planet!" he screamed, eyes burning with tears he refused to shed.

Then something banged inside the core, metal giving way under pressure. The boom that followed rocked the entire structure, as if some giant had given it a thunderous kick from the outside. Up on the ladder, Curtis shouted and Otto looked up to see his brother slip, fingers frantically grasping for the rungs.

Otto shouted his brother's name as Curtis fell. He ran toward the base of the ladder. When Curtis hit the floor, the sound of it froze Otto in his tracks. He knew that noise from childhood—it was the sound of breaking bone.

Curtis let out a cry of pain—just one—and then fell so silent, so quickly that it seemed as if a guillotine had cut off his voice. He slumped there at the base of the ladder with the whole processor rocking and banging around them, more and more steam misting the already hot, close air, and Otto feared he might have died.

Draper shoved Otto roughly aside, saying *shitshitshitshitshitshit* as if in time with his racing heartbeat, and ran to kneel by Curtis.

Yousseff took two steps toward the core.

"Draper, this is not going to end well," she said. "We need to get out of here!"

With two fingers on Curtis's neck, checking for a pulse, Draper turned to glare at her.

"You don't think I know that?" he said. "What's your plan? Try driving in the grit-storm? If we don't wait for it to subside, we're dead out there."

"We're dead *in here* if we don't purge the throat of this beast!" Yousseff shouted.

Otto could barely hear them. He shuffled toward Curtis and fell to his knees beside Draper, shaking his head. His thoughts had been muddled with anxiety and fear for so long—a profound and growing sense that they were all in terrible danger—that it felt strange to have sudden clarity.

"Curtis?" he ventured, and he nudged his brother's shoulder. Curtis did not stir.

Otto's hands fluttered to his mouth and he turned to stare at Draper, breath hitching in his chest, horror spreading through him, eradicating all other emotions.

"Oh God," he said. "I did this. I did this! He didn't want to come to the colony and I talked him into it. This is my fault. I killed my own brother!"

Draper reached up and flicked Otto across the nose. The pain made him jerk backward.

"What the hell is—"

"Have I got your attention?" Draper shouted, and suddenly the sound of the storm sandpapering the outer walls and the thunder of the groaning processor flooded back into Otto's ears, as if he had somehow turned the volume down on the rest of the world for a minute.

Otto nodded.

"Moron's not dead," Draper said, nodding toward Curtis. "His leg's broken from the fall. Banged his head pretty good. If he's lucky, he passed out from the pain, and not brain damage. The big question is, can you do the job, Otto? Can you climb your ass up there and clear those vents?"

Shaking his head, Otto reached out to stroke Curtis's hair.

"Damn it, man, do you know how to do the job?" Draper roared, poking him in the chest.

"No!" Otto shouted, lower lip quivering. "I don't have the first clue!"

Draper turned toward Yousseff.

"I know the storm's causing interference, but you've gotta call us in. Get someone out here in the heavy-crawler!" Outside the wind howled even louder. The grit scouring the metal seemed almost to sing a high, mocking melody.

"No way we're getting a comms signal through this!" Yousseff barked at him. "We've got to go back out, take cover inside the crawler!"

"Keep trying, damn it!" Draper roared. "There'll be a lull in the storm. You'll get through."

Yousseff spun away from them and marched toward the far wall, covering one ear as she slipped on her headset. Otto stared at her, and he knew there would be no signal. They were going to die out here, and Acheron would swallow them up. The grit would strip them to the bone and the bones would be buried in dust and they'd slip down into the hell he always saw in his nightmares—the hell at the heart of this planet.

"I hate this planet!" he said loudly, trembling. He turned to look at the slack expression on his brother's face. Curtis's head lolled to one side and for the first time Otto saw the huge bruise on his left temple, red and swollen.

"Curtis!" he whined, unable to help himself. He shook his brother's hand, nudged his shoulder. "Curtis, please! I'm sorry. I'm so, so sorry!" He rocked back and forth, closing his eyes. "I hate this planet! I hate this—"

His eyes sprang open as Draper grabbed him by the front of his shirt.

"Shut your mouth!" Draper shouted, and he swung his fist.

The blow silenced Otto, bloodied his mouth, and broke off a tooth. Shocked, he stared at Draper, who still held him by the shirt, fist ready to land another punch. Tears sprang to Otto's eyes and this time he could not fight them off. They began to slide down his cheeks as he spit out his broken tooth and then used his tongue to probe the sharp edges in the hole where it had been.

"You're going up there," Draper said, gesturing to the ladder. "You and your asshole brother are inseparable. I don't believe for a second that you don't have at least *some* idea of how to stop this. So you're going up, Otto. Could be my life depends on it, which means you go up, or I shoot you in the head."

Otto's breath hitched. His shoulders shook.

"I hate this pla—"

Draper's fist crashed into his face again. Otto sagged in the marine's grip, sobbing, and spit out a big gob of his own blood. Then he nodded.

At least up on the ladder, he would be out of reach of Draper's fist. And maybe from up high, Curtis would look like he was only sleeping.

Regaining his balance, he went to the bottom rung. With the whole processor clanging and screaming around him, Otto began to climb.

On the third rung he froze, and then he let go, dropping down to land with a thud.

"What the hell are you—" Draper began.

Otto turned to him, tears running freely.

"Shoot me," he said as he flopped back against the wall and slid to the floor, anguish tearing him apart. "If you're going to kill me, just do it. I'd rather be dead than be here."

Draper swore and leveled his gun.

Yousseff grabbed his wrist, gave a quick shake of her head, and then walked toward Otto.

"Curtis is injured, Otto," she said. "If you don't do something, there's a good chance we're all going to die out here—your brother included."

Otto looked into her brown eyes, glistening and beautiful.

"Promise you'll make them send us home—me and Curtis—and I'll do what I can. Promise you'll make them send us on the next ship out."

Yousseff nodded. "I promise."

Otto sneered, nostrils flaring, and turned away.

"Lying bitch. You think I can't see it in your eyes?" he sobbed. And then he screamed. "I want to go home!"

7

TROUBLE IN THREES

DATE: 10 JUNE, 2179
TIME: 1110

In Demian Brackett's experience, the further out from Earth he was stationed, the more likely he was to run into troublemakers. People joined the Colonial Marines for a variety of reasons: some out of a sense of honor and duty, others to escape the patterns of their pasts, and still others because they had violence inside them and didn't want to hurt the people they loved.

What he'd found was that no matter what their rationale for enlisting, once they were in the Corps, they either turned into good marines or walking trouble. Whatever their intentions had been in the beginning, he'd found that most people had the capacity to go in either direction once they immersed themselves in a life as part of the Corps.

The other thing he'd observed over time was that the further from Earth a squad was assigned, the more freedom its troublemakers felt they had to stir things up.

Within forty-five minutes of his arrival on Acheron, Capt. Brackett had stowed his gear in his quarters, held a preliminary meet-and-greet with Al Simpson and the colony's senior support staff, and begun his first squad briefing. The Colonial Marines had a small muster room at their disposal, but it was large enough for the twenty-one men and women now gathered there.

Brackett stood at the front of the room, leaning on a podium that made him think of some sort of religious service, and studied the marines who stood before him. There were chairs stacked against one wall, but since this was his first meeting with the squad, he didn't want them getting comfortable.

Better for them all to stand, himself included.

Brackett kept it simple. Basic introduction and expectations, a hope that they would help him get up to speed, a firm instruction to adhere to protocol, and an appreciation of the welcome he'd already received from Lt. Paris and Sgt. Coughlin, who stood to one side, both slightly apart from the rest of the squad. As he spoke, he watched their eyes. Most of the squad seemed attentive, even curious about their new CO, just there to do their jobs. Several of them, however, did not seem quite as open.

One man in particular kept his eyes slightly narrowed, the corner of his mouth upturned, as if he might sneer at any moment. Pale and thin, with a hawk-like nose, the man radiated rebellion. Brackett had seen the sort before—defiant and hostile, the kind of man who would snicker and whisper and grumble. Hawk-Nose would warrant some attention, but he wasn't Brackett's only concern.

There were three others who stood nearby. While they didn't quite share Hawk-Nose's sneer, Brackett saw the tension and stiffness in them, and thought he caught several silent exchanges.

There were dangers on Acheron, but it ought to have been a relatively simple assignment. Brackett intended to make sure Hawk-Nose and his friends didn't complicate things for him.

"All right, that'll do for now," the captain said, surveying his squad. A tough-looking bunch, most of them alert and responsive. "Over the next few days I'll want to meet briefly with each of you. If we're going to be spending all this time together in paradise, I want to know who I've got watching my back, and I want you all to know that I've got your backs."

It might've been his imagination, but he was sure the slight sneer on the left side of Hawk-Nose's mouth deepened a bit.

"That's all. Dismissed." Brackett glanced to his right. "Lieutenant Paris. Sergeant Coughlin. Stick around a minute, please."

He waited while the squad filed out of the room, several of them unable to wait even until they reached the corridor before the quiet muttering began. Brackett wouldn't hold it against them. They had just met their new CO—it was natural for them to speculate about how much of a pain in the ass he was likely to become. He watched until the last of them had exited, and found himself alone with Paris and Coughlin.

"How did I do?" he asked, turning to them.

"You did fine, Captain," Paris said. "They don't know what to make of you yet, but they'll unclench soon enough."

"Not sure I want them to," Brackett replied thoughtfully. He frowned deeply. "The guy with the hawk-nose… what's his story?"

Paris cocked her head curiously. "Hawk-nose?"

Coughlin knew who he meant.

"That's Stamovich. Not much of a story to him, but if you're asking if he's going to give you a hard time—"

"The answer's 'maybe,'" Paris interrupted, and Coughlin nodded. "Stamovich is a prickly son of a bitch, probably punched his way out of his momma's womb, but he'll behave himself unless Draper tells him otherwise."

"Sergeant Marvin Draper?" Brackett asked, and his eyes narrowed. "I read his file. He's got a couple of black marks for insubordination, but that was years ago. Should I be worried about him, then? I mean, if he's the guy who might tell Cpl. Stamovich what to do…"

"Draper can be managed," Paris said. "He knows he's floating on an ugly little rock in space, and that pissing off the CO is a bad idea. As long as he doesn't directly disobey orders, best bet is to just ignore him as best you can."

Brackett frowned.

"If this sergeant has Stamovich on some sort of a leash, then how am I supposed to re—"

"Not just Stamovich, Cap," Coughlin cut in. "There are a few others who follow Draper's lead."

Eyes still narrowed, Brackett turned to study the muster room, repopulating it in his mind. He tried to summon the faces of his squad, remember where they had all been standing.

"Which one was Draper?" he asked.

Paris shook her head. "None of them. He and Yousseff are out with a survey team."

"Why's that?"

"Standard procedure, sir," Paris replied. "Every time admin sends out a survey team, two of our people accompany them."

Brackett blinked. "Why are Colonial Marines needed on civilian excursions? The colonists have their jobs, and we have ours. We're meant to maintain security for the colony itself, not personal safety for each of its residents."

Paris glanced at Coughlin, but the stout little man just shrugged.

"Just SOP, Cap," Coughlin said. "Been that way since I got here."

"Al Simpson's been here from the beginning," Paris said. "If anyone has an answer to that, it'd be him."

Brackett took a deep breath. He hadn't intended to rock the boat on his first day, but it didn't sit right with him to think that marines were risking their lives on a daily basis, in ways that weren't part of their mission.

"Go about your duties," he said. "I'm going to talk to Simpson, and then get myself settled. Meet me back here at 1300."

Paris and Coughlin saluted, but Brackett barely noticed. His thoughts were on the absent Sgt. Draper. Had his superiors failed to sufficiently brief him on his posting on Acheron, or was the colonial administration utilizing the marines for corporate purposes without the authorization to do so?

He left the muster room and started to retrace his steps toward the administrative hub. The last thing he wanted was to get off on the wrong foot with Al Simpson on the first day of his deployment, but he hadn't spent years with the Colonial Marines—from firefights to bug hunts—and been awarded a Galactic Cross just so he could be some corporate lapdog in the ass-end of the universe.

Brow furrowed, lost in thought, he took a wrong turn and nearly collided with a man and woman headed the other direction.

"Pardon me," he mumbled.

The words were barely out of his mouth when he registered the little gasp that escaped the woman's lips. Initially, Brackett thought the near-collision had startled her, and he began to apologize again. He caught the strange look her companion gave her, but only when he refocused did he realize that her gasp had been one of shocked recognition.

"Demian?" she said, features blossoming into a brilliant smile. "What are *you* doing here?"

All of the tension and frustration slipped away. Brackett returned her smile and gave a delighted little laugh. One hundred and fifty-eight colonists at Hadley's Hope, not even counting the marines, and already he'd practically run her down.

"Hello, Anne," he said.

I'd forgotten how beautiful you are, he almost added. But then he cut his gaze to the left, caught the confused expression on her companion's face, and made the connection that had momentarily eluded him.

Brackett held out a hand.

"You must be Russell Jorden."

"Russ," the man said warily, shaking his hand.

"Captain Demian Brackett, Russ. Very pleased to meet the man worthy of being this one's husband."

"Yeah… thanks," Russ said carefully, but the caution behind his eyes did not disappear. Brackett couldn't blame him—husbands tended not to love having their wives' exes around.

For her part, Anne still wore her smile, but it had gone from bright to mystified.

"Seriously, Demian," she said. "What are you doing on Acheron? I never thought I'd see you again."

In the years since he'd seen her, age had added a few crinkles around her eyes, and the time she'd spent in the savage wilderness of deep space had made her seem somehow wilder herself. But time had only made her more beautiful to him. Tangled curls framed her face, and hard work had made her lean and powerful. Her eyes were alight with the intrepid determination inherent to those who chose life's more challenging paths.

She's another man's wife, he reminded himself. Not that he needed much of a reminder with the way Russ Jorden now studied him from behind slitted, almost reptilian eyes.

"This is my new post," Brackett explained. "The marines at Hadley's Hope are under my command."

"That's… that's…" Anne fumbled.

"Amazing," Russ said, now wearing a polite mask of a smile. "Welcome aboard, Brackett. It's rough living, but we've been out here so long that it just seems like home to us. I guess wherever your children grow up, that's always going to be home, right?"

"So I'm told," Brackett replied. "No kids myself, but I envy you two."

Anne glanced from Brackett to her husband, and a rigid sort of awkwardness descended upon them all. She looked as if she was searching for the right combination of words to alleviate that discomfort, when a voice called along the corridor.

"Captain Brackett, there you are!"

Brackett turned to see Al Simpson lumbering toward them. The man seemed afflicted with a permanent air of disapproval.

"I was just on my way to see you," Brackett said, letting his own tone inform the administrator that disapproval was an emotion available to both of them.

"Good timing, then," Simpson replied. If he'd caught the annoyance in the captain's voice, he didn't show it. "Look, we've got a small crisis on our hands, and it involves some of your people. I've called a meeting in the conference room, and you should be there."

"When's this?" Brackett asked.

"Now."

Anne glanced worriedly at her husband.

"Is this about Otto and Curtis?" Russ asked Simpson. "We were just coming to talk to you."

A flicker of panic passed over Simpson's face.

"The Finch brothers are fine. The storm is hitting hard in that sector, but they've taken shelter. All's well. Now, if you'll excuse us, I need Captain Brackett's consultation on a matter regarding his squad."

Simpson took Brackett by the elbow and abruptly steered him toward the administrative hub. The captain glanced back at the Jordens. Russ was staring after them, but Anne had turned her gaze to her husband, looking worried and pale. For an instant, Brackett regretted having accepted the post on Acheron, but then he shook off the feeling. He hadn't come to Hadley's Hope just to see Anne Jorden again.

Had he?

He shook off Simpson's arm and gave the man a sidelong glance as they hurried along the corridor, across a hallway junction, and into view of the busy, glassed-in administrative hub of the command block.

"You're not a good liar," Brackett said.

"Excuse me?" Simpson snapped, his face pinched with annoyance.

"I don't know who the Finch brothers are, but whoever they are, they're not fine." He paused, then added, "I seriously doubt Anne believed you either."

"She doesn't have to believe me," Simpson said. "She works for me. So why don't you let me worry about my people, and you can worry about yours?"

As they passed the command block and rounded a corner, Brackett studied him more closely. On the surface, the guy seemed like a hundred other low-level management monkeys he'd met, yet he wondered if Simpson was smarter than he looked.

A short way down the hall they paused at a door marked RESEARCH: NO UNAUTHORIZED ADMITTANCE, and Simpson punched numbers into a keypad that admitted them.

"You bring up an interesting subject," Brackett said, "the line that separates your people from mine."

Simpson made sure the door swung shut behind them and the lock engaged, then he set off for a white door a dozen feet along the hall, obviously expecting Brackett to follow.

"Whatever you've got to say, save it," the administrator sniffed. "We've got bigger problems at the moment than whatever dick-waving contest you feel like having to assert your authority."

Brackett quickened his pace, fighting the urge to grab Simpson by the scruff of his neck and smash his face into the doorframe. Then they were inside the white-doored room, and there were too many witnesses for him to do anything. He wouldn't have done it anyway—probably—but he sure as hell wasn't going to bloody the admin's nose in front of some young wide-eyed lab assistants in white coats and several older researchers in civilian clothes.

The lab coats clustered around the trio of older researchers, including a silver-haired Japanese man, a grim-eyed white guy with a wine-dark birthmark on his throat and jaw, and a sixtyish woman so slender that she reminded Brackett of the stick figures he'd drawn as a child.

The only guy in the room who didn't look like a scientist stood a distance back from the table, a deep frown creasing his forehead. An air of disapproval hung over him, like a man waiting for his children to get tired at a playground so he can take them home.

"Captain Brackett, meet Doctors Mori, Reese, and Hidalgo, and their team of brainiacs."

The doctors nodded. Simpson gestured to the guy standing away from the table.

"The moper in the corner there is Derrick Bradford, who's in charge of our ongoing terraforming operations."

"Captain," Bradford said with a nod.

Brackett approached the table for a proper round of handshakes.

"Welcome to Hadley's Hope, Captain—" Dr. Mori began.

"Enough of that," the grim-eyed doctor said, his birthmark flushing darker. "We haven't got time for niceties. Dr. Hidalgo, please bring the captain up to speed."

The stick figure sat up a bit straighter. Brackett noticed she had kind eyes. Worried eyes, at the moment.

"Two of our surveyors, Otto and Curtis Finch, encountered a level five atmospheric storm. They're fairly rare and localized, and the duration is hard to predict," Dr. Hidalgo said. "The Finchs and their marine escort were forced to abandon their vehicle and take shelter in an atmosphere processor."

Here, she shot a withering glance at Bradford.

"This processor hasn't been serviced in at least six months," she continued. "Records are unclear—"

Brackett grimaced and held up a hand.

"Look, I'm not even sure why my people are out there to begin with, but—"

"Later, Captain," Dr. Reese said.

Brackett glanced at Simpson.

"Later," the administrator agreed.

"They're in trouble," Derrick Bradford said, emphasizing the last word to make sure they all had their priorities straight. "The processor is malfunctioning—clogged—and the storm is making it worse. Curtis Finch is the only one with any engineering training among them, and he's injured."

Brackett tensed. "How long before the unit blows?"

"We can't be sure from here," Simpson said. "The storm's interfering, not just with communications, but with the monitoring signal from the processor. That's why we didn't know it had malfunctioned. It's not critical yet, but as far as we can tell, it's getting there."

Brackett stared at him. "You have a heavy-crawler, don't you? Why are we even talking about this? Get someone out there!"

Dr. Mori and Dr. Hidalgo exchanged an indecipherable glance.

Dr. Reese's smile reminded Brackett of a shark's.

"That's why you're here, Captain," Reese said. "There are two Colonial Marines out there, and you people never leave one of your own behind. We assumed that you and your squad would want to mount the rescue yourselves."

Brackett hadn't been at Hadley's Hope for half a day, and already he wanted to throttle most of the people he'd met.

"So, you send marines out to do your errands," he said, "and now you expect us to do your dirty work as well?"

Dr. Mori smoothed the jagged-cut lapels of his tailored jacket.

"While you're out there," he said, "the company would appreciate you retrieving whatever samples the team gathered before this mishap began."

Brackett stared at him, but remained silent. He'd wanted to hit Simpson earlier. Now he gritted his teeth and reminded himself that assaulting an aging Weyland-Yutani scientist would be frowned upon by his superiors.

"Mishap," he said, the word sounding like profanity to his ears.

Blank-faced, all of the scientists in the room just stared back at him. Only Bradford and Dr. Hidalgo had the good sense to look slightly uncomfortable.

Brackett turned to Simpson.

"Get the heavy-crawler outside."

"It's ready to go," Simpson replied.

"Fine. Call Sergeant Coughlin. Tell him he's got three minutes to pick five marines and meet me at my quarters."

He turned and strode back into the corridor.

Mishap, he thought.

Welcome to Acheron, indeed.

8

STORMS SEEN AND UNSEEN

DATE: 10 JUNE, 2179
TIME: 1232

Anne and Russ Jorden strode down the corridor side by side, connected by long years of marriage and a web of tension that chained them to each other even as it forced them apart. Anne hated the sound of her husband's heavy footfalls, the way he seemed to stalk the floor when angry. She could feel the anxiety coming off him in waves, and it made her want to run away.

If only there were some place to which she could have fled, just for a little while, to regain her sense of self. But where could she have gone inside the colony of Hadley's Hope where Russ wouldn't be able to find her? Or where she wouldn't be intruded upon by well-meaning friends?

Nowhere.

"Still want to eat?" he asked, the words short and clipped, as if he'd barely opened his mouth to speak.

"If you're hungry," she replied warily. They'd planned to check with Simpson about the Finch brothers and then go to the mess hall for lunch. Now she had a stomach full of what seemed to be warring factions of butterflies.

"Game room, then?" Russ asked.

Still monosyllabic. Anxiety was giving way to anger. It made her want to punch him. Anne loved her husband from the scruff on his unshaven chin down to his almost comically skinny ankles. Over the years they had laughed so much together. They'd been courageous, and sometimes a little crazy. They'd crossed the galaxy, and had their children so far from Earth that they joked that the kids might qualify as alien creatures if they ever returned to their parents' home planet.

There had been difficult years, but Anne and Russ had been together—a team—and that had counted for something when the sameness of life at Hadley's Hope had started to make them both feel claustrophobic. On the day Russ had confessed that it sometimes felt like a prison sentence, Anne had cried until he'd sworn to her that her love, and the presence of Tim and Newt, were the only things that kept him sane.

They still had good days—wonderful days, even—but they both had frayed nerves. Some nights Anne couldn't sleep, and she felt as if she might be unraveling. Then she heard Newt laugh or saw Tim trying to model his walk after his father's masculine gait, and all would be well.

Not today.

Anne Jorden knew her husband's every tic and gesture. They weren't going to make it to the recreation center. Just as that thought solidified in her mind, Russ ducked into a maintenance corridor and turned to face her. Anne wanted to keep walking—maybe the dropship hadn't left yet—but instead she stepped into that quiet corridor with her husband. A worker passed by and glanced at them without slowing.

"What the hell is he doing here?" Russ whispered, almost hissing the words. He searched her eyes for a moment, and then looked away, as if bracing himself for the answer.

"I have *no* idea," Anne insisted.

His eyes narrowed.

"And I'm supposed to believe that? Think about how far we are from Earth, how many colonies there are now, and how few people had any interest in volunteering to come here in the first place. You want me to believe that this guy you used to sleep with just showed up here? *Here*?"

Anne felt her face flush. Her heart slammed against her ribcage, and she could feel her pulse throbbing in her temples. She took a step forward and punched Russ in the shoulder.

"Hey, what the fu—" he started.

She poked him in the chest once, then again.

"You get your head together, Russell," she hissed back. "Has your brain become so fuzzy after all these years out here that you've lost the ability to think rationally? How the hell would I know anything about what Demian's doing? I haven't had any contact with him since we left Earth." She stepped back and looked at him. "What do you think? That I've been carrying on some kind of intergalactic romance? Sure, that makes sense—its only thirty-nine light years away." She paused, then added, "Are you out of your damn mind?"

Russ just stared at her, fuming with anger and frustration. But then the words sank in, and he ran his hands over the stubble on his cheeks.

"No," he admitted. "Of course not… that's just—"

"Crazy."

"—stupid," he said. "But if this is a coincidence… now *that's* crazy."

Anne took his hand, ran her thumb over the ridges of his knuckles in an almost unconscious gesture. She knew it calmed him, and did it without even thinking, just as he barely recognized the effect it had. Their marriage included a thousand such comfortable intimacies.

"I'm not going to lie to you, Russ," Anne said calmly. "I'm delighted that Demian's here. We have friends in Hadley's Hope, but it's just such an unexpected pleasure to encounter someone who knows me well. Demian and I were together once, but before that we were friends for a long time. Real friends. He's a good man, and I want to learn about what he's done with his life since I saw him last…

"But you're my husband."

Russ exhaled, turned and slumped against the wall.

"I'm sort of an idiot, right?"

Anne smiled softly. "Sort of?"

Suddenly they heard giggles echoing down the main corridor, and then the sound of running feet. Together they turned and watched as several of the colony's children raced past the mouth of the maintenance corridor, scraps of paper in hand. Most of the children were seven years old or less, a band of tiny marauders who darted along in duos and trios. Anne saw the flaming red hair of Luisa Cantrell and then the familiar blond mane of their six-year-old, Rebecca.

"Newt!" she called to her daughter.

The little girl skidded to a halt. As she turned toward the maintenance corridor, she was nearly knocked over by her older brother, Tim.

"Rebecca, what are you—"

Newt smacked his chest.

"Look out, dummy," she said, walking over to her mother and father. "What are you guys doing here?"

Russ grinned. "We needed a private place for some messy kissing."

"Eeewww!" Newt cried, but she followed it with a little giggle. "You guys are so disfusting."

"Disgusting," Tim corrected, rolling his eyes.

Newt nodded. "Exactly."

"You're so embarrassing," Tim told his parents. He had the same blond hair as his sister, but at nearly ten, he had begun to look less like the little boy he had once been.

"We do our best," Anne told him.

Several other children ran past, including Tim's friend Aaron, who shouted out to him that Tim and Newt were going to lose.

"Tim, come on," Newt pleaded, trying to haul her brother away, anxious to return to whatever havoc they were wreaking.

"What are you all doing?" Russ asked. "Aside from running around like lunatics?"

"Scavenger hunt," Tim said as Newt took him by the hand and dragged him back into the main corridor. "Bye!" he called over his shoulder.

Russ shook his head in amusement as he watched the kids rush off. Despite whatever tensions had been growing between them the past few years, Anne's heart still melted when she saw how much her husband loved their children.

"Hey," she said, squeezing his hand as she rose up to kiss his cheek. She stared into his eyes. "There's nothing to worry about, okay? Absolutely nothing. This is home for us, and we're strong together, you and me. Our family is safe and sound."

Russ smiled. "Safe and sound," he said.

Yet she couldn't help noticing a trace of sadness in his eyes. As glad as she had been to see Demian, she knew her husband would continue to be haunted by the presence of her ex.

He let her hand slip from his.

"Hungry?"

"Starving, actually," she confessed. "My appetite's returned."

They walked together to the mess hall, hands by their sides, not quite touching. Russ grew quiet, and Anne could feel the frisson of lingering tension between them. Doubts and fears coalesced, pushing them apart.

Safe and sound, she told herself, not sure if it was a vow or a plea.

DATE: 10 JUNE, 2179
TIME: 1337

The marine driving the heavy-crawler was an aging jarhead named Aldo Crowley. He had skin like leather and gray in the stubble of his buzzcut, but the bright glint in his copper eyes suggested that he might not be as old as he looked.

He was. Aldo Crowley had turned forty-one in January. He was a grunt from a family of grunts, neither smart nor ambitious enough to rise above sergeant, and busted back down to corporal every time he disobeyed the orders of superior officers far greener than he'd been on his first day in uniform.

Brackett learned all of this in the first sixty seconds of the conversation he'd had with Julisa Paris about which members of the squad to bring on the rescue mission. Crowley was the first person she'd suggested, followed by a couple of hard-eyed privates named Chenovski and Hauer, who'd earned a rep for keeping their shit together when a situation turned ugly.

The captain took Lt. Paris with him as well, and the first three marines he could lay eyes on in the frantic moments of preparation—Nguyen, Pettigrew, and Stamovich.

"Not sure why you brought me with you, Captain," Paris said.

Brackett glanced around the vast interior of the heavy-crawler. The others were lined up on benches along the forward compartment. The back of the vehicle was used for equipment storage and cargo space.

He looked at Lt. Paris. With the rumble of the heavy-crawler's engines, and the way it rattled as it churned across Acheron's terrain, none of the others could have heard him if he'd replied. But what would he have said? That he wanted her there because he trusted her, though he'd only known her a few hours? That she knew the topography and the marines and the nature of the atmospheric storms? Any of those admissions would convey a kind of weakness.

Instead he turned the question around.

"Do you have concerns about Sergeant Coughlin's ability to command in our absence?"

Paris furrowed her brow. "None whatsoever!"

"Good, then."

She studied him a moment, the heavy-crawler rocking them back and forth, and then she turned away, trying to peer through the windshield ahead. Visibility had been shitty from the moment they'd rolled out of Hadley's Hope, and it had only gotten worse as they drove toward Processor Six. Aldo had an array of instruments on the dash that provided radar and thermography readings of the terrain ahead. Even so, Brackett had no idea how the guy could see anything at all.

On the bench beside him was an exo-mask. The black masks with their bulbous goggle-eyes made him think of giant, nightmarish insects. They were generally used for brief exposure on planets and moons where the atmosphere had toxins, but was otherwise suitable for humans. Exo-masks were commonly utilized during the worst of Acheron's storms, too, just to keep the grit out of eyes and mouths, making it easier to see and breathe.

"Tell me something," Brackett said, trying to break up the ice that was forming between himself and his lieutenant. "Has anyone ever asked why marines are sent along on these survey excursions? Is it as simple as free labor, or are our people supposed to keep the surveyors from slacking off on the job?"

"I did ask, when I first got here," Paris said. "My first CO on Acheron told me it'd been commonplace since the science team first arrived—we're talking twelve or thirteen years ago, now. But the surveyors aren't just taking samples and mapping topography."

Brackett arched an eyebrow.

"What the hell else could they be doing out on this rock?"

Lt. Paris cast a wary glance at Stamovich and the others who sat across from them. She tucked a stray short curl behind her ear.

"It's Weyland-Yutani, Captain," she said, as if that explained it all.

Brackett settled against the bench, his head bumping the wall as the heavy-crawler dipped into a shallow pit, and then climbed out of it. Maybe the involvement of Weyland-Yutani did explain it all. Standing orders from the corporation would include not only the study of the planetoid itself, but the company's ongoing interest in alien life, whether aboriginal or left behind by spacefaring races. Yet thirteen years after the science team's arrival, it seemed like a ridiculous idea.

If the surveyors had been likely to find anything of interest to their employers, surely they would have found it already. Maybe the Company was sending marines along for security, after all, just as a precaution.

He leaned forward, trying to catch a glimpse of anything at all through the windshield. Aldo never slowed down, no matter how much the heavy-crawler shook or how completely the storm blocked out any visibility.

"Can you see anything at all?" Brackett called to him, raising his voice to be heard over the vehicle's rumbling and the staccato scrape of the windblown debris against its shell.

Aldo glanced back at him.

"That's the trick, Captain," he replied. "You've just got to accept that there *is* nothing to see, and then you're all right!"

Brackett shook his head. "Why the hell did they put a colony on this damn moon to begin with?"

On the opposite bench, Stamovich caught the question and spoke up.

"The rest of the universe needed a place they could point to when things turned nasty and say, 'It could be worse—we could be on Acheron!'"

Nguyen and Pettigrew laughed at that, nodding in agreement. Stamovich high-fived Pettigrew, but the rest of the team Brackett had chosen for this mission didn't seem at all amused. He glanced at Chenovski and Hauer, saw the way they were averting their eyes, and then studied Stamovich.

The guy smiled thinly, an air of arrogance about him. Lt. Paris had told Brackett that Stamovich was loyal only to Sgt. Draper, but now he began to see that there was a deep divide among his squad, and it worried him. That kind of fractiousness in the ranks could get marines killed.

The heavy-crawler tilted hard to the left, and the engine roared as it climbed out of whatever pit they'd rolled through. As they leveled off, Aldo hit the brakes. The crawler skidded in the dust, rocking back and forth for a moment. He locked the transmission, and then turned in his seat to look back at Brackett.

"This is it, Cap," Aldo said. "But I'd make it quick if I were you."

"Is the storm getting worse?" Lt. Paris asked.

Aldo gave a tired laugh. "Nah. The processor's on fire."

9

OTTO'S WISH

DATE: 10 JUNE, 2179
TIME: 1341

Brackett swore and pushed forward, jamming himself between the front seats so he could peer out the windshield.

Off to their right, in the wind-driven swirl of grit, he could see the dark tower of Processor Six. Even from inside the heavy-crawler he could hear the groan and rattle of its core and vents, a kind of mechanical shriek. Black smoke poured out of the vents on top of the unit, and he saw the orange flicker of flames from inside them.

"Son of a…"

He grabbed his exo-mask.

"Move out!" he bellowed. "This thing could blow any minute, and I don't want to be here when it does!"

Aldo stayed in the driver's seat and Brackett ordered Pettigrew to stay inside the heavy-crawler—always good to keep someone back to play cavalry if things went from bad to worse. The rear hatch of the crawler could be lowered to the ground as a ramp, but in the midst of the storm, they exited through a side door and slid it quickly shut behind them.

Masks in place, Brackett and Paris led the other three marines through the blowing garbage, staggering against the wind. One step after another they made their way toward the atmosphere processor. Even inside his exo-mask, Brackett felt as if he were suffocating.

"Listen to that!" Nguyen called.

Brackett listened. Banging and grinding noises came from inside the processor. Every instinct told him to get the hell away from the groaning tower, but the noise bothered him much less than the stinking chemical smoke the storm swept their way.

"Have you started to rethink accepting this post?" Lt. Paris shouted beside him, her voice muffled and almost lost in the gale.

Brackett said nothing. He didn't like to lie.

They hit the entrance seconds later. Stamovich reached it first and released the latch. The wind blew the door in with a clang and Nguyen barreled inside. Brackett knew they were friends of Sgt. Draper's, eager to make sure their friend was all right, so he didn't worry about who had led the way.

Out of the raging storm, the noise level dropped so dramatically that he felt for a moment as if he'd gone partly deaf. Then Chenovski slammed the metal door closed behind them and the captain flinched in the gloom. Only dim emergency lights provided pulsing illumination. Red warnings flickered all over the core, and a cloud of thin black smoke filled the tower, thicker overhead.

Brackett pulled off his mask and glanced upward, but could not see whatever was burning up top.

"Draper! Yousseff!" Paris shouted, and all of the marines glanced around.

There were signs of the stranded team—jackets, a pair of goggles, and strangely enough, a boot—but nothing human in view. The core thundered, shaking so hard that the bolts locking it to the floor seemed to be trying to pull themselves out of their holes. One of the ascension ladders glimmered in red zoetrope shadows on the wall to the right.

"Marv! Sing out, ya bastard!" Stamovich barked. "Where are you?"

Brackett started around the core, nodding to Nguyen to proceed. They hadn't taken two steps when they heard a reply.

"Here! Watch yourselves!"

Then another voice, screaming.

"Send us home!"

Brackett hadn't run another three steps before he saw the burly bearded man lying on the ground. Blood streaked his face and caked in the hair on the left side of his head. His eyes were open and one hand rose to wave them back—or perhaps in a plea for help. He clutched his left leg, and Brackett realized the angle of the limb was all wrong.

Broken bone, and a bad one.

"Curtis!" Lt. Paris shouted.

Three more steps, and the whole scene came into view—it was the last thing Brackett had expected. He drew his weapon before his mind even had time to completely make sense of the dynamics playing out in front of him.

A ginger-haired man with mad eyes stood with his back to the wall, holding a female marine from behind with one arm, choking her as he held what had to be her own gun to her temple. A dozen feet away, deeper in the oily, flashing red shadows of the processor, another marine stood with his feet planted, his gun aimed at the ginger man and his hostage.

It wasn't hard for Brackett to figure out who the players were. If the guy with the broken leg was Curtis Finch, this had to be—

"Otto!" he roared. "Let Private Yousseff go!"

Draper—who else could it have been?—cast a quick glance at the new arrivals, but didn't dare take his focus off of Otto Finch for longer than that. He shuffled a bit to his right, moving toward the other marines. Brackett and Stamovich were side by side now, and rushed up to take position beside him. The rest found cover.

"Back off!" Otto screamed. His voice melded terror with the timbre of a child throwing a tantrum, and he stared around at the newly arrived marines as if the wrong twitch would make him explode. "Stay back or I'll kill her! I don't want to… I didn't ask for this, but I swear I'll do it!"

"Draper, report!" Brackett snapped.

The sergeant glared at him, then shot a questioning look at Stamovich.

"New CO," Stamovich called.

"I've got eyes, Stam," Draper sneered. He took a step nearer to Otto, who shrieked until he moved back again.

Curtis Finch gestured to Lt. Paris, and she raced over to kneel beside him.

"Sergeant Draper, report!" Brackett ordered.

"What does it look like, sir?" Draper barked. "You need me to spell this shit out for you?"

"He wants off!" Yousseff shouted. Her expression betrayed no fear, but Brackett could see it in her eyes. Colonial Marines were tough as nails, some tougher, but no warrior wanted to die a hostage. It looked as if she was having trouble breathing.

"What the hell do you mean, *off*?" Lt. Paris called.

"Off the planet!" Yousseff snapped, then she coughed.

"Just send us home!" Otto shrieked, wild eyes darting back and forth, tears flowing. Snot dripped down over his lips. "I don't care about money anymore! I don't need a dollar of what we've earned up here! Just take me and Curtis and put us on a ship for home!"

The whole tower shook, as if the ground shuddered beneath them. A crack like thunder exploded in the air, and a fissure opened in the shell of the core, black smoke billowing out. An explosion rocked the unit high overhead and Brackett looked up to see orange flames gouting out into the swirling debris of the storm.

A quarter of the roof had just blown off.

"You got it!" Brackett said urgently. "Whatever you want, Otto! You want to go home, I'll make sure you get there!"

"Captain—" Draper warned.

"How do I know?" Otto screamed. "How can I believe *anyone* in this damned place?"

The grinding inside the core grew louder still. Brackett wracked his brain, trying to figure out what he could possibly say that would calm Otto Finch. The man had experienced some kind of psychotic break. There was no way he would believe any promise Brackett might make about getting him and his brother off-planet.

His brother.

Brackett glanced across and saw Paris kneeling with Curtis Finch. Sweat beaded on the man's pale forehead. From this angle, Brackett could see a small puddle on the floor beside him, where Curtis had vomited from the pain of his shattered leg. He looked desperate, gripping Paris's sleeve as if pleading with her.

Is this guy crazy, too?

One way to find out. Brackett ran from cover and slid to his knees beside the lieutenant. In the process he dropped his exo-mask.

Paris turned to him.

"Whatever you're going to do, Captain, do it fast," she said. "Curtis says we've just got minutes before this place tears itself apart."

Otto started shouting again. Brackett saw Draper motion to Stamovich and Pettigrew, who each eased a bit closer, as if they didn't really believe that Otto would kill Sgt. Yousseff. The wild-eyed ginger choked her harder, and screamed at them to stop.

"One more step and she's dead!" he screamed.

"Otto, listen to me!" Brackett said, rising to his feet again. "You won't just be killing Sergeant Yousseff—you'll be killing all of us, yourself and your brother included! Curtis says we've only got minutes before the core explodes. Look around, man! Half the roof is gone, all this fire and smoke… we're dead if we don't go now—"

"Take Curtis out!" Otto shouted, fresh tears cutting clean lines in the soot on his cheeks.

Brackett holstered his gun and held up his hands.

"We all need to go," he said. "Not just your brother."

"Take him out of here!" Otto screamed.

Brackett stared a moment at the profound fear in Otto's eyes, and then nodded, turning to Paris.

"Get him out."

He glanced around. "Nguyen! Hauer! Help Lt. Paris bring Curtis to the crawler!"

As the marines hustled to obey, slinging their weapons, Otto went still. Yousseff tensed as if to attempt to escape his grasp, and Otto jammed the gun against her temple.

"What are you doing?" Otto screamed, not at Yousseff but at the marines moving his brother. "Leave him alone!"

Lt. Paris snapped quiet orders to Hauer and Nguyen. One of the men rushed to a control panel, yanked it open and began to tear it from its hinge as the other helped Paris work Curtis out of his jacket.

"We're going to get him out of here, but we've got to stabilize his broken leg first," Brackett called to Otto, sweat running down the back of his neck. The temperature inside Processor Six continued to climb. "It's a bad break, Otto. He can't walk! Do you want your brother to die here?"

Torn, Otto stared. For several seconds he squeezed his eyes closed and then the words erupted from his mouth.

"Fine! Take him out!"

Paris nodded to Nguyen and Hauer, who worked hurriedly to slip the small metal door underneath Curtis's legs. Then they wrapped his jacket around both legs, tying them to the metal. Curtis cried out several times, and when Nguyen tightened the jacket, he screamed and fell unconscious. Even over the roar and rumble of the failing processor, that scream crawled under Brackett's skin.

"Go, go!" he snapped.

Hauer, Nguyen, and Paris hoisted Curtis off the ground and carried him in a rush toward the exit. If he hadn't already been unconscious, Brackett had no doubt the screams would have been hideous as his broken bones ground together.

"Captain!" Draper barked. "We don't have time—"

Brackett held up a hand to silence him, turning to Otto. He didn't like the look of Yousseff, whose gaze had begun to droop.

"We're out of time, Otto," Brackett said. "We're going to help Curtis, and we can help you too. I will do all I can to get you both sent home, but you've got to let Sergeant Yousseff go right—"

"I need to hear it from the Company!" Otto shouted, his voice cracking. "I want their guarantee!" The desperation in his eyes spoke of a profound fear that Brackett knew he could never assuage. Otto behaved like a man in a nightmare from which he could not wake. But he wasn't sleeping. This was all real, and deadly.

"Otto, we've got two or three minutes!" Brackett called. "Let

Yousseff go now, or we're all going to die in here!"

"Captain Brackett, we're out of options!" Stamovich shouted.

"Damn right we are," Draper snapped.

He shot Otto Finch through the left eye, blowing blood and skull fragments and gray matter onto the wall. In death, Otto's fingers twitched and the gun in his hand went off. Yousseff shouted and pushed back, but the corpse's hand had already begun to jerk away and the bullet went astray, firing up into the smoke-filled darkness overhead.

Brackett stormed across the shuddering floor as the whole processor rocked and clanked around them.

"Dammit, Draper, what the hell was that?"

"Taking action, sir!" Draper called. "You said yourself we don't have time to waste."

Pettigrew and Stamovich nodded in agreement. Furious, Brackett felt his hands close into fists, but he forced them open again. Draper would have to wait until later.

"Move out!" he shouted, gesturing to the rest of them—Pettigrew, Chenovski, and Stamovich—as Yousseff staggered away from Otto's corpse, trying to catch her breath. "But we're taking the body back with us! His brother's going to want to bury him!"

"Screw that!" Draper barked. "Friggin' lunatic nearly killed Yousseff. We're not risking our lives for the guy!"

Despite the mounting danger—the seconds he could feel ticking away on his internal clock—Brackett stared in astonishment as Draper tapped Stamovich and the two of them broke into a trot for the door, with Pettigrew hesitating only a second before following.

Son of a bitch is mine, Brackett thought.

"Captain!" a voice called.

Brackett turned to see Chenovski trying to lift Otto Finch's corpse from the floor. Blood and gore had already baked onto the hot metal wall, but the pool on the ground around the dead man had widened and Chenovski slipped a bit as he tried to hoist Otto up. Brackett ran toward them. Something moved to his left and he glanced over to see Yousseff, who had at last recovered her breath.

Together, the three of them picked Otto up the way the others had carried Curtis, and they lurched for the way out. The whole processor seemed to tilt and they careened off the frame of the open door before bursting out into the darkness and the shrieking grit-storm. The wind swept them aside and they bent into it. Without his exo-mask, Brackett could barely make out the heavy-crawler. The three marines who had disobeyed his direct order were trudging toward it, fighting the gale. Seeing those escaping figures gave him additional motivation, and he shouted to Yousseff and Chenovski.

They made it to the crawler twelve long seconds behind Draper and the others. Aldo met them at the back of the vehicle, where the ramp was down, and helped Chenovski drag Otto's corpse inside, placing him beside his unconscious brother.

"Why did you help?" Brackett asked Yousseff, shouting to be heard over the storm.

Yousseff stared at him. "You gave an order."

Brackett knew that wasn't the real answer. Yousseff was one of Draper's cronies, or she wouldn't have been picked to accompany the Finchs.

"Let's move, Captain!" Aldo shouted, waving them along as he ran back toward the driver's door.

A pair of explosions came from Processor Six. Yousseff turned to stare at the tower, and Brackett followed her gaze toward the gout of flame rising from the shattered roof of the thing. He put a hand on her back, gave a little shove, and Yousseff seemed to snap from her momentary trance. They ran around up the ramp in a stoop, slamming down into seats even as the door ratcheted shut and the ramp retracted.

"Strap in!" Aldo shouted, and the crawler lunged forward, the grit-storm scouring its shell as it rumbled across the rugged terrain.

Brackett found a seat, glanced across the heavy-crawler, and realized he was directly opposite Draper. All eyes in the passenger section of the vehicle were upon him, the other marines wondering how he would react to Draper's insubordination.

Remaining silent, the captain ground his teeth so hard his jaw hurt. His first instinct was to put the bastard in the brig the second they returned to Hadley's Hope, and keep him there until he could arrange for Draper to be transferred away from Acheron. The trouble was that he didn't know how much backup he'd get from his own superiors. If he put Draper in the brig and then had to release him, it would undermine his authority even further than Draper's actions already had.

"Listen to me, you son of a bitch—" Brackett began, leaning forward and pointing.

At that moment, Processor Six exploded. The blast rocked the crawler to the left. Hauer and Pettigrew fell into the space between the facing rows of seats. Even muffled by the storm, the thunderous noise of the explosion made them all wince, and Yousseff covered her ears. Something crashed down on the crawler's roof, and Aldo swerved to avoid a flaming chunk of metal that struck in front of them like a meteorite.

Stamovich swore loudly, and immediately the others began to taunt him for showing fear. That lasted only seconds, as they all returned their attention to the silent hostility crackling in the space that separated Brackett and Draper.

"You were saying?" Draper asked, his voice dry, tone full of disrespect.

"I'm saying it's been an ugly first day at my new command," Brackett said. "But I'm willing to bet the ugliness is just getting started for you, Sergeant. You, Stamovich, and Pettigrew are confined to quarters upon our return, and you'll stay there until further notice. If you think there won't be consequences for your actions today, I can only assume that your previous CO gave you the impression that rank meant nothing out here on the edge of oblivion.

"I'm here to disabuse you of that notion."

The corner of Draper's mouth lifted in what might have been a smirk, but otherwise he had no reply. The others were also wise enough not to speak.

The crawler rolled on.

* * *

They were halfway back to the colony, the storm at last beginning to subside, when Julisa Paris crawled from the rear of the crawler and slid into a seat beside Chenovski.

"Sorry, Captain," she said. "Hauer did what he could. Shock and blood loss took a toll. Curtis Finch is dead."

Brackett let out a heavy sigh and laid his head back against the juddering wall of the crawler.

"Crazy prick wanted off the planet, him and his brother both," Stamovich muttered. "Looks like he got his wish."

"How is that getting his wish?" Chenovski asked, sneering at him. "They're never getting off Acheron now. They'll be buried here. Whoever they've got back on Earth will learn they're dead, and just carry on. This place is so far away from home that these colonists might as well be dead already, in the minds of the people they left behind. If this was more than just a post for me—if I knew I was here permanently—I'd lose my shit just like Otto did."

They rolled on for a minute or two, all of them just taking that in. The marines began to stare at their feet, or tried to see out through the windshield, though Aldo waved for them to stay seated.

Yousseff nudged Brackett with an elbow. He'd been aware of her beside him, but had been too preoccupied with his anger to do more than acknowledge her.

"You asked me why I helped you carry him," she said quietly, so that over the roar of the engine and the whoosh of the diminishing storm, only Brackett could hear.

"It wasn't just you obeying an order," he replied, and it wasn't a question.

Yousseff dropped her gaze a moment, and then turned to face him.

"I could feel his fear," she said. "Otto could be a pain in the ass, but I liked him well enough. The guy just fell apart, Captain. He didn't want to hurt me—he was just terrified. I hate that it ended like this."

Brackett narrowed his gaze.

"What could scare anyone that much?"

Yousseff shrugged. "I don't think it was anything real. Nothing tangible. Acheron just got under his skin. He convinced himself there was something on this damned moon for him to fear, something that was gonna kill him. He was afraid he was gonna die if he didn't get off this rock."

Brackett glanced at Draper.

"I guess he was right. But it wasn't Acheron he should've been afraid of."

10

THE COST

DATE: 10 JUNE, 2179
TIME: 1648

Newt never minded being thought of as a child. She knew some kids who became very angry when grownups dismissed them as *little*, but Newt considered that a pretty silly thing to get mad about. After all, they *were* little. It wasn't as if the grownups were trying to insult them with the truth.

Really, she wasn't in any hurry to grow up at all. Adults were grumpy a lot. They got stressed out over things that didn't seem that important—sometimes about disagreements they assumed were going to happen, but which had not happened quite yet. Her parents were the perfect example. Lately they'd seemed all worried about things Newt freely admitted that she didn't quite understand.

What she did know was that there seemed no point to any of it. Stress made them both tense and edgy, and it crackled between them like that invisible energy that always gave her shocks when she dug through freshly laundered clothes in search of matching socks.

Static, Newt thought, proud of herself. *Of course—that's the word.*

The static electricity that sizzled unseen in the air between her parents over the past few months had kept growing stronger, but it had never been as bad as today. Newt had been in their quarters doing her homework, and had seen the way they navigated their way around the rooms, sometimes avoiding each other… and she'd had to get out of there.

Tim had been playing full-immersion *Burning Gods* and had ignored her when she'd asked if he wanted to go to the kitchen and see if Bronagh Flaherty would give them a freeze-pop. So she had gone without him.

Newt liked freeze-pops. Her favorite flavor was cherry, although there was a cherry tree in the greenhouse, and after tasting the fruit she had never understood why cherry freeze-pops were called cherry, when they tasted nothing like actual cherries.

Lost in such thoughts, she nearly ran right into the man who came hurriedly around the corner near the administration offices.

"Whoa!" he said, holding out his hands.

Only when Newt looked up at him, protecting her cherry freeze-pop from the imminent collision, did she realize it was Capt. Brackett. When he recognized her, the captain smiled.

"Hey! Rebecca, right?" he said, as if he'd somehow solved a riddle. Grownups were so weird. He had a nice smile, though.

"Newt," she said. "Everybody calls me—"

"Right, sorry!" Capt. Brackett said. "And I'm sorry I nearly ran you down. Just too many things on my mind, but that's no excuse for not paying attention." He looked down. "Is that a strawberry freeze-pop?"

He wore a smile, but it seemed tense to Newt, as if he wanted to be kind to her at the same time as he wanted to be angry at someone else. It seemed to create its own kind of static, a sort of cloud of frustration that surrounded him.

"Cherry," she answered. "It's my favorite."

"Cherry's nice," he allowed. "Do they have grape down there, as well?"

"If you ask Bronagh in the kitchen, she'll make you one, even if they don't have them in the freezer."

Capt. Brackett nodded as if this news pleased him very much.

"I'll have to do that," he said. "She sounds like a nice person."

Newt nodded. "Very nice."

He studied her for a second.

"You look so much like your mom. Do people tell you that?"

"It's because I have crazy hair sometimes. My mom has crazy hair pretty much all the time, but mine is only crazy sometimes. I have a doll—my brother says I'm too old for dolls, and maybe I am, but it's just one doll. Her name is Casey. She has crazy hair, too."

Capt. Brackett gave a soft laugh, and Newt noticed that some of the static around him seemed to have gone away. He didn't seem as stressed as he had been when he'd almost crashed into her, coming around the corner.

"Maybe I could meet Casey sometime," he said. "And maybe you could introduce me to Bronagh, too."

Newt smiled. "I can do that."

"Great! I'll track you down later." He looked down the hall. "Right now I've got to go talk to Mr. Simpson."

She gave him a thumbs up and bit the top off her freeze-pop. The icy cherry rush froze her teeth and made her talk a little funny.

"Okeydoke," she said. Her father always said that. "See ya."

"See ya, Newt," he replied, and he started past her, walking toward the command block with his shoulders set in a way that made him seem angry.

"Captain Brackett?" she called after him.

He glanced over his shoulder at her.

"Yeah?"

"You look like you're having a bad first day. I hope it gets better."

Capt. Brackett gave that same soft laugh and nodded.

"Me too, kid. Me too."

Brackett found Al Simpson in his office. Several people had given him strange looks as he strode purposefully toward the colonial administrator's closed door, but only after he had knocked and swung it open did he understand their wary expressions.

Simpson wasn't alone. He snapped his head around at Brackett's intrusion, bushy eyebrows knitted in irritation.

"Can I help you, Captain?"

Brackett stared at him, hand still on the knob, and then took a closer look at the other two people in the office—Dr. Reese and Dr. Hidalgo, the leaders of the colony's Weyland-Yutani science team. The three of them looked to be in the middle of something, but what could be more important than the destruction of Processor Six, and the deaths of two of their surveyors?

"I thought you'd want a report on today's events," Brackett said, without trying to hide the accusatory bite of his words. "Two men died, in case you hadn't heard."

Simpson's gaze went even colder.

"I'd heard, yes," he said. "We were just discussing the failures in maintenance that led to the processor malfunctioning. Making sure nothing like that happens again is my top priority. The cost of replacing Processor Six alone is going to be—"

"Right," Brackett said. "The *cost*."

Dr. Hidalgo glanced away, unnerved by the insinuation, but Dr. Reese stiffened and raised his chin as if preparing for a fight.

"The Finch brothers knew the risks they were taking every time they went out there," Dr. Reese said. "If you wish to remonstrate with Mr. Simpson for his attention to the bottom line, I'll remind you that he is doing his job. Perhaps, Captain, you ought to worry more about your own."

Brackett thought of a dozen ways to wipe the smug expression off the doctor's face. He forced himself to take a deep breath.

"That's one of the things I came to talk about, actually," he said, turning his focus back to Simpson. "We need to get some clarity on exactly what the job is meant to be for the marines stationed with this colony. Before I address that, however, protocol requires that I deliver a report on what went down out there—and that's what I came to do."

Simpson sat back in his chair, tapping his fingers on his gleaming silver and glass alloy desk. The whole office was beautifully appointed with sleek, coldly metallic furniture and swirling light fixtures, unlike anything else Brackett had seen since arriving at

Hadley's Hope. This elegance had to be a perk of the job, and yet Simpson had let the debris of his work pile up on every surface—dirty coffee mugs, cast-aside sweaters, tubes of soil samples, thick old paper files capped by more than one computer tablet. The man treated his surroundings shabbily, and Brackett could only assume that he treated his people the same way.

"Type it up and forward it to me," Simpson said, his fingers ceasing their drumming. "I'll get to it."

The tone implied a dismissal, but Brackett wasn't ready to be dismissed.

"You have two men dead, Simpson. You're not going to be able to sort out the events leading to their deaths without a full report—"

Dr. Reese sighed heavily, as if he tired of dealing with a simpleton. "We've got a full report, Captain."

Brackett cocked his head. "But I didn't file any—"

"From Sergeant Draper," Simpson interrupted.

For a second or two, Brackett could only stare at them. Then he scoffed and shook his head as the significance of the statement sank in.

"Draper is confined to quarters," he said.

"Understood," Simpson replied. "But to my knowledge, you gave no orders that restricted his ability to receive visitors. You weren't immediately available upon your return—"

"I was debriefing my team," Brackett said, standing a bit straighter, his uniform chafing against his skin, "and seeing to the offloading of your two dead colonists. But I expect you knew that."

"Sergeant Draper's report was very thorough, and certainly sufficient for our needs," Dr. Reese said. "I'm sure there's a conversation that we all need to have, Captain Brackett—a conversation about the way operations are conducted here, and how the science team works hand in hand with the Colonial Marines—but I'm afraid it's going to have to wait until later. The destruction of Processor Six leaves us—"

Brackett coughed to clear his throat, which had the advantage of silencing the doctor for a moment.

"Yeah, doc," he said, "we'll discuss it over tea. Meantime, there are a couple of things I want to get straight, and right now. Things that *won't* wait." He held up a finger. "First off, from this moment forward you are to have no direct contact with any of my marines, aside from a thank you if they're polite enough to hold the door open for you in the hallway."

Brackett peered at Simpson, and then at Dr. Hidalgo, who seemed very uncomfortable.

"Captain, you must understand..." she began.

"Must I?" Brackett said. He shook his head. "No, doctor, I don't think so. My squad answers to me, and to me alone—and *you* don't get reports from Draper or anyone else. Sergeant Draper is a problem child. There's always at least one. But from now on I'm going to make him *my* problem."

"Noted," Simpson said, smoothing his shirt over his round belly.

Brackett studied the administrator for a second, then narrowed his gaze as he turned to Reese and Hidalgo. The birthmark on Reese's jaw and throat had turned so dark that it was almost purple.

"What about you two? Simpson may keep the lights on around here, but it's clear that the company has more influence than the government. So I need to hear it from you, as well. Is my message clear enough?"

Dr. Reese glared at him, the man's small eyes glittering with contempt.

"Quite clear," Dr. Hidalgo said.

Reese didn't argue with her. Brackett would've liked a more concrete response from him, given that he was the senior member of the science team, but his silence would have to be enough... for the moment.

"Good. That brings us to the other thing."

Al Simpson tucked his shirt in a bit tighter, as if it would give him greater authority.

"Can't this wait?"

Brackett just ignored him, and remained focused on the scientists. "I'm told that it's standard procedure for Colonial Marines to accompany your survey teams into the field," he said. "That practice ends immediately."

Dr. Hidalgo flinched. "You can't do that!"

"Excuse me, doctor, but I certainly can." He stared at her, surprised at the sudden change that had come over her. She had seemed uncomfortable with Reese's attitude before, but now she'd adopted a similarly flinty air.

Brackett figured they saw him as some bristle-headed lunk in a uniform. Simpson and the scientists thought they were keeping him in the dark, but it didn't take a genius to understand why they wanted marines along on these excursions. Not once he'd had a little time to mull it over.

Most of the major scientific advancements of the past century had been made by organizations that had acquired and studied specimens from a variety of alien life forms. Sometimes it was a government, but most of the time it was a corporation.

Weyland-Yutani had long been on a crusade to find and utilize, monetize, or weaponize any alien species they could get their hands on. The company's efforts were hardly secret. Humanity had learned so much just from their Arcturian trading partners.

Brackett couldn't deny the value of encounters with alien life, but the Colonial Marines had never been meant to play security guards for a bunch of civilian surveyors… or to mount rescue missions for freelance wildcatters.

It had to stop.

"You're right, Captain—it *has* been our standard procedure," Simpson acknowledged. "It's been that way since the beginning of the colony. The marines provide security, and support for—"

Brackett held up a hand to stop him.

"No, we don't. This isn't something we're going to discuss. When I received my orders to take up the post of commander at Hadley's Hope, no mention was made of any such arrangement. The Colonial Marines aren't company employees, Mr. Simpson." He paused, then continued. "As soon as I leave here, I will transmit a query to my superiors. It will take approximately a week for a message to reach Earth, and for me to receive any reply. If I'm instructed to cooperate with your demands, I will of course comply with those orders. But unless and until I receive instructions along those lines, there will be no more marine escorts on these survey missions."

Dr. Reese sniffed, his face like stone.

"I don't think you'll like the answer you receive."

Brackett shrugged. "It's not up to me to like or dislike my orders, Doc. I'm a marine. For the moment, that means I don't have to give a shit what you think."

DATE: 10 JUNE, 2179
TIME: 1844

Hadley's Hope had been designed for communal living. The dining hall—what the marines called the "mess"—served three meals a day, and Anne Jorden would be the first to admit that the men and women who worked there were a hell of a lot more talented in the kitchen than she would ever be.

Russ had some skill with food prep—equal parts inspiration and intuition—but at her best Anne had never been able to do more with a meal than follow basic directions. Even so, at least twice a week the Jordens had a family dinner in their quarters, just the four of them sitting around the little table or sprawled on chairs in their family room.

Most of the colonists took at least a few meals in private each week. Communal living had its pleasures, but everyone needed private time now and again. The trouble of late had been that every time she and Russ had downtime—either alone or with the kids—they found themselves at odds.

Anne loved her husband. She hadn't come halfway across the universe with him on a whim. But the years on Acheron had showed them that living in such a small community meant there was nowhere for their daydreams to take them. Back on Earth, if she was irritated with her mate, she could have fantasized about moving out, getting a cottage in the mountains, and meeting a man who would look at her the way Russ had when they were first dating.

She could still remember that look, the desire and mischief in his eyes.

Here, her dreams had nowhere to run. It made her impatient with him, and sometimes unforgiving.

Not tonight, she vowed, as she stirred the noodles and spices frying in the pan on the small stove. The smell wafted up and made her mouth water. Three kinds of peppers, a cupboard's array of herbs... she might not be the galaxy's greatest chef, but she had perfected this one dish, at least.

Too bad the kids hated it.

Anne sipped her wine as she stirred, and glanced over at Tim. Her son sat in a plush chair, low to the floor, and stared studiously at the small tablet in his hands. Anyone would have thought he was doing homework or reading a book, but she could see the small black buttons in his ears that indicated he was listening to something. He was either watching some kind of vid, or playing a game.

Another day she might have admonished him—tonight, she took another sip of wine, smiled, and stirred the spicy noodles.

Demian Brackett, she thought, her smile soft and full of memories.

No. Tonight wasn't the night to get into an argument with Russ.

She wasn't about to rush off and have an affair with Demian—there'd be nowhere on Acheron she could hide from the consequences of infidelity. But that didn't mean she couldn't muse on the idea for a while. A good man, if a tad too serious, Demian was as handsome as he'd ever been. If anything, the small creases in the dark skin at the edges of his eyes made him even more attractive.

Anne sipped her wine, letting her mind wander. Russ was irritated with Demian's presence. She had wanted to punch him for his childishness earlier in the day. But if she kept letting her thoughts drift in salacious directions, she had the feeling that tonight her husband would be reaping the benefits of her ex-boyfriend's arrival.

Lucky Russ, she thought. *Lucky Anne, too*, because despite their recent tensions, she had a strong, intelligent, handsome and courageous husband who loved their children more than his own life. Whatever they might argue about, she knew they would still be together when the dust settled. Russ Jorden was her scruffy, wild-eyed man, even when she wanted to smack him in the head.

The door latch rattled, and then she heard the familiar creak. Stirring the spicy noodles, she lowered the heat on the burner a bit and turned to smile at Russ as he stepped into their quarters.

"Hey, honey," she began. "Can I pour you a glass of—"

The pale, haunted look on his face froze her tongue.

"Annie..."

She clicked off the burner, a dreadful numbness spreading inside her.

"What is it, Russell?" she said. "I know that look. Crap, I hate that look."

He crossed toward her. Anne noticed Tim's head swiveling to follow him—young as he was, he too must have been troubled by his father's mournful expression. The door still hung wide, open to the corridor, and she wanted to tell Timmy to shut it, but then Russ took her in his arms and held her tightly. He sagged into her, a ship lowering its sails when it had reached safe harbor, and she ran her fingers through the hair at the back of his neck.

"Tell me," she breathed.

Russ sighed heavily, pressed his forehead to hers, and then stepped back to meet her gaze.

"I just ran into Nolan Cale and he gave me the news... Curtis and Otto are dead."

The news staggered her, weakened her knees.

"No," she managed to say, shaking her head. "That can't..."

Anne turned to lean on the stove, shutting her eyes against her grief as a wave of anger swept over her.

"Idiots," she said. She slammed her hand down on the stove, rattling the still-sizzling pan. "Those dumb sons of bitches!"

"Hey," Russ said, taking her arm. "You know it's not like that. They took shelter in Processor Six. They'd have been okay, but Otto went stir crazy. From what I'm hearing, he just... unraveled."

Anne stared at him.

"They shouldn't have been out there in the first place. Those two were always taking unnecessary risks—anything to try to get ahead."

"They were our friends," Russ reminded her.

"Doesn't mean they weren't foolish," Anne said, refusing to be mollified. "The worst atmo-storms can be predicted within hours. Maybe they couldn't have seen how bad this storm would get before they left this morning, but they knew it was going to be a rough day."

Russ took a step back, glancing at Tim, who kept his eyes glued firmly on his tablet.

"But they're dead, Anne. You're going to hate yourself later, for—"

"For what? For being angry because they didn't have to die?" She let out a long, shuddering, tearful breath and dropped her gaze, staring at the ground. "They *didn't* have to die."

Russ touched her arm, slid his warm hand along her skin.

"No, they didn't."

Anne looked up at him, wiping her eyes.

"We're just as ambitious as they were, but we've never taken risks like that. We take our kids out on surveying trips, Russ. Our *kids*. Some of the administrators think we're crazy, but anyone who's ever spent time out there, surveying in the grit and the wind, knows how to figure out when the really bad storms are likely to hit."

"Otto just lost it, hon," he said. "You know he's been on edge."

Anne stiffened, then slowly nodded.

"Falling apart, Russ. The guy was falling apart. I've been worried about him and I've been worried about you, ever since the two of you started spending so much time together, the past few months. Thinking dark thoughts. Wishing impossible wishes."

Russ winced, then shook his head, running a hand over his scruffy chin.

"Now?" he said. "You want to do this right now?"

Anne felt as if she couldn't breathe.

"I don't *ever* want to do this. That doesn't mean I'm going to pretend it doesn't bother me that you and Otto have spent months convincing each other that your lives would've been better if you'd never come to Acheron."

"Wouldn't they have?" Russ barked, throwing up his hands.

"Wouldn't things be better? For one thing, Otto and Curtis would still be alive!"

"You don't know that," she countered. "Otto was never the most stable—"

"Stop!"

"We came here because we dreamed of a life of discovery."

Russ rolled his eyes. "And how's that going for us so far?"

"We're on the far edge of the spread of human civilization," Anne said. "We have a good life. Make a decent living. Every night when I lay my head down, I think of all the people who would never have the courage to do what we've done!"

"None of them are stupid enough to take the risks we've taken."

"You have to take great risks to reap great rewards," Anne said, echoing the words he'd spoken when he had persuaded her to join the colony, years ago. Russ just cocked his head, staring at her as if she had grown two extra heads.

"When we go out on salvage runs, they control every step we take. They know where we are and what we're doing. Even if we found some artifacts, left there by indigenous life forms, or a vein of precious stone, they've got controls in place to cap what we can earn from any of it. That's not even real wildcatting… it's just risking our necks without the safeguards we've got when we're doing work for the company.

"And in all these years, what have we found of any real value? Nothing!" He glared at her. "We're wasting our time on this damned rock!"

Anne felt bile rise in the back of her throat. She wanted to be sick.

"I don't feel like I'm wasting my time here, Russell," she said. "I've got a happy little family and a circle of friends and a job that gives me the occasional surge of adrenaline. That's a good life."

"I didn't mean…" he said, then shook his head angrily. "That's not what I'm saying, and you know it."

Anne glanced at Tim, hunched over his tablet. No way the little black buds in his ears kept out his father's voice—not when Russ shouted.

"If you want to leave the colony so badly," she said quietly, "then do it. If you're that unhappy—"

"Oh, you'd love *that*, wouldn't you?" Russ said. "Perfect timing, now that Demian fucking Brackett has arrived!"

She glared at him. "Crap, you really are ten years old, you know that?"

"Play it off all you want, Anne, but I know you still have feelings for him. I can tell."

Anne covered her mouth with a hand. She didn't dare glance at Tim. What the hell was Russ thinking, having this conversation with their son in the room? They'd had plenty of disagreements with the kids around, but nothing like this. She only prayed that Tim was trying hard not to pay attention, that he had lost himself in whatever he was watching, reading, or playing, as he so often tended to do.

"You should stop now," she said.

Russ blinked and glanced back at Tim, understanding at last, but when he turned to Anne again, the anger still reddened his face.

"You're upset about Otto," she added. "So am I. Let's talk about this later."

"I'm upset, yes. My friend is gone. Otto may have been unstable, but that doesn't mean he wasn't right. This colony is a dead end for me—"

"For you?"

"For all of us."

Anne forced herself to breathe.

"If you want to go—"

"Fuck!" Russ shouted, throwing his arms up. He turned to storm out and they both looked at the door. Newt stood there, her mouth rimmed with a sticky red smear from her favorite popsicles. Her eyes were wide and full of pain and her lower lip trembled.

"Daddy's leaving?" she whispered.

Russ clenched and unclenched his hands, face etched with regret.

"Just for now, sweetheart," he said. "Just for now." Then he walked out.

Anne and Newt and Tim all stared at the door for a long moment, and then Newt ran into the corridor after him. Russ had turned left, probably heading to the rec center, but Newt didn't follow her father. She turned right, and vanished in an instant.

"Newt!" Anne called.

Tim shot up, plucking the buds from his ears and dropping his tablet onto the plush chair.

"I'll go after her," he said. Then he cast a hard look at his mother. "What is *wrong* with you two?"

Anne watched in silence as her son raced out into the hall in pursuit of his sister. She was left alone in the family quarters with her heart pounding in her ears.

The smell of cooking spices had gotten into her hair and her clothes, but she had lost her appetite.

11

NEW FRIENDS AND OLD

DATE: 10 JUNE, 2179
TIME: 1932

Brackett's quarters at Hadley's Hope were no more and no less than he'd expected.

A career in the Colonial Marines meant getting used to living a Spartan lifestyle. Bunk and sink, a chest of drawers, and a small closet if you were lucky. Living his life in uniform made it easier. On his off days, a plain t-shirt and regulation pants or sweatpants were all he needed, and he never had to worry about what he would be putting on—only whether or not he had clean laundry.

He never took a lot of personal items with him when he was reassigned. He had a photo-cube, a tablet full of music and thousands of books, his mother's dog tags, and a small wooden lion. It was a figurine carved by his father. These were the only pieces of his youth that he needed, just touchstones whose physical presence grounded him, so that even out here on the nascent edge of civilization, he was at home.

Brackett opened and closed the cabinets in the galley kitchen, saw glasses and plates and bowls. On the counter were a coffee maker and a toaster, and the sight made him smile. No matter how many things technology changed, certain others stayed the same. A couple of centuries after its introduction, a toaster was still necessary if you wanted to make toast properly. Sure, it had been improved, but it didn't play music for you or do research or boil your dinner—it made toast. In a strange way, he found that reassuring.

"Son of a bitch," he whispered, realizing just how exhausted he was.

Of course you're tired, he thought. On his way to Acheron, he'd had the fanciful idea that he'd arrive and meet the squad and the staff, settle in, have a nice meal, and just get to know everyone. Instead the day had started off ugly, and then turned deadly. He could still hear Otto Finch's desperate pleas as he walked across the anteroom and into his bedroom.

White sheets, white pillows, off-white walls, gray floor. A wave of familiar pleasure rolled over him and he sagged on his feet. Done. All he wanted was to put the grim day behind him and start over in the morning.

Brackett looked longingly at the bed. He needed to transmit a report to his superiors, and a request for clarification regarding the science team's co-opting of marine personnel, but he figured those could wait a couple of hours. He knew he ought to unpack, but what was the rush? His bags lay on the floor in the corner of the small anteroom, courtesy of Sgt. Coughlin.

So he crumpled onto the bed, boots still on, and dragged the pillow under his head. He could feel sleep rising up around him like some magical, enfolding mist, there instantly, ready to take him away. Draper and the other two assholes were confined to quarters, and Brackett decided that for the moment, he would confine himself to quarters as well. Just for a few hours… or maybe for the night. In the back of his mind, he knew he was hungry, but hunger felt disconnected from him. Far away. His thoughts began to blur.

A rapping came at the door.

"Oh, come on," Brackett groaned.

He clung to the pillow as if it were a life preserver, while the moment of almost-sleep dissipated. He'd left Lt. Paris and Pvt. Hauer as duty officers, unable to imagine another crisis rearing its head today. But the rapping came at the door a second time, and he knew he wasn't going to be able to ignore it.

Swearing under his breath, Brackett swung his legs off the bed and rose. Stretching, he twisted his neck until he heard a satisfying crack, and then strode through the anteroom toward the door.

"Who's there?" he called.

"Sergeant Coughlin, sir," came the muffled reply. "I'm sorry to disturb you, Captain, but you have a visitor."

Brackett frowned deeply. A visitor who required an escort? For a second he thought it must be one of the science team, but then he realized that Dr. Reese wouldn't need anyone to show him where to find the commanding officer's quarters.

He paused with his hand on the door latch, and a smile touched his lips.

Anne, he thought. *It must be.*

Unlocking the door, he hauled it open, head cocked at a curious angle. Coughlin stood smiling in the hall and Brackett blinked in confusion when he saw that it wasn't Anne beside him.

It was her daughter, Newt.

"She seemed lost," Coughlin said. "When she told me she was looking for you, I thought you wouldn't mind the intrusion."

Brackett dropped to a crouch so he could be face to face with the little girl. She still had a sticky red smear around her mouth from the freeze-pop she'd been eating earlier. She beamed at him, putting on her best smile, but Brackett could see from her red-rimmed eyes and the salty streaks on her face that she'd been crying.

Coughlin had surely noticed as well, and kindness had driven him to disturb his CO.

"It's no intrusion at all," Brackett said. "What can I do for you, Newt?"

The little girl shrugged. "Nothing for me. It's what *I* can do for *you*. See, I got back home and I thought to myself that you seemed like you really wanted one of those freeze-pops, and I wouldn't mind having another one, so I thought maybe I could bring you over to meet Bronagh right now instead of tomorrow or whenever. My mom always says 'don't put off till tomorrow what you can do today.'"

Brackett chuckled. "Well, she's right about that one." He glanced up at Coughlin. "I'll take it from here, Sergeant. Thanks for your help."

"Of course," Coughlin said. Then he tipped a wink at Newt. "If Bronagh has an extra freeze-pop, you know where to find me. My favorite's blueberry."

"Eeeeww," Newt said, scrunching her nose. "But okay. Mom also says 'don't yuck somebody else's yum.'"

"That's another good one," Coughlin told her, before saluting Brackett and turning to head back along the corridor.

The captain waited until the sergeant had gone before he went down on one knee, meeting Newt's hopeful gaze.

"I do like freeze-pops," he said, "but I don't think that's why you came to see me."

Newt pursed her lips, her brow knitted in disapproval.

"If you don't want one, you can just say so."

"Tell you what," Brackett said softly, "why don't we take a rain check and do that tomorrow, and right now I'll walk you back to your quarters. It's dinner time. Your mother must be wondering where you've gotten off to."

Newt replied so quietly that it took him a moment to realize that she'd spoken at all.

"They were fighting," she said. "I don't like it when they fight."

"I know what you mean," Brackett said. "My parents used to argue all the time. Sometimes it took a while for them to make up, but they always did." He stood up and reached for her hand. "Let me walk you back, and I bet you by the time we get there, all the fighting will be done.

"Tell you what," he added, "since I'm new here, you can show me around along the way."

Newt's lips were still pursed and her brow still knitted, but he saw her mouth tremble and then she nodded. No words, just that nod.

She took his hand and led the way, giving him her own little girl version of a tour of the civilian sections of the colony. Before long he knew which of the colonists had children, which of those children were bullies or babies, which air ducts made the best secret passages for hide and seek, and which of her neighbors made food that smelled disgusting. He almost reminded her of her mother's admonition not to yuck somebody else's yum, but decided not to tease her.

At a junction in the corridor, they encountered Dr. Hidalgo, who had surrendered her lab coat in favor of thick blue cotton sweatpants and a t-shirt. She had a towel around her neck and her face had gone pink from exertion. The aging scientist had appeared thin when Brackett had met her, but in this ensemble, her limbs seemed almost skeletal.

"Didja have a good workout, Dr. H?" Newt asked.

Dr. Hidalgo smiled. "I did, sweetie." She glanced at Brackett. "I see you've made a new friend."

"He's an *old* friend, actually," Newt said earnestly. "Of my mom's, I mean."

Dr. Hidalgo gave them a lopsided smile and glanced at Brackett.

"Small universe, isn't it, Captain?"

Brackett nodded. "Smaller every day. But it hasn't run out of ways to surprise us."

"Let's hope it never does."

Dr. Hidalgo and Newt said their farewells, and then the girl continued to lead Brackett into the civilian quarters. He glanced back at the lanky scientist as she went around a corner and out of sight, and then turned to Newt.

"You like Dr. Hidalgo, huh?" he asked.

She shot him a curious glance.

"Don't you?"

Brackett grunted. "I guess I do," he said, surprising himself. Dr. Reese and Dr. Mori seemed like grim, arrogant, conniving pricks, and Dr. Hidalgo worked with them every day. Whatever they were doing here on Acheron, she was fully involved. But if a sweet kid like Rebecca Jorden liked her, surely she couldn't be all bad.

When they stopped in front of the door to her family's quarters, the little blond girl looked up at Brackett with her big, wise-beyond-her-years eyes, and sighed, steeling herself for whatever lay beyond the door.

"Thanks for being my friend," she said.

Brackett's grin was genuine, and so wide it hurt his grit-scoured face.

"My pleasure," he said. "It's always nice to make a new friend."

Newt turned the latch and pushed the door open. When she stepped inside, Brackett stayed in the corridor, hesitant to intrude. He could hear Anne call her daughter's name, her tone carrying that combination of love and worry and frustration that seemed exclusive to parents.

"You know you're not supposed to run off alone!" she said.

"Mom, I'm always running off alone," Newt replied. "Even when you make Tim go along, he hardly ever sticks with me. Nothing bad's going to happen. I know *everyone*."

A pause. In the hall, Brackett could almost picture the expression on Anne's face. In their time together, he believed he had seen every facet of her features on display. He took a step over the threshold and saw the boy, sitting on a broad plush chair on the floor, rolling his eyes at the fussing over his sister.

Tim noticed the movement and glanced up at Brackett.

"Hey," the boy said, raising a hand.

"Hello, Tim."

"Who's that?" Anne asked, and he heard her footfalls as she crossed their family room.

Brackett stepped into their quarters, leaving the door open behind him. To have closed it would have been presumptuous. As it was, he worried that he might be overstepping his bounds, but he couldn't help himself.

"Demian," Anne said, blinking several times as she brought herself up short, stopping a few feet away from him.

"Captain Brackett walked me back," Newt said happily, taking her mother's hand. The girl beamed proudly, as if she'd brought home an injured kitten to be nursed back to health. "I promised him I'd introduce him to Bronagh and get him a freeze-pop, but he said we should do that another day, that it must be dinner time—"

"It's *past* dinner time," Anne said, without taking her eyes off Brackett.

"Nuh-uh, 'cause Dad's not back yet," Newt said.

The logic seemed reasonable, but Anne flinched. Newt seemed to sense her misstep, and a sadness slid over her features.

Anne let go of her daughter's hand.

"Go wash up for dinner, please."

Newt hesitated for only a second before she thanked Brackett, promised him a freeze-pop the following day, and retreated down a short corridor to a door that must have been the bathroom.

"You too, Tim," Anne said, glancing at her son. Uneasy, uncertain.

Tim took a pair of black buds from his ears and set his tablet aside, then rose and made his way back into that corridor.

"Hello again, Annie," Brackett said once Tim had gone. Careful. Neutral.

Apparently at a loss for words, she opened her mouth to speak, but could only utter a short sound that sounded like half-laugh and half-sigh. She wetted her lips with her tongue and glanced away, shaking her head.

"I shouldn't have come?" Brackett asked.

"To my quarters, or to Hadley's Hope?"

"Neither, I'm guessing. Or both." He shrugged one shoulder. "But I'm here anyway."

Anne rolled her eyes, a familiar smirk on her lips.

"You're an exasperating man, Demian—always have been—but I'm glad you're here. It really is a wonderful surprise. I thought I'd never see you again—or anyone else from home."

He gazed at her a moment, so many things unspoken, demanding to be said. But years had passed, her children were nearby, and her husband might walk in at any moment. So all he did was smile.

"Happy I can still surprise you," he said, and he turned to go.

"Wait!" Anne said, reaching out to grab his arm.

The contact made them both freeze… both look down at the place where her fingers touched his forearm. Anne drew her hand back as if she'd been scalded, her eyes sad and uncertain. Then she gave that same sighing chuckle.

"Thanks for bringing Newt home," she said.

"She's a wonderful kid."

Anne nodded. "She is. A handful, though."

"Just like her mom."

A terrible sadness engulfed him, and he knew she saw it in his eyes, saw the way he deflated.

"Demian," she said carefully, "you knew..."

He waved the words away.

"Don't. I'm fine. I'd be lying if I said I didn't still feel something between us, but I didn't come here for you, and I damn sure have no intention of interfering with your life or your happiness. I just..."

"Just?" she echoed, her voice barely above a whisper, eyes full of history and could-have-beens.

Brackett gave her a lopsided smile.

"I've got to go. You've got beautiful children."

He wanted to tell her that it was impossible for him to look at Tim and Newt and not think that, if only they had made different choices years before, they could have been his. His and Anne's, together. He wanted to tell her that it hurt him, because he could so easily imagine the family they might have had.

But that wouldn't have been fair to anyone. Way back in boot camp, he had learned that sometimes there was no safe path, no decision from which one could emerge unscathed. In those cases, he had been taught to take the path of honor, even if it led to pain or death.

"I've got to transmit a report," he said. "See you around, Annie. Tell Newt I look forward to our date for freeze-pops."

Brackett left without looking her in the eyes again, not wanting to see if there were possibilities there. Not wanting her to see the possibilities in his.

12

NOSTROMO MYSTERIES

DATE: 12 JUNE, 2179

Maybe they're just doing this to torture me, Ripley thought. *But all it's doing is pissing me off.*

She'd emerged from hospital care, only to discover that she had become something of an oddity on Gateway Station—almost a celebrity, with her shockingly long hypersleep and tale of survival. The company had told her not to say anything, of course. Not to discuss anything of her experiences with anyone who might be unauthorized. But there were still whispers and rumors.

There always were.

And now they were showing her the faces of the dead.

She'd seen them a dozen times already today, but still she stared, trying to draw them nearer in her memory. It seemed the right thing to do, but they had all been dead and gone for more than half a century. However recent and fresh her grief might feel, they were fading into history.

Them and her daughter, too. Her whole life was informed by grief.

Screw it.

"I don't understand this," she said, turning around to face the group who had gathered for the official inquiry. "We have been here for three and a half hours. How many different ways do you want me to tell the same story?"

Van Leuwen—another Company man, but smarter than Burke by a long shot—sat at the end of the long table. He was overseeing the inquiry, and sitting on either side of the table were eight others: Feds, interstellar commerce commission, colonial admin, insurance guys… and Burke.

He had tried to school her in how to approach this, what to say.

Bloody weasel.

"Look at it from our perspective, please," Van Leuwen said. He invited her to sit once again, and Ripley, frustrated with the whole process but starting to see that perhaps playing it their way was the way to go, submitted. She sat, slowly, and listened to what she'd already heard several times before.

"Now, you freely admit to detonating the engines of, and thereby destroying, an M-Class star freighter, a rather expensive piece of hardware."

The insurance guy spoke up.

"Forty-two million in adjusted dollars." He smirked at Ripley. "That's minus payload, of course." *I could wipe that smirk off his face,* she thought, a little startled at the image of lashing out at him. He wasn't her enemy. None of these people were. Her enemy was dead, and the most frustrating thing was that no one here seemed to believe it.

The memory of her slaughtered friends demanded that she *force* them to believe. The undercurrent was that something suspicious had happened, something that she was trying to cover up with this outlandish story, and she was determined to put them right.

"The lifeboat's flight recorder corroborates *some* elements of your account," Van Leuwen continued. "That for reasons unknown, the *Nostromo* set down on LV-426, an unsurveyed planet at that time. That it resumed its course and was subsequently set to self-destruct, by *you*, for reasons unknown—"

"*Not* for reasons unknown!" Ripley said, again. *One more time,* she thought. The more she told her story, the less they seemed to believe it, and the more terrible it became to her. "I told you, we set down there on Company orders to get this thing which destroyed my crew. And your expensive ship."

A ripple seemed to pass through the people assembled there. Company people, some of them, but surely not all. She was essentially blaming the Company for what had happened to the *Nostromo*, so she could understand *some* of them feeling uncomfortable with that. Van Leuwen, the woman from the bio division, and that creep Burke.

But *all* of them?

"The analysis team that went over the lifeboat centimeter by centimeter found no physical evidence of the creature you described," Van Leuwen said.

"Good!" Ripley said, standing again. She was tall, imposing, and she liked the way a couple of the guys winced a little when she shouted. "That's because I blew it out of the airlock."

She sighed and looked down at her signed deposition, still feeling as if it lacked something. A story told, yet unfinished. She turned back to the screen to see Lambert staring at her—poor, scared Lambert who had died a dreadful death.

"Are there any species like this hostile organism on LV-426?" the insurance guy asked, turning to the woman from the bio division. She was sucking greedily on her cigarette, and it took her a few seconds to reply.

"No, it's a rock," she replied. "No indigenous life."

Now it was Ash staring at her from the screen, mocking her for being here with these idiots.

"Did IQs just drop sharply while I was away?" Ripley asked. "Ma'am, I already said it was not indigenous—it was a derelict spacecraft, it was an alien ship, it was not from there." She stared at the woman, who had something of a smirk on her lips. "Do you get it? We homed in on its beacon—"

"And found something never recorded once in over three hundred surveyed worlds," the woman said. "A creature that gestates inside a living human host—these are your words—and has concentrated acid for blood!"

"That's right!" Ripley snapped.

She was angry, frustrated, tired and hungry. But she could also see the looks on those faces around the table. Some were gently humoring her. Others looked aghast—not at what she was telling them, but at what they saw as a woman suffering a breakdown. Most of them seemed embarrassed to even be there.

"Look, I can see where this is going, but I'm telling you that those things exist."

"Thank you, Officer Ripley, that will be all," Van Leuwen said.

"Please, you're not listening to me. Kane, the crew member..." She had a flash memory of Kane, laconic and nice, a sweet guy just looking to earn a decent wage to help his family. "Kane, who went into that ship, said he saw thousands of eggs there. Thousands."

"Thank you, that will be *all.*"

"Dammit, that's not all!" Ripley shouted. She couldn't get through to them. Could they not *see*? Could they not *understand*? "'Cause if one of those things gets down here, that *will* be all, and this..." She grabbed the papers, copies of her deposition, evidence sheets. "This bullshit that you think is so important... you can kiss all that goodbye!"

Silence. Some of them even stared. She knew she'd gone too far, but fuck it. Her sweet daughter had died believing her mother was lost forever. Ripley was adrift. And all she had left to do was to make sure no one, *no one*, had to go through what she had been through. Never again.

Van Leuwen sighed and clipped the lid onto his pen. Then after a longer pause, he broke the silence.

"It is the finding of this court of inquiry that Warrant Officer E. Ripley, NOC 14472, has acted with questionable judgment, and is unfit to hold an ICC license as a commercial flight officer. Said license is hereby suspended indefinitely. No criminal charges will be filed against you at this time..."

He went on. Official speak, technical terms. Ripley stared at him, trying to will him to believe her, holding back her anger and grief to prevent herself blowing up one more time. But Van Leuwen's mind was made up. He didn't look like the sort of man who made such decisions lightly, and it would take more than Ripley's gaze to change his mind.

In truth, she even agreed with him, partly. She wasn't fit to fly. She woke up from fresh nightmares two mornings out of three. That sense of dark, heavy dread was still inside her. Sometimes it threatened to pull her and everyone around her into its embrace.

But this wasn't about her.

She turned away, took a deep breath. As the others started to leave the room, the sleazeball Burke sidled up to her. She smelled his aftershave before she saw him, and both made her sick.

"That could have been... better," he said. But instead of responding, she dismissed him, and turned to confront Van Leuwen as he left the room.

"Van Leuwen," she said, doing her best to keep her voice level, to hold the madness down. "Why don't you just check out LV-426?"

"Because I don't have to," he said. "There have been people there for over twenty years, and they've never complained about any hostile organism."

No!

"What do you mean?" she asked. "What people?"

"Terraformers. Planet engineers. They go in and set up these big atmosphere processors to make the air breathable. Takes decades. What we call a shake-and-bake colony."

She slammed her arm on the door, blocking his exit.

"How many are there?" she demanded. "How many colonists?"

"I don't know," he shrugged. "Sixty, maybe seventy families." He looked down at her arm. "Do you mind?"

She let him go. She had no choice. That sense of dread within her was blooming, a terrible secret she should know but could not grasp, could not open.

"Families," she whispered, closing her eyes and seeing her sweet Amanda on those nights when the little girl had come into her bedroom, cold and scared of the dark, scared of monsters.

* * *

DATE: 19 JUNE, 2179
TIME: 1612

Dr. Bartholomew Reese kept mostly to himself.

Years before, at the urging of Dr. Hidalgo, the science team had arranged a weekly dinner, a sort of enforced socialization period for people who tended toward isolation and rumination. Dr. Reese supposed the Monday night rituals were a good thing, even necessary in a way—for himself, at least, he knew that too much time alone made him more impatient and more irritable with the rest of the world than he already was, and that was saying something. Still, he never quite enjoyed the meal and considered it a distraction.

Fortunately, tonight was Thursday—the Monday gathering still days away—so he did not have to suffer the presence of his colleagues, or pretend an amiability he had never felt.

Reese sat in a reclining chair in his anteroom, a glass of Malbec on a side table and a two-hundred-year-old edition of Ray Bradbury's *The Illustrated Man* open in his lap. Most people eschewed the printed book, even scoffed at what they viewed as self-indulgence on his part for carting several boxes of books to Acheron when he had first been assigned here by the company. But in a savage, uncaring universe, Reese had always felt that a glass of wine and an open book were the best way to remind himself what it meant to be civilized.

A soft chime echoed through his quarters. He frowned and glanced at the door in irritation, wondering if he could ignore it. But no… nobody would interrupt him without good reason. He had no real friends, only colleagues, and they would not have come here without an urgent need.

Taking a sip of wine, he set the glass back down on the side table, slid a finger into his book to hold the page, and rose from the chair. As he crossed to the door, the arthritis in his knees singing out a painful reminder, the bell chimed again.

"Hang on!" he called.

He opened the door to find Dr. Mori on his threshold. In all of their time working together, Reese had never seen so wide a smile on the silver-haired Japanese biologist. The grin transformed him, and for a fleeting moment Reese had an image of what Mori must have looked like as a little boy.

"Bartholomew," Dr. Mori said, "may I come in?"

Reese stepped aside and Dr. Mori practically lunged into the room. He steepled his hands in front of his face as if to hide his grin. Dr. Reese closed the door and turned toward him.

"You look as giddy as a lovestruck teen," Reese said, with a hint of disapproval. "Whatever it is—"

"It *may* be the answer to the *Nostromo* mystery," Dr. Mori said, lowering his hands to reveal his smile again. He shook his head with a small laugh.

Reese felt his heart jump, but restrained himself. This might be nothing. Wishful thinking at best.

"Explain yourself," he said.

Dr. Mori nodded. "Al Simpson has just received a special order, copies of which were also transmitted to yourself and to me. In it, a Weyland-Yutani executive named Carter Burke has sent surface grid coordinates with instructions that a survey team be dispatched immediately to investigate the site. With that kind of urgency, Bartholomew, what else could it be?"

Dr. Reese lowered his gaze and stared at the floor a moment before uttering a small laugh.

He nodded.

"We've been here for years," Reese said. "There can only be one rationale for urgency." He narrowed his gaze. "Though you realize it may not be about the *Nostromo* at all. It might be some other indication—an atmospheric imaging array, revealing a geological depression that hints at the presence of ruins."

"Then why the suddenness?" Dr. Mori countered. "Why go directly to Simpson?"

Dr. Reese contemplated Mori's reasoning, and could not find fault in it. Still, he forced himself to breathe. Only a fool would allow himself to become overly excited before they truly knew the purpose for Carter Burke's special order.

Decades earlier, a Weyland-Yutani star freighter called the *Nostromo* had diverted from its course to respond to what the crew believed was a deep space distress call—one which could only have come from an alien ship—and subsequently vanished. It had long been believed that that distress call had come from one of the moons of Calpamos, with Acheron the likeliest candidate.

The science team's primary work with the Hadley's Hope colony had been to study Acheron and the way in which it had been changed by terraforming, as well as attempting to enrich the changing soil to support agriculture. At least, that was what the colonists, marines, and administrators had been told. Their less overt, higher-priority work was to examine all samples for any indication of alien life—native or visitor, past or present—on LV-426.

"Whatever has happened," Dr. Mori said, "new information must have come to light."

Reese nodded, his thoughts racing. He paced back toward his chair, considering the best way to handle the science team's relationship with Simpson. The man would follow instructions from Weyland-Yutani as if they had come from his own government. The government and the company had founded Hadley's Hope together, but Simpson's paychecks bore the Weyland-Yutani logo. He knew for whom he really worked.

Spotting his wine glass out of the corner of his eye, Dr. Reese set down his book and picked up the glass. He swirled the Malbec around for several seconds before taking a thoughtful sip.

"The timing of Captain Brackett's arrival is less than ideal," he said, glancing up at Dr. Mori. "I'm confident I know what his superiors will tell him, but until he is commanded otherwise, his orders on the ground here will stand as he sees them."

Dr. Mori frowned. "Why are you troubled by this?" he asked. "It isn't the marines who ought to be going along on this sojourn, but one of us. I should go with them, or you should. Even Dr. Hidalgo…"

Reese arched an eyebrow. "You want to go and investigate an unknown alien presence without a marine escort? Someone with guns and a willingness to use them, who will die protecting you?"

"Well, when you put it that way..."

"No, let's allow Simpson to send out a team of his wildcatters. Meanwhile, we'll get to work re-analyzing any data we've collected from that area. If the survey team returns without incident, perhaps one of us will go along the next time. By then, Brackett will have been instructed to cooperate, and the risk will be significantly decreased."

Dr. Mori smiled. "I like your thinking. We could toast to it if you'd offer me a glass of that rich red."

Reese's eyebrows shot up. "How rude of me. Apologies, my friend. A case arrived on this morning's dropship, and I don't mean to hoard it."

"Of course you do," Dr. Mori scoffed.

"Well, yes, but not so completely that I can't offer you a glass," he said with a smile. "I don't think we should start celebrating just yet—"

"Of course not."

"—but that doesn't mean we can't raise a glass in hope."

He retrieved a second glass from his small kitchen and poured several mouthfuls of wine for Mori. Reese handed it over and then raised his own glass.

"To the *Nostromo*," he said.

Dr. Mori nodded and clinked his glass against Reese's.

"To the *Nostromo*."

Dr. Hidalgo stood outside Dr. Mori's office, waiting for his return.

The news had torn her away from her dinner, and as she stood leaning against the wall, her stomach growled. She had been compared to a bird many times in her life—a stork, a flamingo—but the most accurate comparisons were to her appetite. She ate small portions, mostly nibbles here and there, but she ate all day long. Tonight she'd been in the dining hall with several of the lab assistants, eating vegetable dumplings with a chili sauce, when Dr. Mori's assistant had come to fetch her.

She'd wheedled the news out of him on the hurried walk back to the office, and now she waited like an errant schoolgirl sent to see the principal.

When she saw Dr. Mori coming down the corridor, she steeled herself for the encounter. She admired Mori for his brilliance and his dedication, but she had never liked him as a person. In her career, Elena Hidalgo had met many scientists whose company she had enjoyed—even here at Hadley's Hope, there were several lab assistants who were thoughtful and kind—but it had been her bad luck to end up working under Bartholomew Reese and the caustic, thoughtless Dr. Mori.

"I need to speak with you," she said as Mori approached. "You and Dr. Reese."

"He'll be along shortly," Dr. Mori said. "Is there a problem?"

"I think there is."

Dr. Mori unlocked his office door and gestured for her to enter. He followed her inside and closed the door behind him. The lights flickered on automatically, sensing their presence.

"Care to elaborate?" Dr. Mori asked, turning toward her and leaning against his desk. Everything about his tone and posture declared that he found her tiresome. "I presume this is about this evening's message from the company."

"From Carter Burke," Dr. Hidalgo said. "Whoever that is."

"Dr. Reese and I were just sharing our excitement about this development, Elena," he told her. "You don't seem as thrilled as I would have expected. This may be precisely the sort of break we've been hoping for since our arrival on Acheron. I don't know about you, but I've harbored a secret fear, almost from day one, that we had spent all of this time and effort, and built the colony in the wrong place."

Dr. Hidalgo shook her head.

"How can there be a wrong place? The colony doesn't exist just as a host body for us to nest upon."

Dr. Mori arched an eyebrow, gazing at her dubiously.

"Are you comparing us to parasites?"

"Of course not," she replied. "I love my work, I'm just… worried. That's all."

"There's nothing for you to be worried about, Dr. Hidalgo."

She thought of the children she had seen earlier, running in the hall; Newt and her little ginger-haired friend, Luisa.

"I'm not worried about myself."

Dr. Mori thoughtfully stroked his chin. The cliché of it—the wise old scientist in silent contemplation—was so condescending that it made her want to scream. But she held her tongue.

"My dear friend," he said, "the Company's had no secrets from you. From any member of our team. Yes, Hadley's Hope would have been built whether or not the Company had co-sponsored its construction, but there was a reason Weyland-Yutani bought into the idea in the first place. It used its influence to choose colony sites which would further its own interests. This is not espionage, Elena. It's business. More importantly, it's science."

She plunged her hands into the pockets of her lab coat, encountering a package of mints on one side and a wad of tissues on the other. Tangible, insignificant things, somehow they made her concerns more real.

"If we find alien life—" she began.

"Living creatures?" Dr. Mori scoffed. "After all these years, with all of the studies we've done of this planet, you know how miniscule the chances are of that. There's been no sign of any activity at all."

"My point is that it's *possible*. For the most part, other encounters with alien races have been benign, but there have been a few violent, bloody clashes. You know that. Our friends in the Colonial Marines must all have stories of friends they've lost. So I can't help but feel some trepidation about making contact with a new alien life form, with a colony full of people—including children—who have no idea that the chance even exists.

"What if the aliens are hostile?" she said. "What then?"

Dr. Mori blinked in surprise, lowering his arms to stare as if her question was the stupidest thing he'd ever heard. Then he frowned, his brow knitting with impatience.

"You know the answer to that question, Dr. Hidalgo," he said curtly. "Our research is too important for it to go to waste. That's why the science team was provided its own evacuation vessel, why we've all been given enough rudimentary training to launch the ship, and trigger the autopilot's homing system.

"You didn't think they were teaching us all of that for their own amusement, do you? Whatever else happens, our findings must reach Earth."

"Right, the evac ship," she responded. "A vessel even the colonial administrator is unaware of."

Dr. Mori flinched back from her, staring through narrowed eyes.

"I'm not sure where you're going with this," he said cautiously, "but I'd remind you about the contracts you've signed—specifically about the priorities the company has set for us. You didn't have to agree to those things. No one put a gun to your head, Elena. You chose this. It's a worst-case scenario—which isn't going to occur, remember." His voice softened slightly. "This is a dead planet. There is no threat here—only history to be unearthed, and perhaps alien remains. But in a worst-case scenario, that evac ship carries us out of here—the science team, our samples, and our data. Nothing more."

"But there are children…"

Dr. Mori glared at her for a long moment, took a breath and let it out slowly.

"Yes, there are," he said at last. "Children whose parents knew that their days and nights would be full of peril, from the moment they set off to join the colony. As did you. If I were you, I'd stop worrying about the worst-case scenario and start focusing on the task ahead of us, the wonderful opportunity we've been given."

He walked around the desk and took a seat behind it, drawing up his chair.

"A word of advice?" Dr. Mori continued. "When we meet with Reese, you'd do well not to bring this up. If he thinks you're not dedicated to the research, he'll cut you out of the process altogether. And then, if we *do* find something, all of the time you've spent on this godforsaken rock, with men you despise, will have been for nothing."

Dr. Hidalgo stared at him. She knew she ought to make some kind of argument, at least tell him that she did not despise him, but she had never been a convincing liar.

Mori opened his tablet and began to tap on a keyboard, perhaps making notes or consulting earlier files. After several long seconds, she turned and left, not bothering to close the door behind her.

In all her years, Dr. Hidalgo had never been more excited.

Or more afraid.

13

A FAMILY OUTING

DATE: 19 JUNE, 2179
TIME: 1857

Anne and Newt sprawled on the carpet playing *Kubix*, a puzzle game they had fallen in love with the previous year. The tiles were colorful, and played musical notes when being connected, but Anne liked it best because of the mathematical element that went into configuring them.

Newt barely noticed that she was learning anything, just enjoying the competition. In the beginning she had rarely won a game, but in recent weeks Newt had improved so much that she routinely beat her mother, which gave the little girl great pleasure.

Tim had gone off to the rec room to meet his friend Aaron, a burly boy with curly black hair and a chip on his shoulder. Anne would have preferred that Tim make other friends, but there weren't many children her son's age at Hadley's Hope, so she resigned herself to hoping Tim would have a positive influence on Aaron, and not the other way around.

Newt placed a triangular tile bearing a fuchsia smiley face into the design she'd been constructing, and a pretty melody began to play, emanating from the chips themselves.

"Yay!" Newt said happily, clapping her hands. "Gotcha!"

Anne laughed. "So you did."

The rattling of the door latch made them both look up, and Anne stiffened. A week had passed since the night they'd had their big argument, but the tension of it had echoed through every interaction they'd had since. She could still hear their angry words. So she drew a deep breath but did not stand up to greet him as the door swung inward.

"Daddy's home!" Russ said, practically bursting inside, a grin on his face. He clapped his hands as he saw them. "Hey, look at my girls. Newt, I hope you're kicking Momma's butt, as usual!"

Newt gave a matter-of-fact nod, eyebrows raised.

"Of course."

Anne realized that Newt had tensed up just as much as she had, and she felt her own relief echoing back from her daughter.

"You're in a good mood," Anne said with a tentative smile.

Russ slammed the door, crossed the carpet and knelt beside her. He took her hands and gazed into her eyes, and she remembered the same look in his eyes the day he had proposed to her.

"You're going to be in a good mood too," he said.

Anne laughed softly. "All right, how many drinks did you and Parvati have?"

"Three," he said. "No, four. Shots included. But it isn't alcohol fueling my mood, sweetheart. It's the promise of money. Simpson came looking for me in the bar. First thing tomorrow morning, you and I are headed out!"

Newt uttered a happy *ooh* and clapped again, her father's excitement infectious. Anne felt it, too.

"Out where?"

Russ snapped his fingers and pointed at her.

"That, my love, is the big question, and the best part. We're not supposed to discuss it, but he's received instructions to send a survey team to some very specific coordinates."

"Specific coordinates," Anne repeated, a pleasurable tremor going through her. "So this isn't random. This time we're actually—"

"*Looking* for something," Russ interrupted, nodding rapidly. He jumped to his feet and started to pace, his thoughts already racing ahead to the next morning. "They're not going to tell us what we're looking for, of course, but the company must expect us to find something out there."

"Native ruins," Anne cried. "It's got to be!"

"Or some kind of ancient settlement," another voice chimed in.

Anne looked over to see Tim standing at the entrance to the hallway, smiling happily. The boy hadn't smiled all day, and it lifted her spirits even further just to see it.

"Exactly." Russ snapped his fingers again and pointed at Tim. "*Non-human* settlement."

"It's like a gift," Anne said, but then a dark thought touched her. "*If* we find something. Let's not get ahead of ourselves, Russ. It might be that we go out there, and don't find anything at all."

Russ nodded. "Could be, could be." But she could see the glint in his eyes—a glint she knew so well—full of hope and plans for the future—and she knew he had already begun to spend the money in his mind.

"I want to come!" Newt said, standing up, her expression adorably determined.

"Rebecca and I *both* want to come," Tim confirmed.

"Absolutely not," Anne said, climbing to her feet.

"You *always* let us come," Newt said, crossing her arms. She turned to her father. "Dad, tell her."

"Well," Russ said, "we don't *always*, Newt. Only when it's not going to be more than a day."

Anne gave him a wary glance.

"Russ…"

He grinned. "Come on, Anne, they're excited. Tell you what, if we wake up tomorrow and the coordinates Simpson gives us are too far away, or if the weather looks ugly—"

"The weather's always ugly," she said, every trace of happiness draining from her as she thought about the Finch brothers. "After what happened with Otto and Curtis, I just don't think it's a good idea."

"Mom, we'll be fine," Tim said. "Come *on*."

"The storm has passed," Russ argued. "I checked on tomorrow's weather, and there's no indication of anything near that level of disturbance."

"That can change in an instant," she said.

"We'll monitor it."

"The calmest atmospheric day on Acheron is still dangerous. The wind and the dust—"

"We've been out with you *plenty* of times," Newt argued.

"Don't whine," her mother chided her.

"I'm *no*-ot."

Russ cocked his head. "Honey?"

Newt and Tim gazed at her expectantly. Anne knew she ought to say no, but their arguments weren't without merit. The storm that had led to the deaths had been an anomaly, and the atmosphere had returned to its ordinary level of violence—which they had all faced many times. Even the kids. And if she and Russ didn't take this job, it would go to Cale or one of the other wildcatters, and if they found anything truly valuable, she'd resent her own decision forever.

Still, she didn't like the idea of spending the next few days in a crawler with her husband. The specter of their week-old argument, and his jealousy over Demian's presence on Acheron, would be hanging over them. That didn't appeal to her at all. Once his euphoria passed, the conversation was sure to go places she didn't want it to go…

Unless the kids came along with them.

"Okay," she said finally. "If the stormcasting program doesn't show any major atmospheric disturbance—not just tomorrow, but for the next few days—then the kids can come."

"Yes!" Tim gave a triumphant fist pump.

Newt came over and wrapped an arm around Anne's waist, nodding her precocious approval.

Russ smiled at her across the room. It was a slow, sweet smile, with a look in his eyes suggesting that he might just have remembered what a great couple they were, and what a great family they'd made.

At that moment her anxiety passed, and Anne felt suffused by a wonderful contentment—a certainty that they had just passed some invisible hurdle. Suddenly she couldn't wait for the next day to arrive.

The coming morning promised a new beginning.

DATE: 21 JUNE, 2179
TIME: 0812

Al Simpson enjoyed mornings in the command block, despite the fact that "morning" was an elusive concept on Acheron. The constant swirl of volcanic ash and loose soil in the atmosphere blotted out any direct sunlight, but on a relatively calm day, morning took on a pleasant, twilight glow.

The colony buzzed with people hard at work. Outside the broad window—its storm shield raised—he could see six-wheeled crawlers moving about, emerging from underground garages and crossing the breadth of the growing colony. Simpson thought of them all as spiders, working together to construct a single web.

He'd been accused of being a curmudgeon, many times, and there was truth to that. But those who worked with him long enough realized very quickly that if they caught him in the morning, on a decent-weather day, and he had a cup of coffee in his hand, he might not bite their heads off.

He turned away from the window and took a sip. After years on Acheron, the shit that passed for coffee up here had finally started to taste good to him. He watched the technicians at their consoles, rushing around, tapping data into computers, and it felt good, especially when he reminded himself that unlike the people of Hadley's Hope, this was just a job to him. The colonists had signed on more or less for life, but Simpson was like the marines in one respect—any time he wanted, he could ask for a transfer.

His gaze drifted purposefully toward Mina Osterman, the most recent hire. She'd arrived two months earlier as a replacement for the plant architect, Borstein, who'd gone to work on a new colony Weyland-Yutani was developing in another sector. Mina had ginger hair and dark eyes, and she held herself always in a sort of relaxed pose that made people feel comfortable around her.

The previous Monday, Simpson had gotten a bit too comfortable with Mina and her reassuring smile and those dark eyes, and suggested certain nocturnal activities that had nothing to do with architecture. Now she seemed to feel his eyes upon her and looked up curiously. A frown furrowed her brow, and she rolled her eyes before returning to the paperwork in front of her.

Simpson took another sip of coffee, but it tasted bitter to him now. He knew he had overstepped with Mina, and it made him feel like an idiot. He turned to head back to his console and saw his assistant operations manager, Brad Lydecker, rushing toward him.

"You remember you sent some wildcatters out to that plateau, out past the Ilium range?"

Simpson grimaced. The Jordens.

And the morning had been going so well.

"Yeah, what?" he asked curtly.

"Well, the guy's on the horn from our mom-and-pop survey team," Lydecker explained. "Says he's homing in on the coordinates, and wants to confirm that his claim will be honored."

Simpson grumbled, cursing himself for sending Jorden out there at all. The guy had been on Acheron as long as Simpson had, and he needed to clarify the rules? Then again, Russ hadn't been chosen for his smarts.

Lydecker, on the other hand, didn't need to know that this was anything other than a routine wildcatting expedition.

"Christ," Simpson said, putting some drama into it. "Some honcho in a cushy office says go look at a grid reference that's in the middle of nowhere, we go and look. They don't say why, and I don't ask. It takes two weeks to get an answer out here, anyhow."

"So what do I tell this guy?" Lydecker said.

Simpson glanced at his coffee, but it had lost its magic altogether. "Tell him that as far as I'm concerned, he finds something, it's his."

* * *

DATE: 21 JUNE, 2179
TIME: 1109

Russ Jorden felt alive. He gripped the crawler's steering wheel, and his heart raced as he hit the accelerator.

The vehicle roared across a shelf of furrowed rock, down a slant, and then blasted through the crest of a high drift of volcanic ash. With the dust eddying around them, it felt to him as if they were surging along the waves of a dead gray sea, with the promised land straight ahead.

In the back of the crawler, Newt and Tim bumped each other and bickered as siblings had done on journeys since time began. His children loved each other and played together daily, but they nipped at each other like growling, overgrown puppies. Sometimes he grew impatient with them, but not today.

"Look at that, Anne," he said, glancing over.

In the green glow of the magnetoscope, she looked ethereally beautiful, a ghostly, wild angel. The memory of their argument from the week before gave him a sudden jolt of sadness, but he pushed it away. They were together, now—really together—partners the way they were meant to be.

"I'm looking," she said, staring at the scope, which pinged again. The tone of the pings altered slightly depending on their proximity to the object they were nearing and the angle of their approach. Right now the sound was loud, and clear as a bell.

"Six degrees west," she told him.

"Six west," Russ echoed, turning the wheel to compensate. The scope kept pinging and he glanced over again, gleeful.

"Look at this fat, juicy magnetic profile!" he cried happily. "And it's mine, mine, mine!"

"Half mine, dear," Anne reminded him with an indulgent smile. His exuberance always amused her—it was how he'd won her over in the first place.

"And half mine!" Newt yelled from the back.

"I got too many partners," Russ joked, although the moment the words were out of his mouth, he knew they weren't really a joke at all. Weyland-Yutani would take the lion's share of whatever it was the scope had picked up.

Don't get greedy, he reminded himself. *This is still the find you've been waiting for.*

Whatever the scope had identified, it definitely wasn't any sort of natural rock or mineral formation. The ping was too strong, too regular, and he knew the terrain around here well enough to know what a huge anomaly they'd found. No, whatever it was, it had been built by someone… or something. Now he just wanted to see it. Sure, the payoff would be lovely, but he couldn't help thinking about what it would mean if he found the ruins of some previously unknown race. His name—their names, his and Anne's—they'd be written in history books, along with Burkhardt and Koizumi and the rest.

Newt poked her head up between the seats.

"Daddy, when are we going back to town?"

Russ smiled. "When we get rich, Newt."

"You always say that," she sulked. "I wanna go back. I wanna play Monster Maze."

Tim nudged her and put his face up close to hers.

"You cheat too much."

"Do not! I'm just the best."

"Do too! You go into places we can't fit."

"So what? That's why I'm the best!"

Frustrated, Anne spun to face them.

"Knock it off, you two. I catch *either* of you playing in the air ducts again, I'll tan your hides."

"*Mo*-om," Newt whined, "all the kids play it."

Russ would have defended them, reminded Anne that if they were children stuck in Hadley's Hope, they'd certainly have spent whole days exploring the system of ducts that crisscrossed the facility. But just at that moment, he lost the ability to put together a sentence—not to mention anything resembling a cogent thought.

All he could do was take his foot off of the crawler's accelerator and lean forward, staring out through the windscreen at the massive shape looming ahead of them in the veil of drifting ash.

"Holy shit," Russ said reverently.

At first glance, the gargantuan object rising out of the ground looked almost organic, as if it were the huge, curving remains of some giant alien beast. As the crawler slowly rolled nearer, he saw that the shape did, indeed, have some kind of organic influence in its design. And there could be no doubt that it *had* been designed.

But not by humans.

"Oh, my God," Anne whispered.

Russ felt his heart hammering in his chest as he pulled the crawler to a stop. They'd never seen anything like the object's horseshoe shape, or its strange, bio-mechanoid construction, but it most certainly was a vessel. A starship. Judging from the way the rocky terrain had been torn up, leaving great piles of debris clustered around it, he felt sure it had crash-landed here, digging up the stone and ash as it scarred the ground on impact.

"Folks," Russ said, "we have scored big this time."

The kids moved out of the way as Anne pulled on her heavy coat, helmet, and the goggles that would protect her eyes from the blowing grit. Russ shut down the engine and followed suit, all four of them keeping up a stream of excited chatter. They wore belts equipped with core samplers, flashlights, and short-range comms that would allow them to communicate without having to shout.

Hefting cameras and testing equipment, he and his wife climbed down out of the vehicle and dropped to the surface. A massive gust of wind buffeted against them and Russ stood to block Anne from the brunt of it. The wind reminded him of Otto and Curtis, and he silently vowed to be more careful than was typical of him, and to watch the skies for any sign that the weather might worsen.

Their breath clouded in the air. The temperature had dropped.

"You kids stay inside," Anne called to them. "I mean it! We'll be right back."

Clicking on his helmet light, Russ set off toward the derelict object, trudging through dust and then climbing onto a rocky ledge that protruded from the ash. Anne caught up to him as he studied the shape and the weird texture of the ship.

"Shouldn't we call it in?" she asked.

"Let's wait until we know what it is," Russ suggested.

Anne gave a soft grunt. "How about 'big weird thing?'"

It was a joke, but she didn't sound as if she was joking. She sounded spooked, and Russ couldn't blame her. Truth was, he was more than a little spooked himself, but he wasn't going to admit it. From the looks of the "big weird thing," it had been out here for ages—maybe centuries. Whatever it had been once upon a time, now it was little more than a creaky old haunted house, silent and remote.

Anne took the lead, trudging down from the jutting stone, through drifts of ash, and up a cascade of rocks beside the hull. Russ ran his gloved hand over the surface, its texture rough and lined when stroked in one direction, but smooth when he slid his palm across it the other way.

They began by attempting to walk the entire periphery of the ship, but just a few minutes after they'd begun, Anne froze up ahead of him.

"What is it?" Russ asked, as he came up beside her. Then he saw the thing that had caused her to halt. It was a large, twisted gash in the metal hull, blackness looming—almost breathing—within.

"What is it?" Anne repeated. She glanced at him, and he could see the wild grin behind her mask. "I'd say it's a way in."

She pointed the light attached to her belt, and turned it on. Russ did the same.

14

DERELICTION AND DUTY

DATE: 21 JUNE, 2179
TIME: 1121

Sgt. Marvin Draper and his cronies had spent Brackett's first week on Acheron testing the new CO's patience. They muttered to one another in the captain's presence, showed up late for duty assignments, and argued among themselves and with other marines. It made him wish he'd kept them confined to their quarters, but he couldn't have left them locked away forever, tempting as the thought might be.

Their latest antics, less than twelve hours earlier, had been to get drunk and enter the livestock pens, so that Cpl. Pettigrew could demonstrate his childhood pastime of "cattle-tipping"—knocking the cows over for a laugh.

All of it was behavior Brackett would have expected from college fraternity boys, but not from Colonial Marines.

He'd had enough.

"You've got a decision to make," he said to the five marines lined up in his office. "Either you fall in line, or you are going to spend the rest of your time on Acheron in your quarters, until I can have you transferred to somewhere even *more* remote than this hellhole."

Draper raised his stubbled chin.

"Sir, *is* there anywhere more remote, sir?"

Nguyen and Pettigrew remained blank-faced, but Stamovich smirked. As far as he was concerned, Draper was the alpha dog at Hadley's Hope, and the corporal had all the confidence in the universe that it would remain that way. Pvt. Yousseff, on the other hand, closed her eyes and pressed her lips tightly together, either furious with Draper and Stamovich, disgusted with them, or both.

Brackett wanted to slap the shit out of Stamovich, but he knew the only way to deal with an ass-kisser was to kick the ass he was so fond of kissing. He focused on Draper instead, moved nearer to him.

"What is my name, Sergeant?" he barked.

"Brackett, sir!" Draper barked in return, cocky as ever.

"Think again!"

"Captain Brackett, sir!"

Pettigrew, Nguyen, and Yousseff all shifted nervously. Stamovich watched the exchange from the corner of his eye, still half-smirking, sure that his asshole idol would win the day.

"Look me in the eye, Sergeant!" Brackett snapped.

Draper sneered as he complied, revealing his true nature.

"I am your commanding officer," Brackett said, quietly now, eye to eye, staring so hard he told himself his gaze was burning the core right out of Draper's brain. "If I order you to lick the floor clean, that's what you will do. If I want you to stand on your head in the corner, and stay there for a month, that's what you will do. If I tell you that you are confined to quarters, with zero human contact, then you will damn well stay alone in your quarters until you gouge your own eyes out with boredom."

Stamovich blinked and shifted a bit.

Draper still seemed too confident, though. Brackett knew he had been foolish to give the man an out, and now he took it away.

"You think it's going to be as easy as transferring out of here if you don't like your new commanding officer?" he continued, glancing at each of them in turn before coming back to Draper. He leaned forward, shuffled nearer, physically intruding on Draper's space until the marine had to take a step back.

"If you want out of here, *I* have to sign that paperwork. I have to be the one to *let* you out. So I'm not just your captain or your CO, Marvin. I'm your jailer. I'm your warden. I'm your personal fucking deity. I can be a benevolent god, or I can be the devil you wish you'd never met."

The pink flush in Draper's cheeks pleased Brackett, but not as much as the uncertainty that appeared in the man's eyes.

"You see it now, don't you, Marvin?" Brackett went on. "You and your friends. The moment I arrived here you made certain assumptions, the stupidest of which was that a young captain with no visible battle scars might just be soft. You figured you could just go on with whatever—"

"Captain?" Yousseff said, voice quiet but firm.

Brackett rounded on her. "You've got something to say, Private? Do you not see me chewing Sergeant Draper a new asshole?"

"Yes, sir," Yousseff said, eyes front, still at attention. "And it's about time, sir. But you should know that this far from home, the company is the tail that wags the dog. They have far more sway than the government. It's been that way forever. We—"

"Maybe none of you is listening," Brackett said, fists clenching and unclenching. "So I'll say this as clearly as I can. I am a marine. I do not work for Weyland-Yutani, and neither do any of you. If the order comes down from above that I'm to reinstate marine escorts on these survey missions, so be it. Until then, we run the show by the book, and the colony's science team will just have to do without us!"

"They've already done that, sir," Pettigrew said.

Brackett frowned. "Done what?"

"Gone ahead without us. One of the wildcatters told me the orders came in from the company—something specific, which isn't how it usually works," Pettigrew replied, chin up at attention, rather than in defiance. "The family went out early yesterday morning, in a crawler."

Icy dread snaked along Brackett's spine.

"What family?"

Pettigrew shrugged.

"Do any of you know?" Brackett asked, scanning their faces.

Stamovich glanced at Pettigrew.

"It was Russ, wasn't it?" the corporal said. "Guy with the scruffy beard and the cute wife?"

Yousseff frowned. "They took their *kids*?"

Brackett stared at her a second, wanting to say something, but the words would not come to him. He had denied it to himself, pretended he was too pragmatic a man to harbor any romantic illusions, but now the truth was stripped bare inside him. He hadn't come to Acheron to steal another man's wife, but had he secretly hoped Anne would realize her mistake, and choose him at last? Put them back on the path they had once shared?

Damn fool that he was, yes he had.

He still loved her.

His decision—not to allow his marines to escort the survey teams—still felt like the right one. But he didn't like it, the thought of Anne and her family, sent out on their own. He could still picture little Newt, her mouth stained with cherry freeze-pop. If anything happened to her because he'd stuck to the rules, he wouldn't be able to forgive himself.

And how had he not known this? It had occurred to him that he hadn't seen Anne, or run into Newt or Tim in the halls—not in the past day or so. But he'd been so focused on getting his squad in line…

Just another reason to be pissed at Draper.

He worried not just because they'd been sent out alone, but because of the circumstances. If specific orders had come in, this wasn't anything routine.

"The order from the company," Brackett said, turning to Pettigrew again. "What did it say, exactly?"

"No idea, Captain," the private replied. "Sorry."

All five marines were watching him now, no doubt wondering why he seemed so troubled by this news. Brackett didn't care. His personal fears were not theirs to know.

"Draper."

"Yes, Captain?"

"For some reason, these friends of yours look up to you." Brackett stared into his eyes again, making it clear that there was no room for debate. "That means that I'm not only going to hold you responsible for your actions, but theirs as well. You've formed your own little tribe here, but you're not part of any tribe. You are a Colonial Marine. I leave it to you to decide whether or not you will begin to behave like one."

Brackett studied them all again.

"Dismissed."

The five of them filed out. He counted ten seconds after the last of them had gone, and then he rushed out into the corridor, shut the door behind him, and went in search of Al Simpson.

He needed answers.

And he couldn't get her out of his mind.

Anne.

DATE: 21 JUNE, 2179
TIME: 1122

When she was nine, back on Earth, Anne Jorden's brother Rick had persuaded her to swim with him in a pond in the dying woodland at the end of their street. The pond had a layer of rotting leaves on top, and a scummy surface tinted a sickly, unnatural green. Mosquitoes flitted across the surface, but never alighted for long.

Aside from the occasional eel they saw nothing else living in the water, certainly no fish. But Anne worked hard to keep up with Rick in those days, fought to be seen by him as his equal, though he was three years her elder. She knew how to throw a punch and climb a tree and fix a car, if the trouble wasn't too complex. And when Rick threw down the gauntlet on a dare, he could be certain his little sister would take him up on it… as long as he led the way.

Anne didn't need her brother to lead the way anymore, but as she stepped through the gash in the starship's hull, a shudder went through her, and she remembered that day at the pond with utter clarity. In only her underpants, she had walked into the water, the silt and muck squishing up between her toes and sucking at her feet. Wading in, she had felt the pond water slide over her skin in an oily, viscous caress. By the time the water was up to her waist, she felt filthier than she ever had in her life.

The interior of the ship reminded her of that pond. The air ought to have been dusty and dry, and the floor near the breach was piled with ash, but even through her heavy jacket she could feel a kind of cold, clinging, damp weight to the air.

"Do you feel that?" Russ asked, coming in behind her.

Anne glanced in either direction along the broad, tall corridor. The floors and walls were made of some otherworldly alloy, tubes like veins running along the ceiling and the innermost wall.

She switched off her helmet lamp to conserve its battery, gripped another light that was attached to her belt, and turned it on. Russ did the same. Streaks of some fluid had dried on the wall in several places. She reached out to touch the stain, but hesitated, then pulled her hand back.

"Yeah. I feel it." She looked to the right, staring along the tunnel. That direction would take them to the tip of the ship's horseshoe design—the one closest to the crawler—which suggested that the more significant finds would be to the left, in the bulk of the vessel.

Anne glanced at Russ.

"We should get out of here," she said, "call this in, and take the kids back to town."

Russ stared at her. His goggles had a mist of condensation on the inside. Even so, she saw the struggle in his eyes.

"We go back, and we'll never know what they really find out here," he said. "Honey, even our little cut of this find could set us up forever. Do you understand? But if we want to protect ourselves, keep the company from fucking us over, we've *gotta* know what it is we've found."

Anne's heart fluttered, but not with fear.

"Is that the only reason you want to go on?"

Russ grinned. "Hell, no. This is what we came out here for…

something just like this! Do you want Mori or Reese or some company asshole to be the first one to see whatever there is to see?"

Nervous, afraid, but more thrilled than she'd ever been, she wetted her lips with her tongue.

"Hell, no," she echoed. "But we'll give it half an hour; no more. I don't want those kids waiting out there forever. I won't do that to them."

Her husband's eyes sparkled.

"Deal," he said.

This, she thought, *is why I married the man.*

She hefted her equipment and turned left, leading the way. The pond-scum feeling never went away. In fact, it increased as they trudged deeper into the derelict vessel. Her skin grew clammy and though the air felt cold, she felt flushed in a feverish sort of way. She would have thought she had fallen ill, except that Russ felt it, too.

Anne tried to keep her bearings, picturing the way the ship had sat on the ground, canted toward the back. It seemed hollow and dead, empty in a way that reminded her of an abandoned church she had entered once, as a girl. The small cemetery in the churchyard had been relocated, the bodies dug up and moved. The tabernacle had been taken out, along with several of the more elaborate stained-glass windows.

The place had felt haunted to her, not by ghosts, but by the absence of life… the architectural memory of voices raised in song and prayer, the echoes of footfalls on the stone floor, the clack of wooden kneelers, and the hope and surrender that always came with worship.

She'd never again felt such emptiness, until now.

Yet this was so much worse. The sense of the unknown, the breath of eons of alien culture slid around her, and she shivered with a dread she did not understand.

"It's just…"

"Extraordinary," Russ said.

"Ominous," Anne corrected. "I feel it in my bones, as if it's welcoming us and yet wants us gone, all at the same time."

"It's in your head," Russ said. "You're projecting. We can't even begin to imagine who the creatures were who built this—they must've been huge, though, far larger than any human. So your imagination tells you that we're intruders."

"We *are* intruders, Russell."

She could hear him laugh softly behind her.

"I don't see anyone sounding an alarm."

Anne flashed a smile, but it only lasted an instant. Her pulse kept racing, adrenaline singing through her.

"To your right," Russ said, voice tight. "Deep shadow. What's that?"

She twisted around and saw the shadowy cleft in the wall. Holding her breath, she edged nearer, and in the light from her belt she could make out an opening that was much larger than she'd thought. Floor to ceiling, it curved into the wall, a wide swath of shadow. Ducking her head into the cleft, she froze.

"Careful," Russ warned.

"It spirals down," she said.

"Their version of stairs?"

"Maybe. Definitely goes to another level, though." The spiral reminded her of the inside of an abandoned seashell, which underlined for her the strange bio-organic feel of the ship, as well as the emptiness that haunted her.

"Keep going. Clock's ticking," Russ reminded her.

Right, she thought. *Newt and Tim*. She had to get over the uneasiness that gripped her, and pick up the pace. Focused on her kids, Anne began to move faster, following her husband now.

"You sure we shouldn't have gone down there, to check out the sub-level?" she asked.

"Maybe, but I'm going to guess that whatever passes for a pilot's cabin is at the crux of the horseshoe. I could be wrong, but we don't have time to think too much about it. Whatever's down there, it'll be more than just corridors."

As he spoke, the ship's inner darkness seemed to deepen. Anne turned her head and shone her light on the wall, revealing scars in the strange metal. She stopped again.

"Anne," Russ prodded.

"Look at this," she said, staring at the pits and gashes in the wall. There were others on the floor. Something had melted right through, which made her stumble back and look up and around to make sure whatever had caused the melting hadn't continued to leak.

"Russ..." she said.

"Later," he told her as he passed by.

Anne fell in behind him again, but she kept her eyes on the walls and floor now, and she saw numerous places where similar scarring had occurred. Not just the melted spots, either. There were scorched holes blown in the wall, as if some sort of weapon had been fired. If not for the obvious age of the vessel, the way the dust and rock had eroded its hull and begun to swallow it, she would have begun to worry.

"Now this is weird," Russ said.

He clicked on one of the more powerful lights they'd brought in with them, hoping to take pictures to help establish their claim. The corridor lit up with a sickly yellow illumination and Anne gasped. The walls were different here. If the ship's construction seemed to hint at the organic, this was something else entirely. These walls were covered with a smooth, ribbed substance, black and gleaming like some mélange of insect cocoon and volcanic rock.

"What the hell is it?" she asked.

"You got me," Russ replied.

She ran one hand over the surface, grabbed a sharp ridge and applied pressure, snapping a small piece off in her hand. Chitinous and hard, its thinnest edges were brittle.

"Let's move on," she said, fascination guiding her. The clammy feeling had grown worse, but somehow she shrugged it off.

When they came to another open cleft, spiraling down to a sub-level, they stopped and stared at it for nearly a full minute. This cleft differed from the first. It, too, had been covered by that chitinous material, as if to adapt it for a different sort of species altogether.

"I don't like this," Anne said.

"Neither do I," Russ admitted. She could tell how hard it was for him to admit it. He sighed. "Look, let's just make it to the crux of the ship, to see if that's the engine room or pilot's cabin or whatever. We'll take footage of it, and then get the hell out of here. As long as we get that far, they can't shut us out entirely."

He started to walk away.

Anne stayed, staring down into that winding cleft.

"What—" Russ began.

"We go down," she said, not entirely certain why. "Whatever might be of value to the company—artifacts, technology, whatever—if it's down there, and we pass it by, we'll regret it forever." She turned and looked at him, letting him see a truth in her eyes that was painful to reveal. "I don't want to be here forever, Russ."

He shook his head with an incredulous laugh, put a gloved hand against his helmet. "Otto and I—"

"Were talking crazy," Anne said. "Abandoning the colony without a backup plan, with no exit strategy… that's foolish. But this… you're right. This could be it for us, the thing we've been searching for. The kids are out there waiting for us and they'll keep waiting. We've left them longer than this, and they know how to entertain each other. It's for their sake that we can't leave here without knowing what it is we've found."

Anne took one more look along the corridor, her light gleaming on the strange ridges and curves of the glassy black walls. A flash of connection sparked in her mind—cocoon to web to spider—and she shuddered at the inference. She didn't like the idea of them trapped inside some kind of spiderweb.

Not a web, she thought, frowning as she studied the walls again. *It's more like a hive. A wasps' nest.*

Either way, she didn't like it.

15

STRANGE CARGO

DATE: 21 JUNE, 2179
TIME: 1131

Brackett caught up with Simpson as he was coming out of the toilet, still in the process of cinching his belt. The man seemed to hear the heavy footfalls coming toward him, and he looked up, tensing immediately. He put his hands up as if he feared an assault.

"I've got a question for you," Brackett said, his voice firm.

"Whatever it is, maybe you'd better take a step back," Simpson said. Nervously, he smoothed his mustache and stood a bit straighter, trying to pretend he hadn't been afraid a moment before.

Brackett leaned in toward him, crowding the administrator so that he was the one who took a step back.

"You sent the Jordens out on a survey—"

"Which is none of your business, is it?" Simpson replied, trying to keep his voice level. "I mean, you made it pretty clear that, in your view, the Colonial Marines aren't to be involved with the Company's field work," he added, eyes narrowing.

"Their kids are, what, six and ten?"

Simpson shrugged. "Something like that."

Brackett tried to remind himself that he would be stationed on Acheron for years, and he had to be able to work with this man. But just the stale smell of Simpson's breath made him want to throw a punch.

"Look, Captain, I'm with you," the administrator continued. "I disapprove entirely of Russ and Anne bringing their kids out on this survey, but there are no rules against it. In fact, this is a wildcat job. Right now they're operating as independent contractors."

"Why now?" Brackett asked. "Why today?"

A pair of technicians hurried past them. They glanced uneasily at Simpson and Brackett, sensing the hostility there.

"It's really not your concern, Captain."

"You received specific orders. This isn't a routine grid search," Brackett said, and he saw the confirmation in Simpson's eyes. "Someone at Weyland-Yutani must have wanted that location surveyed immediately."

Simpson narrowed his eyes, a smirk appearing on his face.

"Presumably that's the case, Captain Brackett, but I'm not privy to the 'whys' in cases like this. Nobody tells me anything. If they *had* told me, however, you can be damned sure I wouldn't share it with you. It's company business, I'll remind you."

"And if something happens to the Jordens?" Brackett demanded. "To their kids?"

Simpson sneered. "Well, then it'll be a damn shame they didn't have any marines along to provide security."

He brushed past, and ambled back toward his office.

Brackett could only watch him go.

DATE: 21 JUNE, 2179
TIME: 1139

Anne led the way into the cleft, and she and Russ followed the spiral down into the lower level of the derelict ship.

Russ said nothing, but she could see from the way he held himself—the cock of his head and the slight hunch of his shoulders—that he felt the dark weight of the ship around him. Just as she did. Her heart beat faster and her breath turned shallow as they wound their way down, helmet lights throwing ghost shapes on the walls.

They found the first dead thing at the bottom of the spiral.

"Holy shit," Russ muttered.

Anne held her breath as she stepped into the corridor, staring at the thing in the juddering beam. She was trembling. In life, the alien had been very tall and powerfully built, with an extended torso and a long head. It seemed humanoid only in the sense that it had two arms and two legs, but otherwise it was entirely *other*. Something about it suggested an insect, which gave her an unnerving connection to her thoughts about the hard substance that coated the walls.

Yet this was no bug.

Its skin wasn't skin at all, but some kind of armored carapace. Richly blue in spots, it had faded to gray in most places, and the carapace looked to have gone thin and brittle. She felt sure the thicker, darker shell was closer to its living appearance. Its tail wound behind it, sharp and skeletal, with a tip that would have made a wicked weapon. Not quite a stinger, Anne thought, but if the alien used it that way it would have killed a person just as quickly.

"It's beautiful," Russ said.

Anne turned to stare at him in disgust.

"What?"

"Look at it," he said. "It's like nothing *anyone* has ever seen. Until now."

"It's horrible," she said quietly, staring at the blue-tinted jaws and the tail. "This thing was born to kill."

"It's been dead for a very long time," Russ said. "But I'll tell you what it was born for… to make us rich."

He gave a quiet laugh and turned away, moving down the sub-level corridor. Anne stared another moment at the dead alien, and then followed. Russ might be right, and she knew this thing couldn't harm her—its cadaver was little more than a shell, not unlike the derelict spacecraft they were exploring. But she couldn't escape the feeling of its presence. When she had first entered the ship, she had been sure its halls were as empty as that abandoned church. Now every shadow felt full of menace, of teeth and slithering, sharp-tipped tails.

The sub-level had been completely taken over by the chitinous walls she'd seen above, but still there were many spots where something had melted through, sprayed and burned its way into the floors and walls. They walked through the darkness, lighting their own way, and at a curve in the hallway they found three more of them.

One had been torn in half, its desiccated corpse a dried and twisted thing, half on one side of the hall and half on the other. Another had an enormous hole through its mid-section, and the floor beneath it had been melted away into a yawning chasm. A draft swept in from there, but whether from outside or from elsewhere in the ship, they could not tell.

There were doors all along the corridor. Some of them opened easily, while others were stuck shut by that strange, hardened, resin-like substance. The first two that Russ opened contained nothing more than dust and small, strange bones. In the next there were thick metal alloy shelves with mounds that were now rot. It was impossible to know what they had been before rotting.

"Cargo, do you think?" Anne asked.

"Of some kind," Russ agreed. "Food or some other materials. Those first two rooms were pens, though. Like stables. Alien livestock or something else… Whatever they were, these creatures were taking them somewhere."

That didn't sound right to Anne. Didn't feel right.

"I don't think so," she said. "Not the things we saw back there."

"What do you mean?"

"Whatever those creatures were, they weren't the ones piloting this ship."

He nodded, but didn't respond.

They continued on, discovering other massive alien corpses in clusters of three or four, perhaps twenty in all. Several minutes later, maneuvering through the claustrophobic underbelly of the ship, they encountered something altogether different. New remains.

Anne froze. Now she understood why the corridors were so high and so wide. They hadn't been built this size for the sake of grandeur, but simply for scale. The remains of this new creature were more humanoid than the first, but even larger than the others—nine feet, Anne guessed. All that remained of its body was its skeleton—bones inside some kind of exo-suit of the same design as the ship, with the same techno-organic texture.

This dead thing had been one of the ship's crew. She knew it.

"Where are the others?" she asked.

"Others?" Russ said. "You think there are other species here?"

"No, no... others like this one. Where's the rest of the crew?"

Russ had no answer.

"How long have we been gone from the crawler?" she asked.

"Dunno," he said, checking his watch. "Thirty-five minutes? Not more than that, I don't think."

Taking a deep breath, she reached out and took his hand, not liking the fact that their gloves kept their skin from touching.

"All right. Let's get some images of this guy and the others, and then we get out of here. Five minutes more," she said.

Russ agreed. They worked mostly in silence, both of them uneasy. Anne felt disappointed in herself—in both of them. By all rights they ought to have been ecstatic. He had been right. This was going to change their lives. Their share of whatever the company made from this salvage—from the ship and its tech, from the alien corpses and whatever Weyland-Yutani might learn from them—meant they would never have to work again. They should have been weeping with joy, screaming in celebration. Instead, Anne felt like she couldn't breathe, felt the weight of the air inside the ship as if it might suffocate her. She just wanted out, and judging from his silence, she knew that Russ felt the same.

It took them ten minutes. When they'd finished in the sub-level, they lugged their gear back up the spiral, then paused together and looked along the corridor toward the crux of the ship. Both of them. They had been married so long, knew each other so well, that no words were necessary for a decision to be made.

"This close," Russ said. "Five minutes or less, we'll be at the crux. See what there is to see. A few images, and we're back outside in fifteen, twenty minutes at most. The kids are probably napping by now."

"I'm sure it's been more than an hour," Anne told him. But Russ knew that it wasn't an argument. They both glanced back the way they'd come, toward the breach in the hull that would be their exit, and then he hefted his gear onto one shoulder and took her hand.

Together they walked toward the crux.

Around the next corner they discovered one of each of the two alien species, locked in a terrible embrace. This bug-like creature was different from its brethren. It was larger, and had a large, ridged plate on its bright blue head that seemed to be a kind of crest.

"What the hell happened here?" Russ muttered.

"War," Anne said. "The question is, where did the bugs come from? Were they on the ship, in the cargo hold, or were they already here on Acheron, and attacked the ship after the crash?"

"And what about this one?" Russ asked. "Why is it so different?"

Anne studied the deadly embrace again, studied that blue crest, and frowned.

"It's a queen."

"What, you mean like with bees?"

"Doesn't this all remind you of a hive?" She gestured at the crusted walls. "Maybe the others are like drones, and this one is like a queen." She shrugged. "Or maybe that crest on its head just makes me think of a crown."

The alien she thought of as a queen had impaled the crewman with its tail, but the crewman had given as good as he'd gotten. He'd thrust his left arm up inside the queen's jaws, as if he had tried to destroy its brain with a bare hand.

"Come on," Russ said. "Let's finish this up. I don't want to be here anymore."

They walked on.

Minutes later, they found a vast chamber where many of the crew must once have been able to gather. The dome curved high overhead, and it was crusted with the same chitin they had seen elsewhere.

"This is just creepy as hell," Russ said. "I feel like I can't breathe."

Anne could only nod.

There was a platform at the front of the chamber. On it stood a massive seat and some kind of gigantic apparatus that she felt sure must have been used to navigate the ship. In the seat was another of the crew, though this one wore a helmet that covered its entire head.

"The pilot, do you think?" Russ asked as they climbed up to investigate.

"Or the navigator."

"Look at its chest," Russ whispered, and she could practically feel his breath at her ear. But Anne had already seen the twisted, mummified bones jutting out of its exo-suit, and the hole behind its ribs.

"That's how they killed him," Russ said. "Must have used a weapon, or maybe one of their tails, like in the corridor back there."

"I don't think so," Anne whispered. She'd seen the way the bones twisted outward. Whatever had killed the giant had come from inside.

She stumbled back from it, nearly slipping off the edge of the platform. Catching herself, she grabbed the side of the navigator's chair and turned to face the back of the cavernous chamber. When they had come in, the platform had been the first thing their lights had illuminated. It had drawn them to it immediately.

Now she saw something else.

Many other somethings.

"Russell," she said quietly. A disquieting feeling came over her, not quite excitement and not quite fear. "Look at this."

Her light played over a low blanket of mist that hung just below the level of the platform. As she looked, she saw that the vapor itself seemed to have some small luminescence of its own. Below it, spread out all around the platform in a recessed area of the chamber floor, were dozens of large pods, each perhaps a foot or eighteen inches high. They were oval, somewhat egg-shaped, though there was something almost floral about the tops of the things. Ugly flowers that would never blossom.

Never, of course, because they had been here for eons.

"The mist…" Russ began.

"It's weirdly humid in here," Anne said. "Maybe the ship is drawing in moisture from the outside, and holding it in this chamber."

"What are they, Annie?" he asked, staring at the pods. "More cargo?"

Anne shone her light around and studied the chamber. A cargo space? It might have been, she supposed. She set her gear on the platform and moved down toward the objects.

"Should we bring one back?" she asked, pushing off from the edge of the platform and sliding down below the upper edge of the fog.

The pods appeared to have a leathery texture, yet they still reminded Anne of flowers yet to bloom. She frowned as she dropped to one knee, and studied the nearest one.

"Are they… pulsing?" Russ asked from behind her.

"I think so," Anne replied. A smile spread across her lips. It wasn't possible for them to be pulsing, of course, because that suggested that life remained in these pods, whatever they were. Centuries or millennia after the ship had crashed and the bloody battle that had killed so many on board, these strangely cool hothouse mists seemed to have kept these pods in some kind of hibernation state.

She reached for the nearest one, her fingers hovering only a foot away.

"Wait," Russ said. "We don't know what they are."

Anne turned to smile at him.

"If the surface is toxic, it won't get through my gloves."

"Let's just set up the camera, take some images, and Simpson can worry about them," Russ urged.

"Now where's *your* sense of adventure?" she asked.

She saw her husband's eyes widen at the same time as she heard a wet, sticky, peeling noise from behind her. Russ grabbed her arm and hauled her toward him.

"Get back!" he snapped.

Anne lost her balance and slumped against the edge of the platform. Beyond Russ, she saw the pod opening, strings of mucous hanging from the four petal-like flaps as it split apart. Something shifted and jerked inside the object.

"Russell…" she said, suddenly afraid.

"It's all right," he told her, glancing over at the pod.

The thing within launched itself at him, latched onto his face, and he tried to scream. The sound became a horrible gagging as he stumbled back into her. Anne cried out his name as she shoved and dragged and urged him up onto the platform. Only there did she see the back of the hideous spider-thing that had attached itself to him.

It's all right, he had said. But it was not all right. Nor would it ever be all right again.

16

BE CAREFUL WHAT YOU WISH FOR

21 JUNE, 2179
TIME: 1207

Upside down on the driver's seat of the crawler, Newt hummed softly to herself. It hurt her neck a bit, putting the weight on her shoulders and the back of her head, but she pushed her feet toward the vehicle's roof, extending her toes, trying to see if she could touch.

"Rebecca, sit normal," Tim instructed.

"This isn't normal?"

"You're upside down."

"Maybe *you're* upside down."

Her brother reached up and whapped her legs. She scrabbled for purchase but went over like a falling tree, tumbling in between the front seats. Her limbs flailed and she felt her right foot kick her brother's thigh. When he called out in protest, she kept flailing a bit longer and kicked him again, smiling to herself.

"Rebecca!" he snapped angrily.

She sat on the crawler's floor between the seats and gave him an exasperated look.

"Why do you always call me that?"

"It's your name," he answered. "And don't kick me."

"You pushed me over. I was falling. And I *don't* like that name."

Tim sighed and shoved himself deeper into his seat. He'd been drawing before, but put his pad aside fifteen or twenty minutes ago.

"Maybe I like being upside down," she muttered, pouting her lips.

"What?" he asked, glaring at her.

"I like being upside down."

He rolled his eyes. "Fine. Just do it in the other seat. I'm going to take a nap."

Newt raised her eyebrows and edged closer to him.

"Wow. You must *really* be bored."

Tim glanced at her. "Aren't you? They take us all the way out here, but then they don't let us do anything. What's the point?"

"I'm not bored," she asserted.

He sat up straighter, scratching at a blemish on his cheek.

"You're telling me you wouldn't rather be back at the colony, playing Monster Maze with Lizzie and Aaron and Kembrell?"

Newt scoffed and blew a lock of her hair away from her eyes. "Sure, that would be more fun than this. But Mom and Dad are here, and so it's okay to be here with them. It's an adventure, remember?"

Tim leaned toward her, cocking his head and studying her as if she were some kind of weird insect.

"Yeah, but it's *their* adventure," he said. "We're just sitting here."

"Maybe you are," Newt said, crawling back into the front seat. "*I'm* thinking."

Shifting around, she put her legs in the air again, propped on her neck and shoulders, and reached for the ceiling with her toes.

"Yeah? What are you thinking, then?"

Newt's stomach gave a little uneasy flutter and she shivered.

"I'm thinking Mom and Dad have been gone an awfully long time."

21 JUNE, 2179
TIME: 1229

Brackett skipped lunch in the dining hall, heated himself a bowl of soup, and then turned to exercise to try to sweat out the worry that was gnawing at him. Two hundred sit-ups, two hundred pushups, and countless squats didn't do the job, so he switched to the pull-up bar his predecessor had installed over the bathroom door. Biceps burning, he drew himself up and lowered himself down, steady and in control of his pace.

His frustration began to leech away as his thoughts blurred with the effort. For the first time in well over an hour, he didn't feel the urge to check the clock on the wall, to count the minutes since the colony's last contact from the Jordens.

Sweat beaded and ran down the middle of his back. His heart thudded in his ears while he tried to remember how many reps he'd done, and decide if he ought to do more. The answer was easy enough—if he stopped now, he'd only go back to watching the time.

Whatever happens, it's not your fault, Brackett told himself, taking hold of the bar again. An image of Newt flickered into his thoughts. Newt, her mouth stained from that freeze-pop, those big eyes so earnest and wise beyond her years.

He hauled himself up again, pull-up after pull-up, trying to blot that image from his mind. It proved just as difficult as his attempts to forget Anne over the years. His life had gone on, and he'd been happy enough. Content enough. He'd thought that he would go the rest of his life without ever seeing her again, and decided that he could live with that.

For a brief period he'd been in love with a pilot named Tyra, but that had all unraveled, partly because of the demands of their careers and partly because each of them had experienced greater love before, and knew that what they had wasn't enough.

Then came his assignment to Acheron. Part of him wished he'd never been posted here. *River of pain*, he thought, remembering the mythological origins of the name. As far as Brackett was concerned, they had chosen it well.

Someone knocked at his door. He dropped down from the bar and grabbed his towel, wiping sweat from his face.

"It's open!" he called. The door swung inward and Julisa Paris stepped inside, straight-backed and formal.

"Captain," she said, by way of greeting.

"You have something for me, Lieutenant?"

"Sorry to say I don't, sir."

Brackett felt an uneasy tremor travel down his spine.

"So the Jordens haven't checked in?"

"That's what I'm told," Paris confirmed, her eyes grim. "As far as I can tell, Simpson hasn't even tried to reach them. He's playing it off as if it's no big deal, and maybe it isn't, but the shift supervisor I spoke to said people are getting jittery."

Brackett cursed under his breath.

"What do you want to do, Captain?" she asked.

"Nothing yet. But be ready. I stood on principle with this matter, and I'll look like an idiot if I throw those principles out the window. But if that family's in trouble, I don't plan to leave them out there. Thirty minutes, Lieutenant. If the Jordens haven't checked in by then, we're going out."

Paris saluted. "Yes, sir."

She turned on her heel and departed. Brackett closed the door behind her.

Where are you, Anne? he thought, as he hurried to the shower. He wanted to be suited up and ready to go if it came to that. The delay in reporting in could have been due to a communications malfunction, or they might be lost in the excitement of discovery. But a dreadful certainty had begun to form in his gut.

Call in, damn it, he thought. *Prove me wrong.*

21 JUNE, 2179
TIME: 1256

Newt sat in the driver's seat, hugging herself.

The crawler's lights had gone on as it grew darker outside. The wind had picked up and it blew against the vehicle hard enough to rattle the windows. Though the heat ran, Newt still felt cold seeping in from outside, and she started to wonder how long the lights and the heat would work. Would the crawler run out of power? Her mom and dad wouldn't leave them here long enough for that to happen, would they?

Not on purpose, she thought.

For the first time, she grew truly worried.

The wind howled even harder as she glanced over at her brother, who had curled up in the passenger seat and fallen asleep at least half an hour before. She wanted to wake him, just so she wouldn't feel so alone, but he would only be nasty to her. Most of the time, Tim was a good big brother. They got along well and they played together and they laughed a lot, but when he was tired or nervous he could be short with her, even mean.

Newt didn't think she could handle him being unkind to her right now.

She sat staring out the window at the huge, curving spaceship. In the swirling dust and the gloom it was hard to get a clear view, but when there was a lull in the wind she could see it all right. The ship seemed quiet now, making it hard to imagine that anyone was alive inside it—walking around, having a Jorden family adventure.

She shifted in her seat, turning away from her view of the big , dark ship. It troubled her now just to think of it, silent and empty. She shifted again, and the wind whipped against the crawler so hard it felt like giant hands were giving the vehicle a shove.

She trembled and wetted her dry lips with her tongue. Tentatively, she reached out and nudged her brother. Tim grumbled and turned away, burrowing into the seat, trying to find a comfortable position.

"Tim," she whispered, shaking him a bit harder. "Timmy, wake up."

She hadn't called him Timmy since she was very little. He didn't like it, now that they were growing up, but at that moment she felt very small. Felt little again.

"Timmy," she said again, and he turned sleepily toward her, eyes opening.

"What?" he groaned.

"They've been gone a long time," she said.

For a second she thought he would snap at her, demand that she let him sleep. Then he sat up a bit straighter, and looked out through the windshield at the darkened landscape, listening to the wind. Nothing so far had scared her as much as the uncertainty she saw in her brother's eyes.

Tim looked afraid.

"It'll be okay, Newt," he said. "Dad knows what he's doing."

Suddenly she couldn't breathe. Tim never called her Newt. Why had he called her that now if not to comfort her, to try to make her less afraid?

Suddenly the door beside her whipped open, crashing against the crawler. Newt screamed as the wind roared in and she twisted just as a dark shape lunged in at her. Shrieking, she pulled back from the shape, her heart about to explode. Then she saw the face and with a shock realized it was her mother, panicked and looking so wild that Newt continued to scream.

Tim's shouts joined with her own as their mom reached inside and grabbed the handheld radio that was tethered to the dash.

"Mayday! Mayday!" her mother called into the radio, shouting over the wind. "This is alpha kilo two four nine calling Hadley Control. Repeat! This is—"

Newt looked past her mother and saw that she wasn't alone, that her father was there, too, but something was wrong with him. He lay sprawled on the ground outside the door and in the light from the crawler she could see there was something on his face. Some kind of disgusting thing that looked like a spider, its many legs like bony fingers, its body pulsing with hideous life.

Her screams turned to shrieks as her eyes went wide. She screamed again and again, her voice merging with the howling wind, so that it seemed as if all of Acheron screamed along with her.

21 JUNE, 2179
TIME: 1257

Brackett strode toward the command block, full of grim purpose. Pride and principle had to be cast aside now. Too much time had passed. The Jordens had to be in trouble.

Lt. Paris walked beside him, perfectly in synch. Proving her wisdom, she hadn't said a word to him about the fact that it had been his decision—his desire to shake things up—that had led to the Jordens being sent out without an escort.

Simpson wouldn't have the lieutenant's discretion.

"You informed Sergeant Coughlin—"

"To gather a team, yes, sir," Paris finished for him. "Aldo will drive. We'll take Hauer and Chenovski—"

"Not 'we,'" Brackett interrupted. "I want you here. Anything goes wrong, I don't want Draper trying to call the shots."

"Yes, sir," she replied. "Only..."

"Only what?" he asked as they rounded a corner. From up ahead they could hear the sound of voices and the beeping of machines.

"It's you who should stay behind, Captain Brackett," she said firmly. "Sorry, sir, but you're the CO here. I'm your junior officer. If there's any risk involved—and we must assume that, until we learn otherwise—it ought to be me who goes."

Brackett didn't look at her.

"Except that you're right, Julisa," he replied. "I'm the CO, so it's my call."

They marched half a dozen steps before she replied.

"Yes, sir."

Simpson emerged from the command block before they'd even reached the door, one of his techs trailing behind him. They were in conversation, both looking deeply troubled, when the administrator glanced up and saw the marines approaching. Brackett knew instantly from his expression that something had occurred, and it wasn't good.

"Captain Brackett," Simpson said, concern turning to a sneer. "I hope you're happy now."

Lt. Paris swore. "You may want to rethink your approach right now, mister."

Brackett held up a hand.

"Stop," he said, glaring at the bureaucrat, who seemed scared even as he puffed himself up with arrogance and disdain. "Tell it fast, Simpson. What's happened?"

Simpson actually glanced around to make sure no one else was within hearing range.

"They found a derelict spacecraft," he said. "Ancient, according to Anne Jorden—"

Anne's all right, Brackett thought.

"—but even so, there was something on board. Some kind of leech, if I understood correctly. Hard to get a clear line with the constant atmospheric disturbance. Russ needs medical attention, and immediately."

"Shit," Brackett muttered. "What about the kids?"

"Okay, for now," Simpson said. "I'm getting a rescue together. Techs and volunteers."

"Forget it," Brackett said quickly. "We've got this. Sergeant Coughlin is gathering a team now. If you hadn't heard from them, we were going out anyway."

Simpson hitched up his belt.

"Oh, you mean it's not too much trouble?" he said. "We don't want to break protocol, after all. Don't want to put you out, Captain."

Brackett ground his teeth together, then took a step forward and poked a finger into the man's chest.

"Later, you and I are going to have a talk about how you could be *stupid* enough to get an order like the one you got from the company—an order that clearly implied a discovery of great importance—and still let Anne and Russ Jorden take their children with them."

He poked Simpson again.

"Until then," he said, "you can go fuck yourself."

22 JUNE, 2179
TIME: 0402

Anne sat in the front seat of the crawler with an arm around each of her children. She had stripped off her jacket as if it had been tainted, somehow, by the vile mist surrounding the pods inside that ship. Sixteen hours after she'd dragged Russ back to the crawler, her ears still rang from Newt's screaming. It had taken forever for the girl to calm down, but she and Tim had finally fallen asleep.

Calmed down? Anne thought to herself. *She's not calm—she's in shock. And so are you, for that matter.*

She hadn't slept a wink. How could she?

Tim rustled in the back seat, coming blearily awake.

"Mom, why are we still here?" He sat up and rubbed his eyes, glancing out through the window at the darkness. "We need to get Dad back to the colony. Dr. Komiskey will help him.

"She *will* be able to help, right?" he added.

Anne kept silent. The words had woken Newt from a restless sleep, and now the little girl looked up. Her lips quivered, and then she buried her face in her mother's chest and began to cry again, a ragged, gasping sob that came and went in waves.

The wind shrieked around the crawler and the door banged because Anne hadn't closed it tightly enough. She shifted forward to look out the window on that side. In the glow of the vehicle's lights she could see the dust sweeping over Russ's still form. His goggles and jacket would protect him from the worst of it, but she'd tucked a blanket under his shoulders and used it to partially cover his face. It flapped in the wind, but so far it hadn't just blown away, and that was good.

Good, because it might keep him from suffocating, if the abomination hugging his face hadn't already done the job. Good, also, because it kept the kids from seeing clearly just what had happened to their father.

"Mom," Tim begged, "it's been too long! We need to just take Dad back ourselves!"

"We can't do that," she said.

"What are we waiting for?" Tim asked, his emotions fraying just as much as hers.

Anne glanced at Newt. She didn't want to have this conversation with Tim, and she sure as hell didn't want to have it with her six-year-old daughter beside her. Newt seemed to be barely listening, though. Even in the midst of her own shock and horror, Anne felt her heart breaking over her daughter's trauma.

You'd better be all right, Russell, she thought furiously. *You* have *to be.*

"It took all my strength to get him out here to the crawler, Tim," she said quietly, nuzzling her son's ear, hoping that Newt wouldn't hear her. "But even if I could get him inside, I wouldn't. And he wouldn't want me to."

"What are you *talking* about?" Tim cried. "He's… you saw him… he needs—"

"Tim!" she snapped, and instantly she regretted it.

Her son stared into her eyes, searching them for an answer.

"I can't have him in here with you and your sister," Anne said, hating the tremor in her voice and the hot tears that began to spill down her cheeks. She swiped at them angrily. "Whatever happens to your father, he would never forgive me if I did that. I don't know anything about that thing on his face—what it's doing to him, or what it might do to you and Newt if I brought it in here with you."

Newt shuddered and mumbled something into her chest, words muffled by Anne's shirt.

"What's that, honey?" Anne asked, glancing again out the window.

"So we have to wait," Newt repeated. Eyes red and puffy, she put on her brave face. "Daddy's going to be okay."

"Okay?" Tim asked. "Did you see that *thing*?"

Newt's breath hitched.

"I saw it before you did. But I also saw Dad when Mom was putting that blanket on him, and his chest was moving up and down. He's breathing, and as long as he's breathing, he's gonna be okay."

Anne smiled wanly at her, hating the screaming of the wind and the rattle of the door, but loving her children with all her heart.

"Of course he is," she said, with a confidence she did not feel. She kissed Newt's cheek, then turned and kissed Tim on the forehead. "Of course he is."

They sat wordlessly, and she clutched them to her.

* * *

"Do you hear that?" Tim asked.

Anne stiffened, listening hard for any sound from Russ or the creature. Then she heard the roar of an engine and her heart leapt. Newt sat up on the seat, facing backward, and headlights washed over her face. Anne whipped around to look out the back window, and saw the lights growing brighter.

Seconds later a heavy-crawler roared up beside them.

Demian Brackett was the first one out onto the ground.

Newt threw her door open, hopped out and ran to him, jumping up into his arms. Brackett staggered back a step but caught her, hugging her tightly. Over Newt's shoulder, he stared at Anne with those strong, reassuring eyes.

"Move it!" Brackett shouted as other marines climbed out of their crawler. He glanced over at Russ, the blanket still flapping over his face like some terrible shroud. "Get him aboard now!"

Anne stared at Russ as the marines went to him, watched the horror on their faces as they got their first glimpses of the thing attached to his face. A cold wave of nausea swept through her as she forced herself not to look at it, not to think about what it might have done to him.

"Sergeant Coughlin!" Brackett shouted over the wind. "Drive the Jordens' crawler back! Hauer, go with them!"

"No!" Newt cried, still in his arms. "You take us! Please!"

Brackett hesitated, cocking his head back to look into Newt's eyes. As the other marines put Russ on a stretcher and lifted him off the ground, Brackett nodded toward Coughlin and carried Newt toward her mother.

"All right," he said, handing Newt up into the crawler. He gave Anne a single nod. "Let's get you all home."

17

NOTHING ALIVE

22 JUNE, 2179
TIME: 2101

Newt climbed out of the crawler and stood between her mother and Tim, watching numbly as the marines drove their larger vehicle into the underground garage behind them.

After so long with the wind and the scouring grit, it seemed strangely quiet in the garage... except of course that it wasn't quiet at all. Techs shouted to one another and a handful of colonists rushed over to talk to Newt's mother. Jiro, the botanist, wanted to know what had happened to Russ. Mrs. Hernandez, who had babysat for Newt and Tim many times, asked Newt's mom if they were all right. Then the nurse, Joel Asher, nudged past them.

"Give them room to breathe," Joel said, focusing on Newt's mother. "Anne, are you all right? Can you talk to me?"

Newt glanced up and saw that her mother didn't seem to have even heard Joel. Instead, she was staring at the marines' crawler as the driver, Aldo, and one of the others climbed up the ramp and into the rear of the vehicle.

"Mom," Newt said, taking her hand. She squeezed. "Joel's talking to you."

Anne blinked, and focused on Joel.

"Just look after Russ," she said. "The rest of us are fine."

"I need to check you all out," the nurse insisted.

"Not now. Just take care of my husband."

"Anne—"

"Not now!"

Capt. Brackett came around the front of the crawler, his eyes sad but kind. He held up a hand to the nurse.

"Please, just do as she asks. Worry about Russ for now," Brackett said, glancing at Newt and then Tim. "I'll make sure these guys come to the medical unit as soon as possible, but they're really fine. You want to make them okay, you need to take care of their father. That's what they need."

The nurse seemed about to argue when they all heard a commotion and looked up to see Aldo and Chenovski carrying Newt's father down out of the heavy-crawler on a stretcher. A ripple of fear went through the garage, and some of the people there recoiled in horror and revulsion from what they saw.

Newt's mother started toward the stretcher, but Brackett caught her by the shoulder.

"You want them to help him," Brackett said. "Let them do their jobs."

She brushed his hand away.

"He needs me."

"Anne," Brackett said, and something about his tone made her turn toward him. "He needs doctors. He needs the science team. You just said you and the kids can look after yourselves, and you're going to have to do that."

Newt watched her mother's face, saw the frustration and grief and even anger there, and she felt her own eyes begin to burn with fresh tears. It upset her—she thought she had been done with crying.

The marines paused at the bottom of the ramp, both of them staring at the multi-legged creature latched on to Russ's face.

"What is it?" Chenovski asked.

Aldo grunted. Newt had heard him talking many times about his past experiences. She thought of him as the bravest of the marines, but she saw the fear in him, and it worried her.

"Let's get it off him first, and then we'll figure out what it is," Aldo said. He glanced at Capt. Brackett when he said it, and a troubled look passed between them.

Newt took the captain's hand, gazing up at him.

"Help my dad."

Brackett went down on one knee beside her. They had ridden all the way back to the colony without any of them saying much, except for Newt's mom comforting her and Tim. Capt. Brackett had spoken kindly to all three of them, but she couldn't remember the words now—only the soothing tone. Mostly he had just *been there*, strong and sure that he could help them.

"I'll do everything I can," he said.

Joel, the nurse, laid a hand on the top of Newt's head.

"We all will."

They stood together and watched the marines carrying the stretcher toward the elevator. A door opened at the far end of the garage, and Dr. Reese came hurrying in with Dr. Mori and two of their researchers. Mr. Lydecker, from administration, strode in behind them. The group pushed past the colonists who had gathered in the garage, and raced to catch up with the marines carrying the stretcher.

Dr. Reese made Aldo and Chenovski stop a few feet from the elevator. He stood staring at Newt's father. Everyone there in the garage had seen the creature attached to his face by now, and all of them had turned away, some twisting their faces in disgust. Dr. Reese was the first person to see the nasty bug-thing with its long spindly legs—to see the way it had clamped onto Russ Jorden—and *smile*.

Lt. Paris walked over toward Brackett, glancing uneasily at Newt and her mother and brother.

"Why is he smiling?" Newt asked, a terrible, sour anger churning in her belly. "Is he happy this happened?"

"Of course not," Lt. Paris said, ruffling Newt's hair. "Dr. Reese is a scientist, honey. This is something he's never seen before. He may be excited about discovering something new, but I'm sure he's just as worried about your father as the rest of us are."

Tim snorted. "Bullshit."

Newt felt sure her mother would punish him for it, but she didn't correct him at all. Maybe she agreed. Or maybe she was just happy that Tim had spoken at all, since he had been so quiet on the ride back.

"Some people smile or laugh when they're nervous," Brackett added.

"I do that sometimes!" Newt said, squeezing her mother's hand, turning to look up into her face.

"He doesn't look nervous," Tim said.

"But he should be," their mother whispered, her eyes wide.

The captain patted Tim on the shoulder, then turned and picked Newt up off the ground as if she weighed nothing at all. Tired and sad as she was, she did not argue with him.

"Come on," he said. "Let's get you all back to your quarters so you can clean up."

Newt's mother nodded, and together they started across the garage toward the far door that Reese and Mori and the others had just come through. Mrs. Hernandez and a wildcatter named Gruenwald walked along with them, but the others hung back and just watched them. It made Newt feel bad to have these people she had known her whole life staring at them as if they were putting on some kind of show, when the only show was her family being scared.

"Simpson's going to be waiting for you upstairs, I'm sure," Brackett said. "He'll have to debrief you about what happened out there, what you saw—"

"I don't know if I can talk about it," Newt's mother said as they walked to the door, their footfalls echoing across the garage.

The captain reached out and squeezed her hand, holding it for only a second.

"You have to, and not just for the sake of the colony and any danger we might be in," he said. "Every detail you remember is another piece of information that might help them help Russ."

"Mom?" Tim said worriedly.

"Okay," Anne said, nodding. "Okay."

"I'll stay with you for the debrief," Brackett went on, "but you should ask a friend to run interference for you afterward, be the gatekeeper, so you don't have to talk to anyone you don't want to talk to."

"Can't you do it?" Newt asked.

Capt. Brackett hefted her a bit higher on his hip and met her eyes.

"I'm sorry, Newt. We're all going to have a lot to do now. That ship out there changes everything for the colony. My squad needs to be prepared for anything, and we need to provide security for the people Dr. Reese and Mr. Simpson are going to send out there, to figure out where it's from and to learn whatever they can about the aliens who built it."

"No!" Newt's mother said, suddenly fearful. "They can't! There are more of those things. A lot more!"

Newt stared at her. A fear she thought she'd beaten appeared in her belly. An image filled her mind of hundreds of those spider things, sneaking around the colony at night, trying to latch onto her face while she slept.

She hugged Brackett tightly.

"How many, Mom?" Tim asked fearfully.

"Did you run into anything else?" Brackett asked. "Larger creatures? Anything that looked more formidable?"

"Nothing alive," Newt's mother said.

Capt. Brackett glanced over at Gruenwald and Mrs. Hernandez, who were walking with Lt. Paris. All of them were paying close attention.

"We'll continue this with Simpson," he said. "Meanwhile, nobody's going to do anything stupid. Precautions will be taken."

Newt watched her mother thinking, saw her nod.

"Okay," Anne said.

"Lieutenant Paris," Brackett said, "post Coughlin and Yousseff outside wherever they're taking Mr. Jorden. Tell Dr. Reese I'm going to want to speak with him as soon as Anne and I are done with Simpson. Then send Draper and two other marines out to the site to stand sentry. Nobody enters that ship without authorization from whoever ends up with operational control of this fiasco."

"Yes, sir."

Newt felt a little safer. The captain's voice—his confidence and determination—reassured her a little bit. She could even believe that her father was going to be all right, if she didn't think about it too much.

She hugged the captain even tighter.

"Thank you," she whispered into his ear.

Then they were through the door and headed up the metal stairs, boots clanking on every step, and they had all run out of words again.

18

DARK TURNS

23 JUNE, 2179
TIME: 1637

Nearly twenty-four hours after she and her family had returned to Hadley's Hope, Newt lay in bed, legs curled up beneath her.

Mrs. Hernandez had come in the middle of the day to look after her and Tim, and had made them a vegetable stir-fry. She explained that their mother did not want them to leave the family quarters.

Even at six, Newt understood that her mom didn't want her overhearing other people talking about what had happened to her dad, or about whatever the scientists and marines might have discovered out at that crashed spaceship. Another day, she would have been angry about being left out. But today she was too distracted by her fears for her father.

The night before, she'd had a terrible time getting to sleep. The memory of her own screams kept ringing in her head, and every time she closed her eyes, she saw the pulsing sacs on the body of the alien creature attached to her father's face. When she'd finally fallen asleep she had slept for ten straight hours without dreaming at all.

Waking, she'd been relieved that she hadn't had any nightmares… and then she'd remembered the day before, and thought about her father in the medical lab. That was when she realized that the real nightmare had been waiting for her to wake up.

Throughout the day, she'd tried to read and tried to nap. She'd tried to eat, too, but could only manage little nibbles. Tim had been sketching, but when she'd asked him what he was drawing, he told her she didn't want to know. Didn't want to see. So she knew exactly what it was he'd been drawing—the same thing she saw when she closed her eyes.

Mrs. Hernandez fussed over them, made sure they ate, but Newt didn't want to talk to anyone, so she retreated to her bedroom as soon as she'd cleared her dinner plate.

"Ssshhh," she whispered, clutching her doll, Casey, to her chest. She kissed the doll's head. "Daddy's going to be okay. Try not to be afraid."

Newt had been giving Casey that advice all day, but her dolly didn't seem inclined to take it. She couldn't make the fear go away, and neither could Newt.

"Just be brave," she whispered.

She exhaled and held Casey even more tightly. That seemed to work. Being brave wasn't the same as not being afraid. Her mom had told her that more than once. Being brave meant you faced your fears, and Newt silently promised herself she would do that, no matter what.

"You and me, Casey," she said. "We're gonna be brave."

She frowned. Had she heard a sound, out in the family room? A thump, maybe. Or a knock. Her pulse quickened and she burrowed deeper under her covers. Then she remembered what she had just told Casey. For a moment she held her breath, then she threw back her covers.

Holding onto Casey, she tiptoed to her bedroom door.

Before she could reach it, the door swung inward. Newt cried out and jumped back, clenching her right fist—ready to fight. Then Tim poked his head into her room. She hissed through her teeth and started toward him, figuring he deserved a punch in the nose just as much as any monster that might've come after her.

"Quiet," Tim whispered, putting a finger to his lips to shush her.

He moved into her room, glancing nervously over his shoulder. "Mrs. Hernandez fell asleep in her chair, and we don't want her waking up right now."

Her hand unclenched. "Why not?"

Tim looked uneasily toward her.

"We need to go, Rebecca."

Newt frowned. "What? Where are we—"

"Dad's awake."

Her heart fluttered. "He's awake? Are you sure? Is he all right?"

A shuffling footstep came from just outside her room and she looked past her brother, noticing for the first time that they weren't alone. Aaron stepped in behind Tim, looking serious and anxious, both at the same time.

Newt held Casey down at her side. Aaron teased her about the doll almost every day, and she didn't know if she could handle it today. A year older than Tim and physically larger, Aaron usually acted younger.

"It's true," Aaron said quietly. No teasing. Not even a glance at the doll.

"I want to see him for myself," Tim said, studying his sister. "But I didn't want to leave you here, not without telling you where I was going, and asking if you wanted to come along."

Newt was confused at first, trying to figure out how they would get there without being discovered. Then she understood.

"Through the ducts?" she asked.

"Of course. We know which lab they're in," Tim said. "We've peeked in there before, when we've been playing Monster Maze."

"I don't know—"

Tim rolled his eyes in frustration. "Newt, are you coming or not?"

"But—"

"C'mon, Tim," Aaron said, "let's go without her."

Newt sat on the edge of her bed, laying Casey on her pillow. Indecision paralyzed her.

"Mom said we weren't supposed to leave our quarters," she reminded him.

Tim glared angrily at her. "I don't care. Aaron heard his parents say that Dad's awake, and I'm gonna see for myself."

"Let's go," Aaron prodded, turning to leave.

Tim followed him. "See you later, Rebecca."

Newt watched him walk out, feeling frozen on the outside but frantic on the inside. She wanted to see her father, too, but their mother had told them to stay put, and she didn't want to make her mother angry. More than that, she was afraid of what they might see if they crawled through the ducts and spied on the medical lab where her father had been taken. What if he wasn't really awake? What if that thing on his face had hurt him, or scarred him?

No way would their dad approve of them spying.

"Tim, don't leave me," she said softly, not wanting to shout for fear of waking Mrs. Hernandez. Taking a deep breath, she stood up, turned, and pointed at Casey, who lay against the pillow. "You stay right there and don't move," she said. "I'll be back."

Slipping on her shoes, she darted silently from her room, glanced once at Mrs. Hernandez napping on the sofa, and then went out the door. She caught up with the boys around the corner, moving down a wide corridor.

"Hey, you guys, wait for me!" she called.

Tim glanced back at her and smiled a little, slowing down until she reached him.

"We're gonna get it if Mom catches us," she said.

"Aw, quit your whining," Aaron snapped.

Tim glared at him, and Newt felt a little better. Her brother didn't always come to her defense, but she hoped with Dad not around they would stick together more than ever before. Aaron could be nice, but mostly he didn't seem to like having a little girl tag along.

Well, it's my *father in there,* Newt thought, *so I don't care what you like.*

She didn't want to get into a fight with him, or to have Tim end up in a fight with his friend. But she had been through too much in the past two days to put up with him being a jerk.

They took a side corridor on the left that was mostly used by maintenance workers. There was a service elevator at the back, and halfway along the hall there was a big vent. Tim and Newt kept watch while Aaron jiggered off the grate, then they snuck in quickly, with Tim bringing up the rear. When they were all inside, he pulled the grate back into place.

Enough light filtered through the vents and grates that they could see where they were going. They crawled quickly along the smooth, rectangular tube for several long minutes, turning this way and that, moving toward the science and medical labs. Usually they kept away from that part of the complex when they were playing—their parents had warned them to stick to the residential areas of the colony. But all of the children of Hadley's Hope had explored far and wide at some point or another.

Still, when they came to a duct that angled downward into darkness, she realized this was a way she had never gone.

"Do we have to go down there?" she whispered.

"What are you, scared?" Aaron scowled, then turned to Tim. "Maybe you oughta send your sister back, before she starts bawling or something." Then he went feet-first down the sloping duct, moving carefully. As soon as he was out of sight, Tim turned to his sister.

"You okay?" he asked. "Look, if you want to go back—"

Newt went head-first without waiting for him to finish. She slid on her belly, dragging the toes of her shoes and using her hands to slow herself, but she still crashed into Aaron at the bottom. He yelped in protest, then clamped a hand over his mouth.

"Sorry," she said, but she said it in a way—and with a smile—that made it clear she didn't mean it.

Tim came down behind them, but managed to stop himself in time. A dim light from ahead gave some gray illumination to the duct, and they quickly moved on. The metal felt cold to the touch, and the chill crept into Newt's bones.

Another few minutes and three more turns, and then Aaron stopped at a vent illuminated by bright white light.

"Here we are," he whispered. "I told you I knew the way. Keep it quiet, now, or they'll hear us."

They took a few seconds arranging themselves so that they could all see through the vent, the boys stretching out in either direction and Newt—the smallest of them—kneeling in the middle. One hand on the duct wall right above the vent, she bent to peer through the slats.

At first she could only see her mother and Dr. Komiskey—a curly haired, fortyish woman who gave all of the colonists annual checkups. But then Newt shifted slightly, cocked her head to the left, and she could make out a third person, sitting upright on an examining table, legs hanging over the edge.

Suddenly Newt grinned, a huge weight lifting from her heart. It was her dad, looking awful silly in nothing but his underpants.

"I know how you feel, Annie, but I just can't let him go," Dr. Komiskey said to Newt's mother. "He's not leaving here until we have a better idea of what happened to him. Even if I was inclined to discharge him, I couldn't. I'm not his physician—I'm just the staff doc.

"Dr. Reese is the director of the science team," she continued, "and there's no way he'd allow it." She looked at Newt's dad. "We're talking about a newly discovered, extraterrestrial, possibly *endoparasitoid* species. As yet, we know nothing about it."

Newt had no idea what Dr. Komiskey was talking about, but then she heard her father laugh quietly, and she grinned again.

Her dad shook his head.

"Honestly, Theodora, it's fine. Honey, tell Theodora it's fine. That thing was disgusting. If it was breathing for me—and it had to be, right?—I'd like to know what, if any, effects it had on me. It had its tongue down my throat, and only Anne's allowed to do that."

Newt twisted up her face, and she heard Aaron chuckle quietly. She elbowed him hard and he glared at her, but she kept her focus on her parents.

Someone coughed, and Newt shifted again, craning her neck the other way. She was surprised to see that Dr. Reese had been in the room all along, with Mr. Simpson beside him.

"Believe me, Mr. Jorden," Dr. Reese said, "we want to get you out of here as quickly as possible—get you back with your kids and back to work. But it'd be irresponsible to do that without making sure you haven't suffered any harm."

"That I haven't picked up some sort of plague or something, you mean," Newt's father said.

"That, too," Dr. Komiskey agreed.

Newt's mother took her father's hand. All this talk of ugly things made her anxious, but it soothed her to see the love between them. They squabbled plenty, but they really did love each other.

"Truthfully, Russ," Mr. Simpson began, "the science team wants their crack at you now. Dr. Komiskey has done what she can for you, but the team needs to study you, and for obvious reasons. Meanwhile, we sent some men out to the site last night. Maybe they can bring back something to work with."

"You sent men?" Russ said, his voice louder. "That's *my* claim, damn it." Newt flinched at her father's anger, glancing away as he went on. "That's an authorized find, and nobody had better get any ideas otherwise."

Dr. Reese strode across the room to a wheeled table, on which sat a metal tray. Newt blinked and a sick shiver went through her as she saw the spider-like legs sticking up from the tray. Gray and dead, the creature lay on its back, stiff, and trailing the tail that had been wrapped around her father's neck.

The doctor picked up a scalpel and pushed back the legs.

"No one's arguing your claim, Mr. Jorden," Dr. Reese said. "But we all have our jobs to do. Try to remember that you had this thing wrapped around your head for nearly twenty-four hours."

Dr. Komiskey turned to Newt's mother.

"Look at him. He's half-dead after playing kiss-face with a lobster, and all he can think about is his claim."

Her father shot Dr. Komiskey an angry look, but Newt realized the doctor was right. He looked pale and exhausted, and more than a little sick. As she watched, her father clutched at his stomach and winced in pain. He groaned and lay back down on the cot, both hands on his belly.

"Please, Theodora," Anne said, "just let me take him to our quarters. I'll watch him every minute."

Dr. Komiskey glanced at Dr. Reese, who shook his head.

"I'm sorry, Annie," Dr. Komiskey said. "We just can't. Why don't you go and get some rest?"

At that moment none of them was looking at her dad, but Newt saw the pain etched on his face. He bared his teeth, and his hands seemed to jerk where they covered his stomach.

"What's wrong with him now?" Tim whispered into her ear.

Newt shook her head. She didn't know.

Her mother hesitated, glancing up at Dr. Reese and Mr. Simpson.

"Go on," Dr. Komiskey said. "I'll stay here with Russ, and wait for them to return from the site. Who knows, maybe they'll turn something up."

At that moment another man rushed into the room, a balding man with a thick brown mustache who Newt recognized as one of the mechanics who repaired the crawlers.

"They're here," the man said, breathing heavy from running. He looked worried and afraid. "They're back…"

Two other men hustled in, carrying someone on a stretcher.

"…and they've brought friends."

To Newt's left, Aaron swore under his breath.

"Oh no," Tim whispered.

Newt felt tears spring to her eyes as a fresh fear took hold of her. A sick feeling started in her stomach and spread from there, because the man on the stretcher had another of those face-hugging creatures attached to him, pulsing and breathing for him. The one on the metal tray was gray and brittle and dead, but this one was very much alive.

"Help me," her father groaned.

Newt bent closer to the vent.

"Tim, what's wrong with—"

Russ screamed and arched his back, roaring with pain. His chest bulged, right at his mid-section. He threw his hands to one side as he bucked again. Newt stared, wide-eyed, as something pushed up from inside him.

"Daddy?" she whispered, tears coming hot and fast now, burning her cheeks.

Her mother spun, staring at him. "Russ!" she cried.

Again he screamed and bucked. His chest burst open with a spray of blood and a sickeningly wet crunch of bone and splitting skin.

"Daddy!" Newt and Tim screamed together.

"Oh shit! Oh my God!" Aaron whimpered. "What is this?"

Then her father lay motionless on the table, but something moved in his chest, rising like a snake from the gory hole. Pale and bloody, it hissed, revealing sharp teeth, its head turning this way and that, eyes shut tight as a newborn's.

Unable to make a sound now, or even to breathe, Newt realized that in some way that must have been exactly what it was. A baby.

The people in the room shouted at one another to do something as the thing slithered out from her father's chest, slid to the floor, and then darted off into a corner where it smashed through a small plastic grate and vanished into the guts of the colony. Still painted with her father's blood.

Newt glanced around at the dimly lit duct.

It's in here now, in the ductwork with us, she thought. *Monster Maze.*

She started screaming again.

And this time she couldn't stop.

23 JUNE, 2179
TIME: 1830

In the small exam room where she usually had her annual physical, Anne sat on the floor with her children huddled on either side of her. They burrowed against her and she held them tightly, whispering to them that it would be all right now, though even six-year-old Newt had to know that was a lie. Their father was dead, cold and bloody and already turning blue in the lab only twenty feet down the hall, where Dr. Reese had evicted Theodora Komiskey from her own med lab.

"Hey," a gentle voice said.

Anne looked up to see Dr. Komiskey standing in the open doorway. She'd been talking to several people, and arguing with

Dr. Mori, but this was the first time the doctor had come in to speak with her.

"Theodora," she managed to say, and then her tears came.

She forced herself to cry quietly, and not to tremble too much, hoping to hide her tears from her children. Newt had fallen asleep against her, exhausted by grief, but Tim looked up at her face, his eyes red but his expression hard and grim. She hated seeing that look on his face—that look that said his world had broken in half, but he expected things to get even worse.

"I guess it's a good thing you didn't let me take him home," she rasped, looking at Dr. Komiskey.

"Can I do anything for you?" the doctor asked. "Reese is in my lab, and Mori and Hidalgo are looking over the others who've been brought in with those creatures on them."

"Have any of the others…" she began.

"Not yet," Dr. Komiskey said. "But they will. And there's been no luck finding the one who… the one that got away."

"Can't they cut the things off? Or do surgery to remove whatever's been implanted in the poor folks with those things on their faces?" Anne asked.

She couldn't believe such questions had to come out of her mouth.

"You know what happened when we tried cutting the one off of Russ. They bleed a powerful acid. Try to remove the thing and the patient is likely to die—never mind the way its proboscis wraps itself around the patient's…"

Dr. Komiskey faltered and glanced away.

"You know what, never mind," she said. "You shouldn't be hearing this. You should take the kids and go back to your place. I'll update you myself if we learn anything."

An icy ball of dread had been growing in Anne's gut, and now it doubled in size.

She shook her head.

"Not going to happen, Theodora," she said. "You've got marines out there. I want to be wherever they are. More of those things means more of the damn creatures in the walls or wherever they're going.

We're in the middle of something no one's ever had to deal with before. With Russ..."

She stopped and glanced at Tim, saw the way his mouth had tightened into a white line as he forced himself not to cry.

"I'm on my own," she continued. "And I'm going to keep these kids safe. That means I want to be where the investigation is taking place. I want to know what you know, when you know it, and I want a marine or two within screaming distance."

She thought of Demian Brackett, but didn't mention him by name. Theodora wouldn't have understood, and Anne wasn't sure that she did, either. Given their history, she ought to have felt terrible guilt over how profoundly she desired his company just then, but she felt nothing of the kind. She loved Russ. He remained her husband in her heart, and she couldn't imagine the day when that would no longer be the case.

But Demian was still her friend, and a Colonial Marine, and she trusted him to do everything he could to look out for her and her children, partly because she knew he was still in love with her. Perhaps she ought to have felt badly about taking advantage of that love, but she was a mother, and her children's safety took precedence over everything.

"How many have been brought back so far?" she asked.

For several seconds, Dr. Komiskey looked everywhere but at Anne.

"How many?" Tim asked.

Newt rustled a bit in her sleep.

"Twelve or thirteen," Dr. Komiskey replied. "With more on the way."

"Are they stupid?" Anne said. "They need to get out of there now, and stay out!"

"From what I hear, they are," the doctor said. "All of these happened within just a minute or so of each other, in two waves... The first ones latched onto the marines who walked in among those eggs—or whatever they are—and the second wave attacked the people who were trying to rescue the first group."

Anne sighed, held her children close, and looked up at her.

"What are they, Theodora?" she asked, not really expecting

an answer. "What the hell have we stumbled upon here? I mean, the company sent us out there, gave us specific coordinates and everything. Did they know what we would find?"

From the haunted look in the doctor's eyes, Anne knew she had been wondering the same thing.

"I wish I knew," Dr. Komiskey said. "But even if we did—"

"What, it wouldn't help?" Anne snapped, disturbing Newt. "If they know *anything* that we don't, I think it's time they clued us in. Don't you?"

The doctor exhaled.

"Whatever I learn, I'll share."

Then she turned and was gone, leaving Anne alone with her children again. They were the Jordens now, just the three of them. Without Russ, she was the only one who could protect them, and she intended to do that.

No matter what it cost her.

19

CAPTURE-FOR-STUDY

23 JUNE, 2179
TIME: 1837

Brackett held tightly to his gun, trying to keep his frustration in check. He led the way for a lab assistant named Khati Fuqua and a surveyor called Bluejay. The origin of the nickname was a mystery the captain hadn't the time or inclination to solve.

Khati carried a three-foot shock-stick, while Bluejay lugged a light mesh soil sifter he intended to use as a net. They were approaching a junction on the basement level of D-Block, beneath the wing that held the med lab and operations. Though the hallway was quiet and abandoned, he was distracted by the voices coming through the comm unit in his ear. Al Simpson. One of Dr. Reese's assistants. Julisa Paris. Sgt. Coughlin.

"Did you join the marines to be a glorified exterminator?" Bluejay asked, his smile rustling his thick gray muttonchop sideburns.

"I'm not an exterminator," Khati snapped. "We're not going to kill this thing. Standing orders are that we take it alive."

"Not my orders," Brackett said.

"You may be stationed here, Captain Brackett," Khati said, "but this facility is under the operational control of Weyland-Yutani, and standing orders from the company are that any newly encountered alien species falls under the capture-for-study edict."

"Unless it represents a threat to human life," Brackett replied.

"There's nothing about that in the handbook," Bluejay told him, darting his head around a doorframe and peering into a bathroom where the door had been left propped open.

"You think this thing presents a danger to the colony?" Khati asked, arching an eyebrow. "From the way Dr. Reese described it, the creature looks like a fat snake with little arms. I don't think it's going to give us much trouble."

"That's if we can find the damn thing," Bluejay sighed. "Hold up for a second." The surveyor dashed into the bathroom, searched the stalls and glanced through air vents.

After the death of Russ Jorden and the escape of the alien parasite that had burst from his chest, Brackett had brought his squad into a room with Al Simpson and two-dozen colonists—some from the science team, and others from the colony staff. Dr. Reese had spoken to them about the parasite, given them a rough description, and asked them to search for it as quickly and as thoroughly as possible. It was vital, he'd said, that the alien be captured alive.

It had been Marvin Draper, of all people, who'd asked the most salient question.

"We catch this thing," Draper had said, "are you going to be able to stop the same thing from happening to those poor bastards we hauled back from that derelict ship?"

Dr. Reese had adopted a sad expression and nodded slowly.

"That is our hope, yes."

Somehow that had turned what Brackett would have expected to be a bug hunt into a search-and-rescue operation. Search for the parasite, rescue those who still had facehuggers attached to their heads.

"Come on, Bluejay," he said, starting along the corridor again without waiting for the surveyor. "We need to be faster."

Khati gave him an approving glance and caught up with him. In the bathroom, a toilet flushed and Bluejay came running out with his net over his shoulder, zipping up his pants. Brackett scowled as he reached the next door.

He rapped lightly on it and waited for a response. Simpson's number two, Lydecker, had gone onto the comm system and instructed everyone in the colony to shut themselves into whatever room they were in. They were to stay there until further notice, and to report anything out of the ordinary.

No answer.

"Open it," Khati said.

Brackett bristled. He needed to have a conversation with this woman. But it could wait.

Supposed to be a quiet post, he thought. *A nothing little colony on the edge of nowhere.* Instead it had been crisis upon crisis since his arrival. *Maybe I'm bad luck.* He thought of Anne Jorden and her children and their grief, and decided he didn't want to take responsibility for any of this—not even jokingly.

"Let's go," he said, turning the latch and pushing the door open.

Khati went in first, shock-stick held out ahead of her. Brackett and Bluejay followed, scanning the floor of what appeared to be some kind of stockroom. Lights flickered on as they entered, and Brackett crouched to look on the lower shelves as Khati and Bluejay did the same along aisles of lab and med supplies.

"Is this stuff manufactured here?" he asked.

"Some of it's brought with our monthly supply run," Khati answered. "The rest we make."

Brackett swore, peering into a vent.

"We've got maybe sixty people looking for this thing when it could be anywhere in the complex. No way are we finding this little bastard if it doesn't want to be—"

A scream tore along the corridor. Brackett ran for the door, but Khati beat him to it. Out in the hall they darted to the right, racing toward the source of the scream—a cry that had been abruptly cut off and now echoed only in his head.

Bluejay followed, but Brackett felt as if he and Khati were in a race until he grabbed her shoulder and shoved her back a step.

"What the hell—"

He turned on her. "That sounded like danger to me, which means you hang back, and I will investigate."

"Those aren't my instructions," she barked.

"They are now." Without waiting for a response, he hurtled down the corridor, gun at the ready, with Khati and Bluejay in his wake. At the junction he paused, trying to sort out whether the scream had come from the left or right, a question solved almost immediately by the sudden appearance of Sgt. Coughlin and two unfamiliar faces coming along the corridor from the left.

"You heard that, Captain?" Coughlin asked.

Brackett ignored him. The new arrivals were coming from the left, which meant the scream—that one, horrible, lonely scream—had come from the short corridor on the right. It ended in two broad, swinging double doors.

He ran toward them, and then stopped short. Khati raced up beside him again. Hot, humid air emanated from behind those doors, along with the thrumming vibration of machinery.

"What's through here?" Brackett asked.

"The laundry."

He signaled to Coughlin, who ran up to stand beside him. With his left hand, Brackett counted off three fingers, and together they burst through those double doors, gun barrels sweeping the room in opposite arcs. The churning noises of the washers assaulted them and the hot, damp scent of industrial cleaner made his eyes sting.

"Stay lively," Brackett said, motioning Coughlin forward and then holding up a hand to indicate that the others should stay back.

"For fuck's sake," Khati said, "it's an alien snake, not the bogeyman."

Brackett shot her a hard glance and she rolled her eyes, but did not advance.

The two marines moved into the vast room, where soiled clothes and linens stood in wheeled baskets below open ducts that Brackett realized must allow for dirty laundry to be dumped into hatches on the upper levels. An open doorway on the far side of that room led to another chamber, the source of the thundering machine noise.

Brackett and Coughlin hurried toward it.

Suddenly a laundry cart moved and a figure lurched up toward them. Brackett swung his gun around, finger on the trigger as he saw the wide, terrified eyes of a tall, white-haired woman staring back at him.

"What—" Coughlin began. Before he could react, the woman pushed past him, bolted past Khati and the rest, and vanished out into the corridor. The fear in her eyes was intense.

An alien snake, *Khati had said. The thing might be ugly as hell, but to inspire that kind of fear, it had to have done something terrible.*

At the broad open doorway that led into the humming, thundering room full of laundry machines, Brackett and Coughlin paused for a moment. Then Brackett nodded, and they went through.

At first he wasn't sure just what he was looking at. Machines washed. Machines dried. Machines folded and stacked. But stacks of clean laundry that must have belonged in carts like the ones out in the duct room had spilled onto the floor.

"Captain," Coughlin said, pointing at one of the huge folding machines.

White sheets made their way through the machine, stretched and creased and folded and then folded again. But one of the sheets wasn't purely white—it had a long red streak down the middle—and the next one had been soaked through with crimson.

Brackett's heart sped up. An ugly little parasite had done this?

"Move," he said, voice low, and he and Coughlin hurried around the other side of the huge folding machine.

Both of them froze as the machine started to whine and clank. Two huge rollers attempted to draw in the body of a slender man whose left arm and shoulder had been chewed up by the folding mechanism. The hole in his forehead, however, had not been made by the machine.

Blood and gray matter spilled onto the floor.

A second corpse lay fifteen feet away, near one of the thumping, swirling dryers.

"How many people normally work down here?" Brackett asked.

"Could be as many as four at a time," Bluejay said.

"Spread out!" Brackett shouted. "You see anything, don't approach. Just sing out."

The six of them moved among the various machines, the thrum and churn creating a blanket of gray noise that made it all the more vital for them to use their eyes. Brackett aimed his weapon up into the mechanical workings of the bloody folding machine, and then moved on to the other, while Coughlin began to search between and behind the dryers.

"Captain!" Bluejay shouted.

Brackett followed his voice, joining him in a corner where a massive fan in the wall drew superheated air out of the room. There were half a dozen of these spread out across the laundry. There were other large vents, as well, and Bluejay was staring at one of them.

"It's the return," he said. "Pushes cooled air back into the room."

Brackett stared. The grate had been destroyed, the metal latticework torn apart from within. The parasite had come through here.

"There," Bluejay said, pointing to the floor nearby.

But Brackett didn't need the surveyor to draw attention to the object that lay there, just a few feet from the torn grating. It was a bloody shoe, left behind. A sick dread knotted itself up inside his gut—no "little parasite" could drag a fully grown human into an air vent.

Weapon aimed at the ruined grate, Brackett backed away.

"All civilians, out of here right now!" he barked, glancing over his shoulder at them.

Khati shot him a dark look. She'd been moving around the huge washers, probing the shadows between and behind them with her shock-stick. Now she started toward him, that insatiable curiosity lighting her eyes.

"What've you found?" she called.

Brackett turned to Coughlin.

"Get them out of here," he said. "I'll call Paris, and get some reinforcements down here."

"If it went into the vents it could be anywhere," Bluejay said.

"Just go," Brackett said.

The surveyor held up his one free hand.

"You don't have to tell me twice. I don't wanna end up like those poor bastards."

Coughlin snapped orders at the two civilians who had accompanied him and ushered them—along with Bluejay and Khati—toward the duct room. Brackett kept his eyes on the torn grating, and backed further away. Had he seen something moving in the darkness there? Somehow they were going to have to flush the thing out, but he had no idea where to begin.

He tapped the comm link on his collar.

"This is Brackett. I need Simpson on the line."

This time, the scream came from behind him.

Brackett spun, and saw one of the civilians dive back into the laundry room. The captain ran for the open doorway. A woman shouted frantically, and then Coughlin's gun barked, rapid-fire.

"Khati!" Brackett shouted as he barreled into the room, weapon up.

Something dark and swift scrambled up a shelving unit standing against the wall. He took aim and fired, bullets punching the wall and pinging off the metal shelving. Coughlin ran over beneath the alien and fired at it from close range, spattering blood onto the floor, where it hissed and smoked and burned straight through. Coughlin screamed and dropped to the floor, tearing off his left boot.

The creature leapt up into a laundry duct, and was gone.

Brackett took two more shots at the metal duct, and then he could only stand there, Khati at his side. She was whispering something that sounded like the most profanity-laced prayer he'd ever heard.

Turning to survey the room, Brackett saw Bluejay lying in a sprawl on top of a spilled cart of filthy towels and sheets, blood pumping out of a hole at the center of his chest. His eyes fluttered once and then glazed over, dark with death.

On the floor, Coughlin scrambled backward from beneath the duct and tore off a thick sock with a cry of fresh pain. He sat staring at his foot. Bloody, raw stumps were all that remained of his last two toes—the acid had burned right through his boot.

"Whatever that thing is, it's no snake," Khati said.

Brackett nodded. In the space of a few hours it had grown to the size of a large dog or a chimpanzee, though it didn't look anything like those creatures. It now had black skin, like a shell, along with a whipping, ridged tail, and its head was huge. He'd caught a glimpse of teeth in its mouth, and felt as if he'd seen something that belonged only in nightmares.

It's like a demon, he thought. But demons only existed in stories, and this alien creature was all too real.

How big would it grow? The question snapped him out of his shock.

"Simpson?" he said into the comm. "Simpson, this is Captain Brackett, are you there?"

"I'm here, Captain," the voice came back, weary and arrogant. "Doing my job. What can I—"

"How many are there now?" Brackett demanded. "How many people with those facehuggers on them?"

"There were thirteen," Simpson said. "Only nine now. Why?"

"What do you mean, 'only nine now?'"

"Four of the things have fallen off and died, just the way it happened with Russ Jorden," Simpson said. "We're keeping a close eye on them. Now, do you want to answer me?"

"You need to do a head count of the whole colony," Brackett said anxiously. "Make sure everyone is accounted for, top to bottom, and warn them to keep an eye out. We've seen the alien, down here in the laundry room. It's killed at least three people that we've seen, but I think it's taken others."

"Taken?" Simpson said. "What do you mean—"

Brackett silenced his comm and turned to Coughlin.

"Get to the med lab, right now. Keep watch over the patients there. If any of them have these things come out of them, you kill those damn snakes before they can get into the ducts, like this one."

Coughlin stood at attention, grim eyes gleaming through the pain. "Sir, yes, sir."

Khati bristled. "You can't—"

"Did you not see that thing?" Brackett snarled. "Fuck if I can't."

* * *

23 JUNE, 2179
TIME: 1903

On his way to the med lab, Coughlin passed the research laboratory used by the science team, just as one of Dr. Reese's assistants came out through the door.

The sergeant glanced inside and stopped short, staring through the gap in the door as it swung closed. In a cylindrical glass tank in the middle of the room—one of a row of such tanks—one of the facehuggers floated in a bubbling bluish liquid. Just before the door clicked shut, Coughlin saw the thing twitch, saw its coiled tail snap out and strike the glass of the tank like a scorpion's sting.

The lab assistant gave him an admonishing glance.

"You're looking at *me* like that?" Coughlin asked. "What's going on in there?"

"Need to know, Sergeant," the young man said. "And you—"

"Yeah, whatever," Coughlin interrupted. "You're running tests on the thing, maybe to try to help, or maybe just because Weyland-Yutani wants their damn data. But what I want to know is *how* did you get it? From what I hear, there's no way to get one of those things off someone without killing the patient. Did you manage to get one of those eggs back from the derelict or did you murder someone for science?"

The assistant frowned disapprovingly.

"Every single one of those people with the stage one Xenomorphs on their faces is as good as dead already."

Coughlin clenched his fists. "What are you saying?"

The assistant smiled thinly. "I'm saying you don't need to know, Sergeant."

The guy walked on.

Coughlin wanted to shoot him.

When he reached the med lab, the sergeant found Dr. Komiskey sitting in a chair near the door with her arms crossed like a petulant child, but Coughlin could see why. Normally Komiskey's domain, the med lab had been taken over by the science team. Dr. Mori hovered over patients while Dr. Hidalgo went from cot to cot checking vital signs. One of their assistants sat on a cot, putting some kind of ointment on a nasty, ragged wound on his own arm.

Coughlin stared at the injured man and swore under his breath. Dr. Hidalgo looked unnerved, even frightened, but Dr. Mori's eyes were lit with a strange excitement.

"Pardon me, doctors, but Captain Brackett has assigned me to—"

"We've been informed," Dr. Mori said coldly. "Come in and stay out of the way."

But Coughlin didn't move. He counted seven patients with facehuggers, and two without.

"Where are the other four?" he asked.

"The morgue," Dr. Hidalgo said, blanching as she spoke.

"Son of a bitch," Coughlin whispered, cupping a hand to his skull. "And the parasites? Did you kill them, or stop them at least?"

The scientists said nothing, but Dr. Hidalgo glanced at the man who was now wrapping his wound. At least one of them had tried to stop the parasites from escaping.

"You people are lunatics," Coughlin said, shaking his head. "Don't you understand? The things growing inside them… they come out of there small, but they grow—fast. And now we've got, what, five of them out there? We're going to have to get everyone together for their own safety, or at least group them in certain locations, and with armed guards."

Dr. Hidalgo used forceps to touch the long, spindly legs of the facehugger that covered Saida Warsi's eyes, nose, and mouth. The thing slid off and flopped to the floor, dead, the trailing proboscis sliding from her open mouth as she coughed herself back to consciousness and began to scream. Coughlin wondered if she had been aware of what was going on around her, of the hideous fate that awaited her.

"Well?" Dr. Mori said. "What are you waiting for? Get hunting."

"Oh no," Coughlin said, raising the barrel of his gun, ready to kill anything that emerged from these poor afflicted bastards. "I'll call it in to Captain Brackett. Me? I'm staying right here."

20

THE WORST QUESTION

23 JUNE, 2179
TIME: 2209

All uncertainty had left Demian Brackett's mind.

He moved along the basement corridors of F-Block with the military precision that had been drummed into him from the first day of training for the Colonial Marines, back to the wall, sweeping the barrel of his weapon in short arcs. Across from him, Pvt. Yousseff did the same, alert and on point. She might be one of Draper's cronies, but she'd proven more than capable of thinking for herself. Her eyes were alight with intelligence, courage, and just the right amount of fear to keep her on her toes.

Hours had passed since Bluejay's death and information had been coming in fast and furious. Coughlin had reported the activity in the med lab, the little science project Dr. Reese had going on. When this was all over and the aliens—what the science team were calling the Xenomorphs—had been eradicated, Brackett intended to have an ugly conversation with the doctor about how they had acquired the living facehugger. If there had been any misconduct—if Reese had endangered lives—Brackett would take the son of a bitch into custody himself. Weyland-Yutani might give their scientists a lot of leeway in accomplishing their goals, but not even they could countenance negligence that led to the death of innocents.

A quiet cough made Brackett glance back. Khati had stayed with him after Bluejay's death, still carrying her shock-stick. Yousseff shot her a withering glare.

"Sorry," Khati said. "I don't know why we have to be so quiet, anyway. If they hear us, these things aren't going to go scampering off. They're going to try to kill us."

Brackett grunted and turned to Yousseff.

"She has a point."

Still, they moved on in relative silence, traveling quickly from room to room, checking shadowed corners and behind furniture, carefully peering through grates and vents. Every time Brackett looked into one of the air ducts he felt sick to his stomach, knowing that Newt and the other children had routinely played there. Some parts of that air circulation system were wide enough for the growing Xenomorph, but other sections were narrower, and he thought the aliens would have trouble getting through there.

"Control, this is Brackett," he said into his comm. "I need a schematic of the ventilation system."

Static on the line, and then a voice.

"Captain, this is Lydecker. We've got it open now, actually. As we've been evacuating sections of the colony—isolating the population in more easily protected pockets—we've sealed off other areas as effectively as possible. Once your team has completed its sweep, you'll be able to access those areas one by one."

Brackett and Yousseff turned and entered an enormous concrete room full of pipes and chemical odors. Water dripped from poorly sealed pipe joints and stained the floor, and the smell of earth and growing things mingled with the chemicals.

"I owe your team an apology, Lydecker," Brackett admitted. "I underestimated you guys."

Static again, then a different voice.

"Save the hugs and kisses for later, Captain," Lt. Paris said. "I've got reports from three different relocation details. We've got the population temporarily settled into four locations, but there are people unaccounted for."

"Shit," Brackett muttered. "How many?"

No answer.

"Lydecker!" Julisa Paris snapped over the comm. "How many in total?"

Static. Then Lydecker replied.

"Fifteen."

The number stopped Brackett short. He froze inside the room with the dripping pipes, and tried to just breathe.

"What is it?" Khati asked.

Yousseff—who was on the same communications channel as Brackett and had heard the exchange—turned to her.

"Trouble."

Brackett exhaled and glanced around at the dripping pipes.

"What the hell is this room?"

"We're underneath the greenhouse," Khati replied.

Okay, Brackett thought. *That explains a lot*.

"Lydecker, this is Brackett," he said into his comm. "We're going to keep hunting, but hunting isn't enough. Once you're sure you've sealed off the population groups, I need you and Simpson to get Dr. Reese and his team in a room, and work on the only question that's going to matter pretty soon."

"What question is that?" No static this time.

"Where are they taking these people?" he replied. "There's got to be a reason they're taking them off somewhere, instead of just killing them and leaving the corpses. I'm going to guess that means they're all gathering in one place, like a nest or a hive or something. We need to figure out where that is, and take the fight to them there."

Many seconds passed with the crackle of static in Brackett's ear. He gazed at Khati and then at Yousseff.

"You think they're using those people to breed," Lydecker said at last. "But we're fairly certain none of the aliens have left the colony—none of the outer doors have been opened or breached in any way—and they'd have to go back to the derelict to reach those… eggs, or whatever they are."

"We don't know that," Youssef chimed in. "We've never encountered this species before. We don't know what they're capable of."

"Those people might still be alive," Brackett said grimly. "So when you know the rest are safe, you start looking. If they can be saved, we've got to try."

"I'm with you, Captain," Lydecker said. "Mr. Simpson just came in and he wants me to assure you that he is with you, as well."

"All right," Brackett said. "Completing the sweep of F-Block's basement level and then moving upstairs to—"

Krrkk. A burst of static on the line. Then shouting.

"—got one! I've got one of the fuckers right here! Level one, northwest corner—"

Krrkk. Screaming in the background.

"Draper!" Youssef shouted into her comm. "Backup's coming!"

Brackett was already in motion, racing out of the pipe room. Northwest corner of level one was practically right above their heads.

"Stairs?" Brackett called. Khati ran beside him with her shock-stick, a pitiful looking thing.

"Turn left, the door's on the right, next to the lift! You can't miss it."

Youssef caught up, still shouting for Draper but receiving no reply on her comm. She swore several times. Brackett gritted his teeth, trying to remember who else had been paired with Draper for the sweep. They skidded around the corner, and he spotted the door with a huge B painted on it.

"Watch your ass!" he said. "There's more than one of these things."

Brackett turned the latch and banged the door open. Youssef charged through, weapon ready, but the stairwell was empty. They raced up two steps at a time in the flickering, failing light, and could hear the shouts and screams before they reached the door into level one.

"Again!" Brackett said, grabbing the door and dragging it open.

Youssef went first and Brackett burst through behind her, with Khati bringing up the rear. They nearly tripped over the bloody and broken corpse of a marine only recognizable by his uniform. For half a second, Brackett thought it was Marvin Draper, but then he heard the roar of a man's voice, and he and Yousseff ran to the corner.

Weapons up, they rounded the corner.

"Holy shit!" Yousseff barked.

Marvin Draper had braced his body against a door to keep one of the aliens from coming through. He had only a handgun for defense, his rifle on the floor half a dozen feet away. He roared profanities at it as the Xenomorph—so much bigger than it had been only four hours before—clawed at the door and slammed its head and body against it, knocking Draper back half a foot before the marine threw himself back again.

The alien hissed, spindly arms reaching through the gap. On the floor of the corridor, a man in a gray jumpsuit sat screaming and staring at his left arm, leg, and abdomen, where the alien's acid blood had eaten through flesh and even now eroded bone. Smoke rose from the wounds.

Brackett ignored the screaming man—he would be dead in minutes at best.

The alien banged its head through the gap, twisted and hissed. From within its jaws came a second set that slid out, punching toward Draper's face.

"Motherfucker!" Draper shouted as he darted aside. He jammed his gun against the alien's mouth and pulled the trigger, then spun away, using the door to shield himself from the acid spray before slamming against it to keep the furious alien from crashing through.

He'd never be able to hold it back for long.

"Draper!" Brackett shouted. "Let it out!"

He expected an argument, but he saw the flicker of understanding in Draper's eyes, and the marine gave him a nod.

"One!" Yousseff shouted, taking position beside Brackett. "Two!"

"Three!" Draper called, and he backed away from the door, darting along the corridor.

The alien crashed through, stood its ground, and glared at the newcomers.

Brackett and Yousseff opened fire. From a safe distance, Draper did the same. They blew the alien apart and it fell to the floor, twitching but dead, its blood eating through the floor in seconds.

Draper whooped triumphantly and shot the alien again. Brackett couldn't celebrate—not with the dead marine behind him and the dying civilian only fifteen feet away. The civilian lay on the floor now, bleeding out, eyes dull and glazed. He'd breathe his last breath at any moment. There wasn't a thing they could do for him, and Brackett didn't even know his name.

The man exhaled, a damp rattle coming from his throat, and then slumped.

His pain had ended.

"He got a few shots in with Valente's weapon after Valente went down," Draper explained. "Too close, though. The blood."

"We know," Yousseff said, turning to look back at the corner, beyond which Valente's corpse lay. "Damn it, Jimmy."

"He was a good marine," Draper said.

In Brackett's mind, that was the only eulogy any of them could hope for.

"Good timing, sir," Draper said, holstering his weapon and giving Brackett a salute.

Brackett casually returned the salute.

"Nice job staying alive until we got here." They stared at each other for a moment, united in mutual dislike, but both, Brackett thought, understanding that each had underestimated the other. From what he'd seen, Draper was a hell of a marine.

"What do they want with us, Captain?" Yousseff asked, approaching the dead alien, staring at its remains. "If they just want us dead, or want to eat us, why not just do that instead of taking people away?"

Khati walked over to the dead Xenomorph, studying it as closely as was safe.

"Now that we've got one to examine, maybe we'll start to figure that out." She noticed Brackett staring at her shock-stick and gave it a shake. "Yeah. I think I'm going to get myself a gun."

21

INCUBATION PERIOD

25 JUNE, 2179
TIME: 0954

Coughlin liked Dr. Hidalgo. She could be cool and clinical, like any scientist he'd ever met, but she also treated people with courtesy and had a kind smile. She seemed to *notice* people, which her contemporaries never did.

Yet as he stood in the med lab and watched her work, he wasn't so sure. The doctor and her assistant—Wes Navarro—monitored the life signs of the people who still had those alien spider-things attached to their faces. But the medics made no effort to save lives. They had given up on the seven people who were still afflicted, surrendered them to imminent death, and it made Coughlin sick. One thing his parents had taught him as a kid was that you never surrendered, never gave in to despair.

Dr. Komiskey sat in a chair between two cots, drinking tea. The patients who'd been on those cots were dead now, carted off to the morgue by Volk, the orderly.

"You're just gonna sit there?" Coughlin asked. "These people are gonna die. Zak Li there, he can carve a flute with his own hands, and he plays the hell out of a guitar. Mo Whiting is like an exo-biologist or something, right? Nice lady. And you're just gonna let them die?"

Theodora Komiskey did not glance up from her tea. Her sorrow hung around her like a cloud.

But Coughlin wanted a reply, and so he forged on.

"All of you people with your medicine and your science, acting like you know everything, and you're not even going to try—"

"Sergeant!" Dr. Hidalgo snapped.

Coughlin looked up to see the older woman glaring at him. She had a small metal canister in one hand. Navarro had stopped, too—he held a pair of forceps and a steel tray. They were standing on either side of Zak Li, as if they'd been about to do something more than just observe.

"Let up on Dr. Komiskey, Sergeant," Dr. Hidalgo said. "We've all gone days with only a few hours' sleep. She's done all she can for these people—everything we can think of. Do you know the term 'triage?'"

"Of course. It means you figure out who's injured the worst, and in what order you need to treat them. We do the same thing in the field."

Dr. Hidalgo nodded slowly, gesturing at the half-dozen patients who lay on cots around them.

"It also means you treat the people who have a chance of surviving, and learn to recognize the ones who don't. We're in triage mode, Sergeant. We can't save these people. If we're to have any chance at all of saving the rest of the people in this colony, we need to learn everything we can about the aliens, and find a way to defeat them."

Coughlin stiffened, but as he glanced at Zak and Mo and the other people with those alien *things* on their faces, he began to see them not as patients, but as casualties. Only one of them—a fellow marine named Joplin Konig—had already lost the facehugger. He'd woken briefly and started to scream, his eyes wild, until Navarro had gotten a needle into him. Now Joplin was heavily sedated.

"That sucks," he muttered.

"I agree," Dr. Hidalgo replied, but she had already resumed what she had been doing. She bent over Zak Li and sprayed something from the canister onto two of the spidery legs on one side of his face. The legs turned white with frost, as did the patch of Zak's cheek that was visible between the alien's legs.

Liquid nitrogen, Sergeant Coughlin thought.

"Go," Hidalgo said.

Navarro used the forceps to pry one of the frozen legs away. It snapped off, and everyone in the room went still.

"No blood," Navarro said.

Dr. Komiskey stood up, sipped her tea, and crossed toward them.

"Might be a way to get the damn things off them safely after all..." she said cautiously, "but you've just killed the flesh on Mr. Li's cheek, as well."

The monitor began to beep loudly, and then to peal.

"Damn it!" Navarro shouted.

"The alien's cut off his oxygen," Dr. Hidalgo said, grimly resigned. "Back away. There's nothing we can do for him now."

So they stood there—the doctor, the scientist, her assistant, and Sgt. Coughlin—helpless to do anything. As the frozen portion of the alien's spidery legs began to thaw, the stub of the snapped one began to bleed. Acid blood burned through Zak's cheek, down through the cot, and into the floor beneath it.

Zak Li couldn't even scream.

"That's it," Coughlin said, lifting his weapon. "There *is* something we can do for these people, a way to stop their suffering. If they're going to die anyway, then let's put them out of their misery and kill these alien cockroaches all at the same time."

Dr. Hidalgo lunged forward, putting herself between Coughlin's gun and the patients.

"You'll do nothing of the kind!"

Coughlin frowned. "Why not? So you can continue studying your precious Xenomorphs?" He shook his head. "Do it without these poor bastards. I know Mori and Reese are over in the research lab, doing God knows what. Go join them, Dr. Hidalgo, and let me worry about the human end of things here. As far as I can see, it's something you and your team aren't very good at."

Navarro cleared his throat.

"Um, folks?"

Dr. Komiskey hurried over to Mo Whiting's cot. She took a pen from her pocket and used it to nudge the alien that was straddling Mo's face, and the spidery thing slid off, trailing the long dried gray proboscis that had been down her throat like it was some kind of withered umbilical cord.

Coughlin felt sick.

Fuck, he thought. *That's exactly what it is*.

"I've got a second one off over here," Navarro said. "We've got no consistent gestation period as yet, but these two are going to wake up soon. Someone's going to have to have 'the talk' with them."

On his cot, over near the door into the testing room, Pvt. Joplin Konig began to choke and jerk. Unconscious, he started to moan, and his body shook as if in a seizure.

Coughlin tapped the comm on his collar.

"Captain Brackett, do you copy? This is Coughlin."

Crackle on the line, and then Brackett's voice.

"Copy, Sergeant. Go ahead."

"It's going down now!"

"Do not let another one of these things leave that lab alive," Brackett snapped over the comm.

"Yes, sir!"

Navarro snatched up a complicated-looking device that he'd rigged with a net, still determined to catch the parasite as it burst from Joplin's chest.

"Back away, Navarro," Coughlin said. "This isn't a capture situation."

"Sergeant—" Dr. Hidalgo began.

Theodora Komiskey put both hands up, trying to referee, as if they had time to discuss it. Too many people were trying to keep Coughlin from doing his job. He needed reinforcements. He'd left Ginzler in the hall, guarding the lab from outside.

As Konig bucked on the table, eyes flying open as he gasped for air, Coughlin backed up to the automatic door and slapped the panel that slid it open. As he heard it shushing open, he spun to call for Ginzler.

An alien stood on the other side of the door, seven feet tall, ebon-skinned and ridged as if designed by some mad architect of the flesh. Stinking, viscous drool slid from its jaws as it reached for him.

Coughlin shouted in terror and brought up his weapon, but too late. As it grabbed him, its grip crushing his arms, he pulled the trigger and bullets tore into the floor and wall and killed Zak Li on his cot. Then the alien brought its tail around and impaled his heart with the precision of a swordsman.

Dying, Coughlin heard Dr. Hidalgo scream.

In his mind, he called for her to run, but he had neither words nor breath remaining to him.

Darkness claimed him.

Dr. Hidalgo shut her mouth, her own screams echoing in her mind. Fear surged through her, a terror unlike anything she'd ever known, but she shut it down.

The alien withdrew its blood-dripping tail from Sergeant Coughlin's chest with a sickening crunch of bone and the wet suction of a killing wound.

Navarro spouted frantic profanities and staggered backward, tripping over Mo Whiting's monitor and falling to the floor. The alien stalked toward him, almost bouncing with each step, its motion vaguely birdlike in a way that sickened her.

"Oh my God," Dr. Komiskey said. "Ohmigod." Her voice came from behind Pvt. Konig's cot, where she huddled now, thinking she could avoid death. A second creature crept through the door, stepping over Sergeant Coughlin's corpse.

The first one moved toward Mo Whiting, and Navarro screamed and jumped up, trying to flee. The creature caught him by the hair and dragged him back, regurgitating a thick liquid into his face. Navarro choked and flailed but quickly became sluggish, and the alien kept dragging him toward the door.

The second alien leapt onto Pvt. Konig just as the man's chest burst open and the newborn creature slithered out. The two monsters ignored each other. The parasite slithered off the cot and darted across the floor, just as the adult alien reached for Dr. Komiskey.

Dr. Hidalgo backed away slowly, keeping them in view. Gradually she picked up her pace. As the second newcomer stabbed its tail through Komiskey's shoulder—not a killing blow—the first paused and turned toward Dr. Hidalgo, and she froze a moment. It had no eyes that she could discern, but it cocked its head as if evaluating her, then hurried about its business with Navarro, dragging him from the lab.

Heart hammering inside her chest, barely able to breathe, she turned and fled toward an adjoining testing room, slapping the pad. When the door swished open, she darted inside, closed and locked it, and ran to the intercom on the wall. She held down the red button there, heard a wash of crackling static, and forced herself not to scream.

"This is Theresa Hidalgo in the med lab," she said quietly, the hushed words coming over the speakers above her head—and on every other speaker throughout the colony. That was the purpose of the red button.

"They're here," she rasped, her lower lip quivering as she glanced toward the door, wondering how long it would be before they came for her.

"Please, someone help."

25 JUNE, 2179
TIME: 0954

Brackett reached the med lab with Yousseff, Hauer, and two other marines in tow. Silent and smooth, practically vibrating with adrenaline, he gestured for them to take up positions around the open door. Blood smeared the floor and had spattered the walls in patterns he read immediately.

Two dead, at least.

He scanned the corridor in both directions but saw no sign of aliens or any other personnel. The science team's research lab was at the far end of the corridor. He gestured to a tall, brutish marine whose name he hadn't even had time to learn, indicating that the man should check on the research lab. The door down that end was sealed up tight, but with the aliens using air ducts to travel, he thought it best to be sure.

"Cap," a low voice said, and he turned to see Hauer crouched in the elevator alcove fifteen feet away. Brackett held a hand up, palm out, to indicate that the private should stay put and wait for him.

With a nod to Yousseff and the other marine—a scarred, unshaven career grunt named Sixto—Brackett stepped into the med lab, sweeping the barrel of his gun in an arc across the room.

"Oh, man," Sixto whispered.

"Search it," Brackett said, and the three of them spread out.

They checked behind machines and kicked cots over, stepped around puddles of blood and shone lights into dark vents. There were three corpses in the room, Coughlin and two colonists who'd had facehuggers on them, but now had big holes in their chests. The rest of the people who'd been there, patients and doctors and marines, were all missing.

"Captain Brackett," Yousseff said, "what the hell is *this*?"

She knelt on the floor near a cot, touching a small pool of thick, sticky, resinous liquid that stretched between her fingers. With a grimace of disgust, she wiped her fingers on the cot.

Brackett heard a thump and glanced around to see Dr. Hidalgo looking at him through the small window set into a door at the other side of the room.

"Fuckin' miracle," he whispered as he rushed to the door and tried the latch.

The doctor stared at him through that little window, eyes wide, and it seemed to take her a moment to realize she had to open the door from inside. She shook her head as if coming out of a daze, and then worked the lock so that the door shushed open, sliding into a pocket in the wall.

"How are you alive?" Brackett asked her.

"Tes... th' tsst..." Dr. Hidalgo tried to speak but faltered, one hand fluttering up to cover her mouth. Her eyes filled with moisture, but as he watched, she seemed to force the tears not to fall. Steeling herself, taking slow breaths, she stood a bit straighter.

"The testing room," she explained, clearly now. "I said I was in the testing room." The words sounded like some kind of accusation, and Brackett frowned. They'd all heard her on the compound's intercom system, but Yousseff had told him that meant the med lab. Was the old woman angry that they hadn't come directly to her before searching the lab for threats?

Maybe she wasn't thinking clearly.

"I don't understand," he admitted.

"It's a sealed area. Sterile," Dr. Hidalgo said, hand still shaking as she tucked a gray strand of hair behind her ear. "My guess is that they couldn't get my scent in there."

"Or they got what they wanted, and didn't want to stick around and wait for the odds to shift against them," Pvt. Yousseff said, kicking at the desiccated body of a dead facehugger. "They dragged everyone else out of here, including the ones who were incubating more of the damn parasites."

Static crackled in Brackett's ear.

"This is Simpson for Captain Brackett. Do you read me, Captain?"

"Hang on, Mr. Simpson," Brackett said, poking his head into the testing room. He glanced around, then turned back to Dr. Hidalgo. The woman was tougher than she looked, but he could see she was still shaken. "Are you sure you're okay?"

Dr. Hidalgo exhaled. She reached out and put a grateful hand on his shoulder.

"Not even close, Captain, but thank you for asking. And for coming. I don't think I'd ever have left that room otherwise."

Brackett shifted his gaze back toward the interior of the testing room.

"Might turn out that you were safer in there." He turned to Yousseff. "Private, please stay with Dr. Hidalgo. I'll be back in a second." Then he headed into the corridor, where Hauer stood guard near the elevator alcove.

"I've got a feeling they're growing too big for the air ducts, Cap," Hauer said.

Brackett walked over and stared at the elevator doors, which had been forced open and now sat jammed at wrong angles inside their frame. The darkness of the elevator shaft yawned wide, a coldness emanating from within. He kept his weapon trained on the opening, but did not venture any closer.

He tapped the comm on his collar.

"Simpson, this is Brackett," he said. "You rang?"

"You sound pretty cavalier, Captain."

"I've had about six hours' sleep in three days, so I'm a little punchy. I've lost track of how many we've got dead, and how many have been abducted, and I'm trying to count up how many of these aliens we might be facing now. Everyone in the med lab is either dead or missing, except for Dr. Hidalgo—"

"Shit."

"—so it won't be long before their numbers rise significantly. We've got to locate these things, and I mean *now*."

"What about the research lab?" Simpson asked.

Brackett glanced along the corridor. The marine he'd sent to check on Reese and Mori walked out of their lab. He gave Brackett a thumbs up.

"All clear," Brackett said.

"Okay. All right, listen," Simpson went on, static fuzzing his words. "I want you to call in all of your people. We're moving all of the personnel together. I want your squad there protecting them." He paused, then added, "When the aliens come for us, you can kill them then."

Brackett scowled, staring into the dark maw of the elevator shaft.

"You're out of your mind, Simpson. They're breeding right now, and the ones already in here with us are growing bigger… stronger. We need to hunt the bugs down and wipe them out before there are more of them. It's our only hope."

"I disagree," Simpson said through the static.

"Yeah? Well, I've got a question for you," Brackett said, turning to see Dr. Hidalgo emerging from the med lab, stepping into the hallway. "Are you sure it's a good idea clustering everyone together? 'Cause if my squad can't track these bastards down, I think you may just be setting the table for dinner."

25 JUNE, 2179
TIME: 1107

Anne jerked awake in the dark, gasping from a nightmare, her memory already splintering and skittering off into the recesses of her mind.

She caught her breath, felt the clammy sweat on her skin, and then exhaled as she realized it had been a dream. Glancing around, she saw Newt and Tim sprawled on a blanket that had been thrown on the floor, jackets and sweatshirts and seat cushions for pillows, and she remembered it all. The derelict spaceship and its abhorrent cargo, and what had happened to her husband.

"Russ," she breathed, eyes welling with tears that she quickly wiped away. She had to be stronger than that, for her kids.

Others slept around them, nearly a dozen people she had known for years but who seemed distant from her now. Some of these people were her friends, others her neighbors or co-workers, but her only priorities were Newt and Tim.

And Demian, she thought. No matter what else their past had held, once he had been her dearest friend. Whatever she intended to do, she ought to include him.

In the back of her mind she was aware that Demian Brackett hadn't made the rank of captain in the Colonial Marines without proving his mettle. She and her kids would have a much better chance of survival with him than without him.

"Mom?" Tim asked quietly. "Are you okay? You made a sound."

"Just bad dreams, sweetie," she said, hoping she sounded calmer than she felt. "Go back to sleep."

"I haven't been sleeping. I can't. Every time I close my eyes..."

You see your father die, she thought.

Whimpering softly, she grabbed her son and hugged him tightly.

"I know, Timmy. I know."

They'd been holed up in clusters for almost two full days, waiting for Simpson and Demian to give the all clear. From what Anne had heard, the reason that hadn't happened was that no trace had been found of the colonists who had gone missing, nor of the aliens that were presumed to have grown from the parasites. Then, last night, someone had noticed that some of the livestock were missing.

The door opened abruptly and she and Tim both flinched away from the light that knifed into the room. The two mechanics near the entrance jerked upright, aiming weapons at the figure that barged in, silhouetted by the glare from the corridor. Then the figure snapped the lights on, and the room flickered into illumination, people grumbling and shielding their eyes.

"Everyone up!" Lydecker said. "We're relocating all personnel immediately." He pulled the two armed mechanics aside for a private word while everyone began to rise, picking up bedding and pillows and other belongings. There were two other children in the room, and they had games and books with them. Anne wished she had brought such distractions for her own kids.

Food and drink had been brought to them over the course of the two days, and much of the detritus of those meals remained. Anne would be glad to leave the confined space.

"What's going on?" she asked, lifting a sleepy Newt into her arms, where the girl snuggled against her and went back to sleep. Two marines waited in the corridor, standing guard. A fresh wave of dread swept over Anne, and she pushed toward Lydecker with Tim trailing behind her.

"Brad, what's happened?" she asked.

Lydecker glanced at the others, saw they were mostly busy gathering their things, and bent to speak softly into her ear.

"Two of the groups were attacked," he said. "Four casualties, but everyone else is safe. Simpson and Brackett both think it'll be easier to protect everyone if we're all in one place. Everyone who can be armed will be, and it'll be easier to seal us off from the rest of the colony, as well."

Anne stared at him.

Safe, he'd said.

"Oh, my God."

Four casualties. She wondered who they were. Each would be someone she knew, perhaps a friend, but at the very least someone with whom she had shared a meal or a laugh over the years. Then Anne realized that she didn't want to know. *Four casualties*, she thought again. Better just to think of them that way. Better… because there would be more.

"Come on, Tim," she said. "Stay with me."

Anne and her kids were among the first people out of the room. She glanced around constantly as they followed Lydecker, but she stuck close to the marines, thinking that would make them safer if the aliens came for them.

With every step she was planning.

Help must be coming, she thought. *They'll have to have sent a report by now, a distress call. But how long would it take for anyone to arrive?*

The colony had a spaceworthy excavator ship on hand to mine asteroids, should the need arise. The question was whether or not the *Onager* had been here on Acheron when the shit hit the fan, or whether it was off-planet. She didn't know the answer, but she realized that she needed to find out—and quietly, because if everyone else had the same thought, there would be a huge rush to get away.

She wondered how far it would take them. Just to another moon, or out of the system? No chance for hypersleep on an excavator ship, she figured, but if they could just get to a safe orbit, they could wait in space for help to arrive.

And if the *Onager* wasn't there, there were always the crawlers in the garage. Out on the surface of the planet, she and her kids would have only whatever food and water they could bring with them, and they'd have to watch for storms, but at least they'd be away from the aliens.

Could they gather supplies and make it to the hangar without being caught? Without the aliens killing them or dragging them off? If the excavator ship wasn't there, and she ransacked the other crawlers for whatever supplies might be in them, how long could they survive if she drove out to one of the more distant processors? Long enough for help to arrive?

"I need to talk to Captain Brackett," she told one of the marines, a Pvt. Stamovich.

"He's a little busy right now," the private sneered.

Anne clutched Tim's hand in her left, carrying the sleeping Newt against her hip with her right.

"As soon as you get us all where we're going, I need you to contact him," she said firmly. "Tell him I want to talk to him."

Stamovich rolled his eyes and moved away, aiming his weapon around corners and through open doors.

The other marine was Boris Chenovski, who sidled up next to her.

"I'll make the call for you, Missus Jorden," Chenovski said. "But it may take a while for the captain to get back to you. We're in the middle of a bug hunt, y'know?"

"I know," she said quietly, leaning her head against Newt's as she walked. "Just please do what you can."

But in her mind, a clock had begun to tick.

22

SAFETY MEASURES

25 JUNE, 2179
TIME: 1212

"Will we really be safe?" Newt asked.

Anne held her daughter's hand as they moved down the stairs, surrounded by fifteen or twenty others. Her heart fluttered wildly in her chest, but she forced herself to smile.

"Newt, I love you very much. I'm not going to let anything happen to you."

"Promise you won't leave me?"

Anne could barely breathe. Her smile thinned as she squeezed the little girl's hand.

"Promise."

They reached the next level. The door had been propped open and people were flowing through, joining others who were already in the hallway, streaming in the same direction. She caught a glimpse of Al Simpson walking by, pale and disheveled but still in charge, barking orders.

"Come on, sweetie," she said, picking Newt up again as she hurried to push past the crowd. Anne glanced over her shoulder and spotted Tim. "Let's go, little man."

Tim frowned. "I'm not little."

"No," Anne agreed, thinking that with his father gone, Tim would have to grow up very quickly indeed. "I guess you're not."

There was a pair of marines in the corridor, helping to guide people and make sure everyone got where they were going in an orderly fashion, but Anne saw the way they watched the vents and the doors and the way they held their guns, ready for trouble.

"See, Newt," she said, "these guys aren't going to let anything happen to us."

A group of mechanics, surveyors, and engineers had been busy welding doors and barricading them, closing off an entire section of D-Block not far from the med lab. Two doors had been left unwelded, but they were guarded by marines, and now most of the surviving colonists were moving to the huge storage area in D-Block, where they would hole up together until the marines and volunteers destroyed the aliens, or help arrived.

Anne tried not to think about the third option.

Tim hurried to catch up and moved in front of his mother and sister as if to shield them.

"Don't worry, Mom," he said grimly. "You and Newt can count on me to look out for you." Anne bit her lip and tried not to sob. She had no fear for herself, but the thought of her children trapped with these monsters made her want to scream. *Monsters we found*, she thought. *Monsters we brought back.*

"I feel better already," she said. "How about you, Newt?"

"Uh, sure," the girl said noncommittally. Her gaze darted around, on guard, just like the marines, and not for the first time Anne realized just how sharp her daughter was. Newt clutched her Casey doll to her chest, and clung a little tighter to her mother.

She caught up with Simpson a moment later. Flustered and sweating, he saw her coming and tried to ignore her.

"Mr. Lydecker," he said into his handheld comm, "do you have anything on the scans? Anything to help pinpoint their location?" This close to Simpson, Anne could hear the crackle of Lydecker's response.

"Not yet, sir. If there's a hive or something… well, we're working on it."

"Keep the doors sealed, Brad," Simpson said. "Stay safe."

Anne switched Newt to her other hip and stared at him as they walked. She wasn't about to let him avoid her.

"Do you really think we'll be safe in the storage area?" she asked.

"If we stay separated, those things will pick us off one by one," Simpson said. "Our best chance is to use all of our resources to secure this area, and hold out until help can arrive."

Anne felt a shiver go through her.

"Seriously, Al. Who could help us?"

"I've sent a message to Gateway," Simpson explained, puffed up and proud, as if he himself had just delivered them all to salvation. "They'll send more marines."

"But that will take weeks!" Anne said.

People turned to look at her. At her side, Tim glared at them until they looked away. Newt hugged her a bit tighter, upset by her distress.

Anne slowed down, letting Simpson get ahead. With her children, she dropped back to walk beside a marine.

"Can you tell me where Captain Brackett is?" she asked. "I really need to speak with him."

"I'll let him know, Mrs. Jorden. But as you can imagine—"

"Just tell him, please," she said. "Tell him it's important."

"Is Demian going to help us, Mom?" Newt whispered in her ear.

"Maybe *we'll* help him," Anne replied, wondering again how long she could afford to wait for Demian before making a break for it… and how long they could survive out on the surface, in the grit-storms, in a crawler.

"We can't stay here," she said to the marine. "There's got to be a way off this planet."

"The only way out of this is to fight," the marine said.

Anne glanced at Tim, so brave and handsome… so like his father. *Yeah, fight and die*, she thought, kissing Newt on the temple.

But perhaps the marine was right—maybe they could still get out of this. With everyone gathered together, there would be a limit to how many new hosts the aliens could abduct. The wildcatters were tough and most of them were armed. *Between us and the marines*, she thought, *maybe we can kill them all. Get back in control of the colony.*

Hour by hour. She decided that was the only way to evaluate their situation. *Hour by hour and day by day.* If Simpson and the rest of the staff could get them all settled in the storage area, Anne would give it a little time.

Is that hope, Annie? she asked herself. In her mind, it was Russ's voice she heard. The answer came to her immediately. It wasn't hope that drove her decision, not now. Her kids were exhausted—and not only the kids. Grief and fear had sapped all of the vitality from her. So for now, they would rest and put their trust in others.

Tomorrow morning she would reevaluate the situation.

Come on, Demian, she thought. *We need to talk, you and I.*

We need to run.

One thing Anne knew for certain, though. If she decided it was time to go and Demian disagreed, or she hadn't been able to find him by then, she and the kids would go it alone.

26 JUNE, 2179
TIME: 0717

Newt's eyes flickered open. She rubbed the grit of sleep from them, and blinked as she stretched into a yawn that rolled her Casey doll out of her grasp.

The floor beneath the blanket was cold and hard, but somehow she'd been sleeping with her mom's jacket balled under her head for a pillow. Grimacing with disgust, she wiped drool from her mouth and realized some of it had gotten on the jacket. As she sat up, she tried to rub it off. Then it struck her where she was, and why she was there.

A terrible weight settled over her heart as she glanced around at the dozens of people who had gathered in the storage area. Only a handful were still sleeping, there at the back of the room with her. The rest were sitting together in frightened conversation or standing in worried clusters. A few marines and wildcatters were scattered around the chamber, carrying weapons. One of them—Chenovski—stood a few feet away from Newt, talking quietly with Tim and his friend Aaron.

"...think they're too big now to come through the air ducts?" Aaron asked.

Chenovski nodded. "Depends how long since they were hatched or whatever, but yeah. That's what we're thinking."

"Some of those ducts are pretty big inside," Tim said, glancing anxiously at a grate high up on the wall. "We've been in them."

"This is a storage area," Chenovski said. "It doesn't usually have anyone living in it. The vents will give us air, but they're really just there for ventilation. The ductwork leading here is narrower than most other parts of the colony. But don't worry, guys..." He slapped his rifle. "We're still on guard. You're protected, okay?"

Tim and Aaron glanced at each other, looking unconvinced. Newt didn't blame them. She had seen the thing that had punched its way out of her father's chest. She glanced nervously at the grating up on the wall, picked up her Casey doll, and hugged her.

She crossed her legs and just sat there, feeling so small with all of those people milling about. Her eyes roved over the many familiar faces and some not quite so familiar, and her heart began to quicken as she scanned in search of her mother. Her eyes darted from side to side and a terrible fear ignited inside her, burning higher and brighter with every passing second.

Newt closed her eyes for a second, but in the darkness inside her head she saw her father bucking as the alien creature burst out of his body, and she heard his scream of pain... the last time she had heard—or would ever hear—his voice.

How many familiar faces were missing now? Dead, like her daddy?

"No," Newt whispered, lip trembling as tears sprang to her eyes. She rose to her feet, holding Casey against her. "Mommy?"

She spun toward Tim and Aaron and Pvt. Chenovski.

"Where's Mommy?" she asked, but her voice came out too soft. She felt as if she were invisible to them.

Her breath hitched in her chest as she set off in a panic, pushing past people. Tim called her name and started after her but Newt didn't want her brother anymore, she wanted her mom. She bumped into legs and hips and backs, calling for her mother, but even as she did she caught sight of faces and tried to figure out who wasn't there in the storage area, and if they were dead. Where was Daddy's friend, Bill? Where was the cook, Bronagh, who always saved her a freeze-pop or a piece of cake?

"Momma?" Newt called.

A hand clutched her arm. Face flushed with heat and wet with tears, Newt tried to pull free but could not. She heard her name, words gently spoken, but she shook her head and turned angrily... desperately. All she wanted was her mother. Instead, she found herself looking into the brown eyes of Dr. Hidalgo. She had lines around her eyes and they seemed to have deepened, as if she had grown much older just in the past few days.

"Newt," Dr. Hidalgo said again. "It's all right. Listen to me. Your mother is helping to bring food and supplies to us. Just a few minutes ago she asked me to look after you when you woke, but I got caught up in conversation. I'm so sorry that you woke up alone."

The words seemed to come from far away.

"She's... she's alive?"

"Yes, dear. She's fine. I promise you." But something dark flickered across Dr. Hidalgo's face and Newt understood it, heard the hesitation in the scientist's voice.

"Someone else died, though," Newt said.

Dr. Hidalgo nodded. "Several were taken while we were getting settled here last night. Quietly."

Quietly, Newt thought. She knew she was young, but she would have been the first to declare that being little didn't make her stupid. Quietly meant the aliens weren't stupid either. They were sneaky and smart.

Tim and Aaron caught up to her.

"Rebecca," her brother said, "what are you doing? You can't just run—"

"I wanted Mom," she replied, wiping her eyes. That same heavy weight settled on her heart, and she felt suddenly as cold and hard as the floor she'd slept on. "I want Dad."

As Aaron glanced away, Tim nodded.

"Me too."

Newt felt herself going a little numb.

"Who else is gone?" she asked Dr. Hidalgo. "Who else is dead? Is Aldo okay? What about Lizzie Russo? Is Mrs. Flaherty here?"

Dr. Hidalgo blinked, taken off guard by the last name, and Newt knew there would be no more pieces of cake set aside for her in the kitchen. No more freeze-pops. Bronagh Flaherty was gone. She squeezed her eyes shut for a second, and again she could hear her father scream.

Newt turned to her brother and slid into his embrace. Tim hugged her tightly.

"I want Mom," she said.

"I know," her brother replied quietly. "She's coming."

23

ESCAPE ROUTES

26 JUNE, 2179
TIME: 1111

Dr. Reese hesitated on the steps while Pvt. Stamovich opened the door and stepped into the corridor, gun at the ready. Stamovich looked pale and exhausted, but the man practically vibrated with potential violence.

Most of the morning had come and gone and there hadn't been an attack from the aliens since the middle of the night. Stam wanted to shoot something. Dr. Reese wanted a man who was ready to kill to protect him, but he did worry a bit that the private's itchy trigger finger might end up finding the wrong target.

Stam glanced back into the stairwell. "You're clear, Doc."

Reese followed him into the corridor and Stam led the way toward the storage area where most of the colonists were holed up.

"You sure they're not going to attack during the day?" Stam asked.

Dr. Reese frowned. "Not certain, of course. There isn't enough data. But aside from the 'births' of the newborn aliens, their appearances have mostly come at night."

"Mostly," Stam echoed.

"I don't think we can be sure of anything with the Xenomorphs, Private. In time, we'll know more about them."

"I don't know that we've got much time, Doc. And I gotta tell ya, I don't need to know much except how to kill 'em."

Dr. Reese tensed, but he nodded.

"We're working on it."

"I know, man," the gruff marine said as he swept his gun barrel in an arc that took in the corridor ahead of them, as well as behind. "Meantime, I still think we ought to be moving in larger groups. Just the two of us together..."

"I have work to do," Dr. Reese said. "And Captain Brackett has most of your squad searching for the creatures. If I had an entire army to protect me, believe me, they would be here now."

It troubled Dr. Reese that they had not yet found the alien hive. There had to be many of them now, and more gestating. Dozens of colonists had been taken away—far more than most of the people knew—and they hadn't just vanished. The aliens would be taking them to a place where there were eggs. His research had shown conclusively that one of the earliest facehuggers had been slightly different from the others. Dr. Mori theorized that its egg must have been selected by the aliens on the derelict, and bathed in special nutrients secreted in similar fashion as the cocooning resin the aliens produced from their throats.

But Dr. Reese did not concur. That meant one of those who'd gone inside the derelict would have had to encounter the one queen egg. The odds against it were overwhelming, and required far too much coincidence. Reese suspected some form of self-determination through biological imperative, where the facehugger itself underwent a metamorphosis in order to produce a queen, and perpetuate the species.

Whatever the case, the number of aliens that had already appeared inside the complex was the only evidence he required. Somewhere in the colony, the aliens had a queen that had matured to adulthood and had begun producing eggs with astonishing speed—yet another dramatic display of biological imperative. From what little they had already learned, it was clear that these Xenomorphs were the most extraordinary creatures he had ever encountered. They lived to perpetuate their own species, and were single-mindedly savage in the process.

A thump came from behind them, and they both swung around, Stamovich ready to shoot. Dr. Mori stood in the hallway with his arms up, his face almost as white as his hair.

"No, no!" Dr. Mori cried. "It's only me."

He seemed out of breath. Dr. Reese nearly barked at him for risking death, but then the stairwell door opened again and their lab assistant, Khati Fuqua, emerged along with a gun-bearing mechanic who had offered to defend them. The man thought he was doing a great service for the colony, since the science team was attempting to figure out a swifter way to kill the aliens.

Which, of course, they were not.

"Jeez, Doc," Stam said to Mori. "That's a good way to get a bullet to the head."

Dr. Mori exhaled loudly as he lowered his hands and hurried toward them.

"Dr. Reese, we need to speak."

Reese gestured to Stam.

"Lead the way, Mr. Stamovich. Give Dr. Mori and myself some privacy, please."

Mori gestured to Khati. She and the mechanic followed Stamovich toward the storage area.

"What is so urgent that you raced after me?" Dr. Reese asked quietly, glancing forward and backward to make sure they would not be overheard.

Dr. Mori knitted his brows. Reese might have been his superior, but he had never liked being spoken to in a tone that reminded him. Not that Reese much cared what Dr. Mori liked or disliked.

"I've only just learned how many of the colonists have been killed or taken," Mori said quietly. "It is time, Dr. Reese. I've done a computer model of the outcome here, but we didn't really need that, did we? You must make the call now. It is time for us to leave Acheron. The specimens are ready to be crated up for transport, and I have saved all of the data. We have everything we need—"

"Not everything we wanted, though," Dr. Reese said with a sidelong glance, eyes narrowed in irritation. "The company will want a living Xenomorph—one of the ovomorphs at least."

"And how do you propose we bring one of those back?" Dr. Mori hissed.

When Dr. Reese ignored him and kept walking, Mori grabbed his arm and forced Reese to face him.

"The model is clear—"

"I am in control of this situation, Dr. Mori," Reese said, jaw tight with anger at the other scientist's presumption.

"What you call control is an illusion," Dr. Mori whispered, both of them aware that Stam, Khati, and the mechanic had all paused to stare at them. "Time is running out. If we are going to save the data and ourselves, we must go."

"Soon," Dr. Reese promised. "Trust me."

26 JUNE, 2179
TIME: 1117

Anne walked into the storage area carrying an enormous crate of fresh fruit from the greenhouse.

She'd spent nearly two hours picking fruit and vegetables with the greenhouse supervisor, Genevieve Dione, and a handful of other volunteers, and it had been among the most frightening times of her life. Despite the fact that they'd had a marine and two armed wildcatters along to watch their asses while they did the work.

She'd been proud to volunteer, glad to be able to help these people. Part of that, she knew, was guilt at the prospect of abandoning them. Some of them were her friends, and even those who weren't were still a part of the family the colony had become.

Now, though, she had done her duty. Her skin had crawled the whole time she'd been in the greenhouse and even on the walk back, waiting for the aliens to attack. She had expected the sensation to fade when she was back among her people, but no such luck. She set the produce basket down and glanced around, pulse quickening at each glimpse of a barricaded door or a dark vent where bars had been screwed in.

The thought of the *Onager* was like a bright ember burning in her mind. She glanced around and wondered who else might have thought of it, as well. Derrick Bradford, Nolan Cale, and Genevieve Dione were standing in a conspiratorial cluster, faces etched with determination. They were planning something, but she couldn't be sure what.

Most of the colonists would have discounted the excavator ship, even if they'd thought of it, knowing that it couldn't get them far. Others, however, must have realized that it all might come down to time, that floating around in orbit would buy them the precious days or weeks needed for rescue to arrive.

If it's even there, she thought. If it wasn't, there were always the crawlers. She could get her kids out of here in one of those metal beasts, should the need arise. But she didn't want to leave without Demian, if she could help it.

The clock was ticking.

"Mom!"

Anne turned to see Newt racing toward her, the Casey doll trailing from her left fist, clutched by its blond hair. She smiled and opened her arms, and Newt leaped into them.

"Hey, sweetie," Anne said, the shadows in her heart retreating for just a moment. "I'm glad you're up."

Newt pushed off so that Anne had to put her down, then punched her mother in the hip.

"Don't leave me alone again!" she said angrily. "You promised!"

"I was only..." Anne began, but she saw that her daughter was angry and afraid, and she cut herself off. "Okay. I'm sorry." She looked around. "Want an apple?"

Newt didn't want to be distracted or appeased, but after a moment's consideration she relented.

"I might like an apple," she admitted.

"Where's Tim?" Anne asked.

"Playing with Aaron," her daughter said, with obvious disapproval.

Anne's breath caught. "Not near the—"

"No, Mom," Newt said. "Not Monster Maze. Boys are dumb, but not *that* dumb. Besides, Private Chenovski has been watching them. I was playing with Luisa for a little while, but then her mom wanted her to eat something, so I've just been waiting."

Anne nodded as she bent to fetch an apple from the basket. As she handed the fruit to her daughter, she glanced over and saw Dr. Reese and Dr. Mori come in with several others, including Pvt. Stamovich. Her eyes narrowed. As Newt bit into the fruit, Anne fought the urge to confront Reese, to try to force him to tell her what he knew about the aliens. What had they learned?

Perhaps more importantly, what did Weyland-Yutani know about the creatures? Had the company known in advance what she and Russ would be walking into when they were ordered to investigate the coordinates where they'd found the derelict?

At the very thought, anger blossomed in her.

"Newt, do you see Dr. Reese right over there?"

"Sure."

"I need to talk to him for a minute. So I'm not leaving. I'll just be right over there—"

"I'll come."

"No, honey," Anne said. "It needs to be in private."

Newt looked suspicious for a second, then glanced over to gauge the distance between herself and the doctors.

"All right. But don't leave without me."

"Never," Anne said, kissing the top of her head. "Jordens forever."

Newt nodded once, firmly.

"Jordens forever," she said, with a mouthful of apple.

Anne strode across the storage area, moving around piles of goods and supplies that had been stacked up to make room for the colonists. Dr. Reese and Dr. Mori were talking to Al Simpson. She was so focused on Reese that when Demian Brackett came through the guarded door just beyond the scientists, also headed for Reese, she didn't immediately register his presence.

When she did spot him, she quickened her pace. It would be a mistake to reveal her plans in front of the scientists, so she would have to be wary. But she couldn't allow Brackett to leave before they'd spoken.

"Demian," she said, intercepting him. "We need to talk."

He must have seen the urgency in her expression, for his eyes filled with concern.

"What is it?" he asked. "Are the kids all right?"

The strength and kindness in him caused a wave of regret to wash over her. She knew she had made the right choice in marrying Russ—otherwise Newt and Tim would never have been born—but a pang of sadness filled her as she allowed herself to wonder where a life with Demian would have led.

"They're okay. I just..." She faltered as Simpson, Reese, and Mori approached them. The cacophony of voices in the storage area seemed to swell, and any hope of having a private conversation seemed like foolishness. "When you're done here, I need a word before you run off again."

Brackett gave her a solemn nod.

"Absolutely. Can you give me a minute?"

Anne started to reply, but then Simpson was there, looking aggrieved.

"Captain, what are you doing?" the administrator asked. "Have you found the nest?" His mustache quivered as he spoke.

"Not yet—" Brackett began.

"Then why are you here?" Simpson said angrily. "More than a few people are blaming the overnight losses on your refusal to dedicate your entire squad to the protection of this shelter. You told me those were unavoidable—that the most important thing was to track and kill the aliens—but you haven't accomplished that yet."

"Simpson," Brackett said, his voice low but dangerous. "I didn't come to talk to you. I'm here for Dr. Reese."

The administrator muttered something under his breath, preparing a retort, but Brackett silenced him with a glare.

"What can I do for you, Captain?" Dr. Reese asked.

"I received a communiqué from my superiors—one that I wanted to share with you," Brackett said.

Dr. Reese smiled thinly. "Please, go on."

"I asked about my squad being used as security detail on colonial surveying missions, making my objections clear. The reply came from Marine Space Force, Eridani command, on Helene 215," he continued, "informing me that my orders are to provide security for the colony itself—and that the safety of individuals traveling beyond the boundaries of the colony would *not* be the responsibility of the USCMC."

Dr. Mori sputtered. "That's absurd. We've always—"

"Hush," Dr. Reese said, holding up a hand. He looked grimly confident, and Anne didn't understand why. "Continue, Captain Brackett."

Anne looked at Demian's face, and she saw the anger there.

"Two hours after I received those initial orders, they were overridden by an eyes-only communiqué issued jointly by the command staff at O'Neil Station—"

"From the highest authority in the Marine Corps," Reese interrupted.

"Yes," Brackett acknowledged. "Jointly with the Chief of Operations for Gateway," he said, glancing at Anne to make sure she understood. He turned back to Reese and Mori, still ignoring Simpson. "I'm now instructed to put myself and my squad at your personal disposal, Dr. Reese. Whatever plan you devise to deal with the Xenomorphs, I am to support it in every way possible. And I will follow those orders, because I am a marine.

"But," he added, "I will continue to voice my opinions, and first among those is that the government and the company are far too cozy.

"I don't trust you, Doctor."

Anne watched Al Simpson deflate. The normally blustery administrator had just lost the last vestiges of whatever leadership he'd ever exerted over the people of Hadley's Hope. Blunt and snappish as he could be, she had always respected Simpson for his hard work and determination, but any control he'd had over the colony had always been an illusion. Everyone knew that Weyland-Yutani called the shots, and that meant that Dr. Reese had *always* been in charge. Brackett's new orders had only formalized the truth.

"What the *hell* is wrong with you?" she asked.

All four men turned to stare at her, the scientists blinking as if she had been invisible to them before. Several colonists had gathered around, spectators to the strange little power struggle going on.

"People are *dying*." Anne glared at them. "My friends and I… my kids… we don't care which of you is in charge. In fact, I'd venture to say that at this point, none of us gives a shit which of you *thinks* he's in charge. This place is falling apart. My husband is dead, along with a lot of my friends, and dozens are missing. The aliens are hard to kill and their number is growing. If you don't figure out a way to eliminate them, nobody will be left alive for any of you to order around.

"So stop standing around measuring your dicks."

A cheer went up around her, and a round of applause began.

"Mommy?" she heard Newt say, and she blushed, realizing her daughter had heard what she'd said. Anne glanced back and saw that Tim had his hands over his little sister's ears, and she smiled at both children.

"Mrs. Jorden is right," Simpson said, looking around at the gathered colonists. "We're already doing everything we can to protect you all, to track down the aliens, and retrieve our missing friends."

Retrieve? Did any of them really believe that? Anne heard grumbling voices around her and knew the colonists would not let Simpson go unchallenged. They were all afraid, and grieving, and there were no words that would soothe them. Only results would calm their nerves.

She glanced at Brackett, but he only stood stiffly beside the scientists as Dr. Reese muttered something to him.

"Are we all gonna die?" Luisa piped up, her red hair a messy tangle around her face.

Brackett's expression melted and he stepped forward.

"No, honey. I'm not going to let that—"

A commotion at the doors startled them all. People recoiled in surprise and fear, some calling out in alarm, but then Lydecker came bustling in with several other members of the administration staff. He saw that he'd frightened them, and apologized before hurrying over to Simpson, taking his boss by the arm and walking him into an isolated corner.

One of the people who'd come in with Lydecker was a young, clean-cut man named Bill Andrews who had often been responsible for assigning survey teams. Anne and Russ had gotten to know him well, and now she approached him.

"Bill… what's going on?"

He glanced around, clearly uncertain as to how much he could share. But then he blinked, as if remembering something he should never have forgotten.

"Annie, how are you holding up?"

She glanced over at her children. Newt and Dr. Hidalgo were seated on plastic crates, engaged in an animated conversation, but Tim sat alone on the floor, an air of sadness around him. When he was looking out for his sister he seemed all right, but when his thoughts weren't otherwise engaged, they naturally drifted back to the horror of his father's death.

"I'm doing okay," she said, exhaling slowly. "But I'm scared for the kids. I keep wondering when the nightmare will end, y'know?"

Bill cast a quick glance at Lydecker and Simpson, and lowered his voice.

"Maybe soon," he said, and she looked at him curiously. "We were stupid before, just not thinking properly. All of us have our PDT implants, and we finally realized we could track the missing folks that way."

Anne clapped a hand to her forehead. Every colonist had a subdermal implant—a personal data transmitter. In the years she'd been at Hadley's Hope, she'd only seen them used twice—when wildcatters had gone out of radio range and run into mechanical trouble—but still, someone ought to have thought of it earlier.

She should have thought of it.

"We think we've located the creatures' nest, underneath Processor

One," Bill said. "Mr. Lydecker figures the marines will send an armed party over there now."

He smiled. "It won't be long."

Anne nodded, not daring to hope.

"One way or another."

26 JUNE, 2179
TIME: 1221

"I don't think you understand me," Dr. Hidalgo said, tucking her hair behind her ears and fixing her colleagues with a grim stare. "I'm going with them."

Dr. Mori bared his teeth in a sneer of disapproval, but Dr. Reese seemed genuinely shocked. Dr. Hidalgo liked that—liked being able to shock him.

"That's not acceptable, Theresa," Reese said.

She laughed softly.

"Do you think I care what you find acceptable?"

When she had seen the clutch of conversation between Lydecker and Simpson, and then watched those two men approach her colleagues on the science team, she'd known that some sort of breakthrough had taken place. Then Anne had come back to collect her children, and told her that the alien nest had been found.

Dr. Hidalgo had known then that she couldn't stay here with the colonists. Not when she knew they were soon to be abandoned. So she had drawn her fellow scientists away from Simpson, Brackett, and the others for this conversation. It had gone about as well as she had expected.

"There is only one way to do this," Dr. Reese said. "The marines have to kill all of the aliens. One of the idiots suggested that they try to overload the processor core and hope that it will explode, just like in the accident involving the Finch brothers… the explosion that destroyed Processor Six."

Dr. Mori gaped at him. "But the entire colony would be destroyed."

"Precisely," Reese sneered.

Dr. Hidalgo nodded. "That's why Al Simpson volunteered to go along. They need a tech—someone who can guide them, and let them know what's safe and what isn't. He's gambling with his life, in the hope that he can help save the rest of these people." She peered at them intently. "I'm willing to do the same."

Dr. Mori gripped her arm roughly, fingers digging in as he came close to her, whispering intently.

"Are you dense, woman?" the silver-haired scientist asked. "We're taking our data and samples, and we are leaving Acheron."

But she shook her head.

"I can help them," she said. "I know enough about medicine to treat injuries, and I can advise them regarding the alien."

"Theresa," Dr. Reese said curtly, "if the marines seem unable to do the job, we are leaving, with you or without you."

Dr. Hidalgo hated even to blink. Every time she did, she saw the aliens murdering people in the med lab, then dragging others off to be used for incubation.

"Do what you have to do, Dr. Reese," she said, and then turned to Mori. "I'd tell you to look after yourself, but really, it's what the two of you have always been best at."

24

ALL FALL DOWN

26 JUNE, 2179
TIME: 1332

Breathe, Julisa, she told herself. *You're armed and dangerous.* Even attempting to walk quietly, Lt. Paris thought her footfalls sounded like thunderclaps in the abandoned corridor.

Normally the thought would have made her smile, but smiles were in short supply this afternoon. So, for that matter, were marines. She wore MX4 body armor and a ballistic helmet. A VP78 pistol hung in the holster on her hip and she carried an M41A pulse rifle in her hands, with a battle rifle slung over her shoulder as a backup, all of them loaded with high-velocity rounds. She had enough firepower to take on an army by herself, but none of it would do a damn bit of good if one of those aliens got to her before she could kill it.

And that acid blood… she didn't even want to think about it.

Capt. Brackett had taken Draper, Pettigrew, and ten other marines off to hunt down the aliens in their hive, or whatever the hell it was, leaving her in charge of safeguarding the colonists in the sealed-off wing of D-Block. She'd stationed the rest of the squad around the inside of the perimeter, not just at every potential entrance into the storage area, but at every junction leading that way.

She herself had been patrolling the inside of the perimeter for the past hour, checking welds and barricades and the guards who were covering the two unwelded doors. She'd passed the door to the storage area a couple of turns back—left it guarded by three marines armed even more thoroughly than she was—but overall, they simply didn't have enough bodies to effectively guard the colonists if the aliens showed up en masse.

Her skin crawled every time she passed a doorway or approached a turn. As she approached the next corner, she whistled the signal she'd arranged. From around the turn came the reply, the same two notes, and she exhaled and quickened her pace. She rounded the corner to find Aldo Crowley leaning against the wall with his weapon cradled in his arms.

"Damn, Aldo," she said, "you look way too relaxed."

Crowley straightened to attention, but only for a moment before he chuckled and leaned back against the wall.

"Lieutenant, I'm one grunt with a gun. Those things come after us in force and I'm in the way, the best way for me to serve you is screaming like a little girl. Give the rest of y'all some warning."

She would have argued with him, but he wasn't wrong.

"Suit yourself," she said. "I'm not going to make you march in place out here. But I'll tell you this… these things *can* die. You just stand there with your thumb up your ass, you're liable to end up pregnant with one of their babies, or whatever the fuck that's about. Me? I'd rather be dead."

Lt. Paris walked on, but she noticed Aldo wasn't leaning against the wall anymore. He had his weapon in both hands, watching the corners and the shadows of the corridor ahead that branched off toward the command block.

Sixty feet further on she came to Pvt. Yousseff and a man called Virgil, who wore a face mask as he used a hand-welder to melt and seal the bolts on the stairwell door. That would leave only one door still unwelded—one way for Brackett and the others to get in and out.

Virgil had started from the bottom, liquid metal sparks flying out in all directions. The metal turned white-hot where the flame struck it.

"Anything?" Lt. Paris called over the noise of the welder.

Yousseff shook her head. Virgil didn't even look up.

Paris rose on her toes and peered through the small square windows set into the stairwell doors. Shadows and light played across the steps on the other side, but she saw nothing moving.

"You think they're going to be able to pull it off, Lieutenant?" Yousseff asked.

"I hope so," Paris said, then she grinned. "The new CO is easy on the eyes. I'd rather he not get his face bitten off."

Yousseff laughed and nodded.

"I'm right there with you."

Lt. Paris walked on, continuing her circuit of the perimeter, surprised that after serving with Yousseff for nearly two years, they'd finally found something they had in common. She thought about Brackett, off with that asshole Draper, and hoped they both came back alive. They'd already lost too many marines, like Coughlin, and she didn't want to lose any more.

Approaching the next corner, she whistled the signal.

Three more steps and she halted, frowning deeply. Breathing in and out, listening to her own heartbeat. She lifted the pulse rifle and took two steps nearer the turn. Then she whistled again.

The sound that came back was a wet gurgle, followed by the slap of flesh on floor.

Fuck.

Quiet and swift, she hurried to the corner. Back to the wall, she peered around the edge, leading with the rifle barrel.

The alien crouched above Chenovski, who lay on the floor, alive but somehow paralyzed. His face and body armor were covered with a thick layer of fluid, some kind of mucous, but his eyes were wide and aware as the alien dragged him toward another branching corridor.

Paralysis, she thought. *But he'll know it when they put him in front of one of those eggs and let a damn facehugger implant a parasite in his chest.*

She had kissed Chenovski once, drunk and maudlin because she was alone on her birthday. Mostly their friendship was based on her cheating at cards and him letting her get away with it.

Paris stepped out from the corner.

"Hey, shithead!" she barked.

The alien snapped its head up. If it had eyes, they stared at her.

"Lieutenant?" Yousseff called from off to her left, back the way she'd come.

Paris shot the alien twice in the chest. It staggered back, acid blood spilling to the ground, hissing as it ate through the floor. The acid spray hit Chenovski's legs and he moaned, but it could've been so much worse.

"Back off!" she shouted, taking a step forward, trying to scare it away from Chenovski while he was still alive.

It didn't look scared.

Instead, it advanced on her as if daring her to fire again—daring her to spill more acid onto her friend. Paris felt a nauseous twist in her gut.

How smart are these things?

She fired several times into the wall just beside the thing. From her left she heard Yousseff shouting... running her way... and then Aldo Crowley, coming as well, all the way from his post at the next corner, seventy yards away.

The alien didn't flinch. Its mouth opened and its jaws slid out, thick rivulets of drool spilling from its lips. Paris wanted to scream. Wanted to throw up. But mostly she wanted to kill it.

She pulled the trigger, a single shot aimed right at the center of its head. It twitched to the left so that the bullet punched through the carapace and struck its skull. It rose up as if in righteous fury, coiled its tail behind it, and Lt. Paris readied herself for it to charge, thinking that if she could open up with a full salvo from the pulse rifle, she could kill it before it reached her and maybe—just maybe—its blood would fall nearer to her, and Chenovski would live.

The alien drove the knifepoint of its tail through Chenovski's skull with a wet crunch.

Paris screamed and opened fire as the alien charged toward her. It took a dozen rounds as it lunged, and she backpedaled, slammed into the wall, and kept shooting until she blew its body apart. Its blood flew and she dove aside as it spattered and burned into the wall.

Sliding onto her belly, combat rifle clacking against her helmet and pistol jamming into her hip, she found herself on the floor as Yousseff reached her.

"Get up, Loot," Yousseff snapped. "There may be more."

As if Paris didn't know that. She scrambled to her feet and swung her plasma rifle up again.

"I don't know how it got in past the sealed-off door down that way, but it had to have come from that side corridor," Yousseff said, gesturing with her weapon. "No chance it got the drop on Chenovski approaching any other way."

Thirty feet along, the opening to that side corridor yawned wide. The two marines exchanged a glance. Neither of them wanted to go down there, but they had no choice. There seemed no question that the aliens knew exactly where the colonists were holed up, and were attempting to take out those who were guarding them.

Or they don't care, Lt. Paris thought with a shiver. *Maybe they just look at our storage area as* their *storage area now… And however that one got in, they figure they can come and get us a few at a time, whenever it's convenient.*

"With me," she told Yousseff, and she took a single step.

A crash reverberated along the corridor.

Aldo Crowley shouted filthy profanities to his God.

Paris and Yousseff whipped around to see Virgil on his ass with the welder in his hand, his face mask still down, almost obscenely impersonal. Another crash and the stairwell doors began to buckle on the top. The weld on the bottom, though still warm, held as the upper parts of the doors began to bow inward.

An alien slammed its head into the widening gap.

"Shoot it, Aldo!" Lt. Paris shouted as she and Yousseff raced back along the hallway. "Open fire, damn it!"

Aldo pulled the trigger, spraying the doors with plasma rounds that blew out the windows and stitched holes into the metal. The alien crashed into the doors again and the hinges shrieked, then began to give way.

Virgil sat up, scrambled forward, thrust his welder through the opening and let loose a stream of concentrated blue flame.

Lt. Paris heard the alien scream. She liked the sound.

Then the alien crashed through the doors. One tore completely free and fell on top of Virgil, knocking the welder from his hand. Its flame cut across his body as the door blocked their view of him, but Paris and Yousseff could hear him roaring in pain.

The alien ripped the gun from Aldo's grip and hurled the weapon aside, even as it punched its extended jaw through his forehead.

As Aldo slid down the wall, dead, Paris and Yousseff opened fire, blowing the alien apart with dozens of rounds.

When they let up, the echo of gunfire ringing in their ears, Paris held her breath. They stared at the open maw of the ruined stairwell doors. After a few seconds they hurried past, not looking at Aldo, stopping only a moment to check on Virgil, who'd ended his own life with his welding torch.

They aimed into the darkened stairwell, lights flickering inside, and then hurried on to the corner that had until moments ago been Aldo Crowley's post.

Together, the two marines stood guard, watching the carnage-strewn corridor for sign of any further attack.

For the moment, the hallway was quiet.

"We are so screwed," Yousseff breathed.

Lt. Paris said nothing. Instead, she prayed that Brackett and Draper could get the job done. She had known the risks when she joined the Corps, but she had decided that she was firmly opposed to dying on Acheron.

26 JUNE, 2179
TIME: 1339

The enormous structure was labeled Atmosphere Processor One. The place was the size of an old-time sports stadium, at least fifteen stories high and several levels deep. Its inner workings included not only the most significant atmospheric processing units, but an energy reactor providing power to the entire colony.

A wide service tunnel ran from the main floor of the colony complex at an angle that led underground and connected up with sub-level one of the massive processing station. Walking through that tunnel, Brackett and his team saw clear evidence that the aliens had been using it to travel back and forth to the complex. The sticky, hardening resin that the demons secreted was everywhere, and they found streaks and puddles of human blood along the way.

Lydecker's staff had tracked the PDTs to a place under the primary heating stations, down in the guts of Processor One—sub-level three. The aliens were building their hive in the hot, humming belly of the place. As the captain led his team into the massive structure, he tried not to wonder how many of the monsters would be waiting.

Sub-level three was accessible via two elevators and long, narrow stairs. Brackett and Draper stood guard as Cpl. Pettigrew took Stamovich, Hauer, and seven other marines into the huge freight elevator. He didn't like splitting their numbers, but the speed of the elevator provided made it the best option. Taking the stairs all the way down offered too many dark corners from which the aliens could come for them.

Too many doors, as well, whereas the elevator only had one.

"Pettigrew, when you reach the bottom you sit tight unless you are under attack," Brackett said. "You read me? No one goes exploring. Just secure the area around the elevator and wait for us. We'll be right behind you."

"Yes, sir," Cpl. Pettigrew said. With the helmet hiding his blond hair he looked older. Or perhaps it was fear that had aged him.

"If you see any nasties, run faster than the other guys," Draper suggested, a mischievous glint in his eye. "The ones at the derelict."

Stamovich barked laughter, but then his face darkened.

"Hey. I'm one of those guys."

"Yeah," Draper said. "I know."

Brackett scowled. "All right, move along. We'll see you down there."

He stepped away from the elevator as the doors slid shut. As it descended, he glanced over to Al Simpson, who stood with Dr. Hidalgo by the other elevator. Simpson held a scanning device tied into the command block's systems. It showed a schematic of the sub-levels, pinpointing the location where sensors had picked up the cluster of PDTs.

"Go ahead, Mr. Simpson," he said.

Simpson hit the call button for the second elevator, and they heard the rattle and hum of its ascension. Dr. Hidalgo peered through the cage that formed the shaft, and watched the empty lift rising toward them.

When the elevator arrived, the cage and the inner doors slid open and they all stepped inside. The elevator rumbled and clattered as the doors closed and it began to descend. It occurred to Brackett to wonder just how smart the aliens might be. Were they capable of separating the sound of the elevator from the other industrial noises that filled this subterranean heart of the colony?

He thought they probably were.

When they reached the bottom—Brackett's thoughts drifting to *Paradise Lost* and the ninth circle of Hell—Pettigrew and the others had secured the area. Brackett was the first to step off the elevator, with Al Simpson a quick second. The administrator didn't so much as glance up, despite the danger they all expected to face. Brackett found himself developing a grudging respect for the man.

"That way," Simpson said, pointing across an open space toward a broad corridor that led between two massive generators. The lights were high up on the ceiling and provided little illumination, such that shadows were far more plentiful than the splashes of light.

"Can't we just let them have the place, and get our asses off-planet?" Hauer asked, a hint of seriousness in his voice. "Dust-off is my middle name."

"I thought your middle name was pussy," Stamovich muttered.

Several of the marines laughed.

Brackett swung his weapon up and aimed it toward the place Simpson had pointed.

"Maybe you assholes want to keep it down?" he suggested. "Y'know, on the off chance they don't already know we're coming?" That shut them up. Several of them took aim at the shadowy space between the generators, the way the captain had.

"Look, this is pretty simple," Draper said, glaring at Brackett. "We kill these things, or they kill us and everyone upstairs."

Brackett nodded. "For once we agree on something." He turned to Pettigrew. "Corporal, keep that elevator on this level, doors open. Dr. Hidalgo's going to stay here with you—"

"Oh no I'm not," the woman said, chin raised defiantly.

"You want to help anyone who's wounded," Brackett said. "Best way to do that is to stay here, because when we're done, this is our exit. Anyone gets hurt, we'll bring them to you on the way out."

Dr. Hidalgo turned and put a comforting hand on Pettigrew's arm.

"No offense to the corporal, but he's just one marine. You may not want to take me into their hive, but realistically, I'm safer with a dozen marines than I am with one." She peered levelly at Brackett. "I'm coming with you, Captain. Like it or not."

Draper scoffed. "And what are you gonna do when one of these things tries to drag you off, and plant you with a baby? No sterile room for you to hide in down here."

The pain in her eyes was unmistakable. She put on a smile that fooled no one.

"Why, I suppose I'll die, Sergeant Draper," she replied. "Though if you'd do your best to prevent that..."

Draper swore and glanced away.

"Aw, Doc," Stamovich said.

Brackett studied her. He knew plenty of women who were formidable warriors, but Dr. Hidalgo was an older woman who had spent most of her life contemplating the universe instead of fighting.

"You know how to fire a gun?" he asked.

"Basically," Dr. Hidalgo said. "My father taught me when I was a girl, but it's been years."

Brackett unholstered his sidearm and handed it to her, butt first.

"Don't shoot anyone human."

When she took the gun from him it hung in her hand with a terrible weight, but then she adjusted her grip and nodded at him.

"I'll do my best."

25

SECRETS AND LIVES

26 JUNE, 2179
TIME: 1346

Simpson led the way with his tracker, its green light casting a ghastly glow on his face. Brackett and Draper flanked him as they made their way deeper beneath the main cooling towers, moving toward the primary heating stations.

Lights flickered and generators clanked. The ceiling was so high down here that the darkness swallowed what little illumination the piss-poor fixtures gave off. Furnaces groaned as their fires kicked up higher, pushing heat through the ducts. Brackett wiped sweat from his forehead, just beneath the rim of his helmet, and wondered if the heat had attracted the aliens—if it made a better breeding ground in which to nurture their eggs.

"Eeh, nasty," one of the marines muttered behind him.

"Cap, take a look at this," Stamovich said. "This shit is disgusting."

Brackett gestured for Draper to stay with Simpson and dropped back to shine a light on a thick, sticky fluid on the floor. The marine who'd stepped in it lifted his boot, and strands of the stuff stretched like a spiderweb between floor and heel. Brackett glanced up at Dr. Hidalgo.

"Science lesson later," she said, mopping her brow with a sleeve.

"Try not to let them vomit on you."

The marines all reacted in revulsion, but nobody said a word. The one who'd stepped in it wiped his boot as best he could on a dry section of floor, and they kept moving. A short time later, Draper pointed at the walls and Brackett shined his light around to discover that the resin had been spread everywhere. In places it seemed to have hardened.

"It looked like this inside the derelict," Draper whispered, "but way more extensive."

They really are building some kind of hive, Brackett thought.

Abruptly Hauer let out a cry of alarm, loud enough that it could be heard over the furnaces and generators.

"Hauer, what's… shit! They're here!" Sixto shouted.

Brackett spun to see Hauer being hauled upward, feet kicking. One of the aliens had its tail wrapped around his waist. In the flickering light Brackett could make out its silhouette in the darkness, on top of a rumbling generator. The alien drew Hauer toward it, wrapped an arm around him, and began to slip away.

"No!" Stamovich screamed, and opened fire, strafing the generator and the darkness above it with bullets.

Several others lost their cool and let loose with battle cries and volleys of bullets, shooting into the shadows above and around them.

"Cease fire!" Brackett roared. "God damn it, cease fire!"

Draper grabbed the barrel of Stamovich's gun and aimed it upward, shouting into his face.

When the gunfire died, Draper shoved Stamovich back.

"You idiot, you could have killed Hauer!"

Stam gaped at him. "Killed him? That thing just—"

"Took him," Draper said. "You don't know we can't get him back alive."

"You didn't even *like* Hauer!" Stamovich snapped.

"I don't know about you," one of the other marines said, "but I'd rather be dead than have one of those things on my face. You're dead anyway."

Brackett whipped around, swinging his pulse rifle in an arc, shining his light into the darkness. Simpson and Dr. Hidalgo moved closer to him, fear and doubt etched in their expressions. The captain nudged Dr. Hidalgo back toward the other marines. Simpson glanced down at his device. Beyond him, where a huge door led through into the reactor, the darkness began to unfurl.

"Movement!" Brackett shouted. "Twelve o'clock!"

They all began shouting then, as the shadows came alive. Stamovich screamed as an alien dropped from the ceiling and landed on top of him. Brackett turned, firing in bursts. He saw a marine die when one of the bugs impaled him from behind, throwing his arms out wide as if he'd been crucified.

Draper ran at Brackett, taking aim with his plasma rifle.

"Get down!"

Brackett hurled himself down and toward Draper, twisting as he landed on the floor, bringing his own gun up as the black contours of an alien lunged toward them. Draper shot the hell out of it, acid blood spattering the floor, its carapace cracking with a brittle crunch at every impact.

"Shit, it was there all along!" Brackett shouted. He'd been fifteen feet away from the thing, and it had clung so cleverly to the side of a furnace that he'd thought it was a part of the machinery.

Dr. Hidalgo appeared at his side, trying to help him up. She had his pistol in her hand and it looked pitifully small, totally useless. He glanced up into her eyes and saw a strange calm.

"There's something you need to know," she said loudly.

"Can't it wait?" he shouted, thinking she had lost her mind. They were in the middle of a firefight, people dying around them. *Marines* dying—his squad.

Brackett scrambled to rise as gunfire hammered at his eardrums, blocking out all other sound. How many aliens had been waiting for them? He tried to make sense of it, and while he did, he saw Al Simpson turn and run. An alien crept out from behind a generator to block his way. Simpson shouted and tried to backpedal, but too late. It took him, dragging him back into the darkness of the labyrinthine machinery.

Brackett shot him dead before the two figures could vanish. The demon dropped his corpse and whipped toward the marine captain, hissing. He and Draper both opened fire on it, but the alien ducked into the shadows. Brackett heard a clanking and scratching, and he caught a glimpse of its tail rising. The damn thing scaled the side of the generator. From up there, it could drop down on them any time.

"Fall back!" he shouted, waving for the squad to retreat. "Let's move!"

A quick scan showed him six marines still standing. Sixto held his side, blood spilling between his fingers, but he was still alive. They'd killed at least three aliens but there were others… the darkness seethed with their presence.

He turned to take Dr. Hidalgo's hand, and saw an alien standing behind her. She must have seen the shock in his eyes, because she spun around, took aim, and fired three bullets into its head. Blood splashed her, hissing as the acid ate into the flesh of her chest and right arm and shoulder.

Brackett bellowed, partly to block out the sound of Dr. Hidalgo's agonized shrieking. He wrapped his left arm around her waist and dragged her backward as he blew the alien apart.

"Go!" he shouted to Draper and the others.

They were marines. Retreat wasn't in their blood, but they went, swift and careful, firing shots into any darkness that might hold an enemy. Dr. Hidalgo staggered alongside Brackett and he helped her tear off her jacket and the body armor she'd been given. The acid had been slowed by the armor, but not stopped, and as he watched it sizzled into her flesh. The stench would stay with him for as long as he drew breath.

"Listen…" she said.

"Shut up!" he snapped. He slung his rifle over his shoulder and lifted her into his arms. She weighed almost nothing. That thin, birdlike body, chest rising and falling so quickly, made him want to scream again.

Brackett ran with her in his arms. Draper and the other marines shouted to him, exhorting him to hurry. As he ran, he looked down at her face and saw a single spot on her right cheek where the alien's blood had hit her. A hole had formed and even now it hissed and smoked, the acid eating down through her face like the slowest bullet in the universe.

She was going to die.

"Listen to me," she rasped.

More shouts came from ahead. The machinery vanished as he stumbled toward the two service elevators. The clanking and groaning continued but now all he could see was Draper and the others waving him forward. His heart hammered in his chest as he raced toward them, the dying scientist in his arms, and counted the heads of his surviving marines.

Six. Draper included. No sign of Pettigrew. They had left him behind to guard the elevators and the aliens had taken him.

Of course they did, Brackett thought. *I might as well have handed him over.*

Dr. Hidalgo began to choke. The acid on her chest had burned its way down into her lungs. She rasped and coughed.

"You... have to... *listen*!" she said.

Draper raced back to them, covering them as they moved toward the open elevator. The other marines were already inside, one of them keeping the doors from closing.

"There's a... ship," Dr. Hidalgo said, her eyes rolling in her head. "Science team... the company gave us... a ship. Authorized personnel door... between the med lab and..."

Brackett looked down at her.

"Here on Acheron? There's a ship here?"

He glanced up at Draper, who stared at her.

"An evac ship? Holy shit!" Draper said. "That son of a bitch Reese! How much room, Doc? How many passengers can she hold?"

Brackett felt her sag in his arms, and her head lolled back as she exhaled her last, rattling breath. For the first time it occurred to him that the acid might not stop, that it could eat its way through her and into him, and he dropped to his knees and placed her gently on the floor.

An evac ship, he thought. Somehow Weyland-Yutani had known. *Hell*, he thought, *maybe that's why they picked this place.*

No, they hadn't known for sure, he realized, or they would have brought a thousand people to scan every inch of the surface. But they'd had an inkling that somewhere in this system they might find something ugly. They'd given their science team a way off of this godforsaken moon, with the intention that everyone else—children included—was expendable.

Newt, Brackett thought. *Anne.*

They didn't have the firepower to destroy the aliens, not when at least a couple of dozen had already bred. The odds against *anyone* leaving Acheron alive were growing... anyone who didn't have an evac ship.

He was a marine. He had a mission and a duty to these people and the Corps. But if he could save the lives of a handful of them—including the woman he loved and her children—surely that was more noble than letting them all die here.

He touched Dr. Hidalgo's left cheek, wishing that she could be aboard that evac ship, silently thanking her. Now he understood the guilt he'd seen in her eyes earlier.

Brackett staggered to his feet and turned just in time to see the elevator begin to rise.

Draper gazed back at him through the cage, his eyes stone cold.

How many passengers can she hold? he had asked.

Brackett couldn't blame him really. Marvin Draper had proven his courage in combat, but if Brackett could have made a list of people to bring off-planet on that evac ship, Draper wouldn't have been on that list.

The elevator rattled upward and vanished into the upper levels.

Brackett hit the call button for the other elevator and peered up through the shaft.

Behind him, the darkness came to life.

26

ONE BY ONE

26 JUNE, 2179
TIME: 1346

When Anne heard the hammering at the storage area door, she knew things had gone sideways. Half of the colonists flinched and scrambled away from the entrance, but she recognized it as the sound of a fist pounding to be let in. Aliens didn't knock.

Newt clutched her Casey doll and grabbed a fistful of her mother's shirt.

"Stay with Tim, honey," Anne said.

"Mom, no!" Newt cried, reaching out for her. "You said—"

"Just one second!"

Anne raced toward the door. Several people shouted for her to stop. Lydecker darted forward and beat her to it.

"What the hell are you doing?" he demanded.

She ignored him. Palm flat against the door, she called out, "Who's there?"

"Lt. Paris!" came a voice.

A twist of sick dread knotted itself in her belly, and her heart began to gallop. She swore under her breath as she shoved aside boxes that had been piled up, and ratcheted back the double locks. Lydecker didn't argue. He'd heard Paris's voice and knew the woman was alive and desperate, or she wouldn't have come knocking.

Anne threw open the door and Paris backed in, with Pvt. Yousseff behind her, both women training their weapons on the corridor behind them. Dressed in full body armor and helmets, they had sweat streaks on their faces and their eyes were wide with urgency.

"Any word from Simpson or Captain Brackett?" Paris demanded, turning on Lydecker.

The man shook his head.

Lt. Paris glanced around, cursing under her breath and not caring who heard her.

"Where the hell is Dr. Reese?" she demanded. "This is his show now, so where the hell is he?"

"Gone," Anne told her.

Yousseff snarled. "What do you mean, *gone*?"

"He and Dr. Mori said they had vital data that needed to be secured," Lydecker explained. "You want to tell me what the hell's going on?"

An icy shiver ran up Anne's spine as she saw the desperate confusion in Paris's eyes. Then the lieutenant slung her plasma rifle over her shoulder.

"Yousseff, the door," Paris said, and the other marine set about locking it up tight, sliding the crates back in front as a barricade.

"Listen up," Lt. Paris called, drawing the attention of the dozens of colonists clustered in the storage area. "None of the other marines set up around the sealed perimeter are answering on comms. At least three are dead that I know of, and we have to assume the aliens are inside the perimeter, picking us off one by one. They're taking their time, removing the people who were protecting you, and then they're coming in."

"How?" One of the wildcatters spoke up. "All but one of the doors have been welded and barricaded." He hefted a heavy shotgun, and frowned. "I'll blast the shit out of any one of those ugly bastards that tries to come near me or mine."

"Maybe you'll get lucky, Meznick," Paris said, "but I'm not sure your shotgun can do you much good. I'm telling you, I don't think this place is secure enough."

Anne felt like she couldn't breathe. *This* place wasn't secure enough? Where else could they go, where so many people could wait for rescue—where they could sleep and eat?

She glanced at her kids. Tim stood with an arm around his little sister, and she thought how proud Russ would have been of him.

People shouted questions at Paris. Some refused to go anywhere without word from Dr. Reese or Al Simpson. But when Yousseff glanced nervously at the door they had just barricaded, practically vibrating with the fear that the aliens would be coming through at any moment, Anne knew there was no more time for hesitation.

"I'm going," she said, dashing toward her children. "Kids, come on."

"I'm scared," Newt cried.

"Me too, Rebecca," Tim said. "But we'll be okay. I'll protect you," he promised.

"Anne, don't," Bill Andrews said, taking her arm from behind.

She shook him off.

"Don't be stupid, Bill," she replied. "Don't you see the fear in the eyes of these marines? You think Lieutenant Paris is wrong? This is a more comfortable place to hold out for rescue, but if we're dead when it arrives—"

"Where do we go then?" Andrews demanded, turning to Paris.

"We have a couple of ideas," the lieutenant said.

Anne lifted Newt into her arms, and then took Tim's hand as she barged toward the freshly barricaded door.

"Up one level and a hundred feet along the southwest corridor," she said. "The surveyors' operations center. It's right above the med lab, but it's basically a big box. One way in and out. We get in there and weld ourselves in—"

"And we starve to death in days," Meznick said.

"So carry what you can," Anne snapped, "but at least there we'd have days to try to figure something out. Better than dying here tonight."

"I ain't goin' nowhere," Meznick retorted. "We make a stand here, wait for Simpson and the others... far as we know, Brackett's team has exterminated the whole damn hive."

"Suit yourself," Anne said.

"What about Demian?" Newt whispered in her ear.

Anne swallowed hard but said nothing. All of her grand plans had gone up in smoke. She'd never make it to the hangar or the garage now—not with the kids, not if the marines who'd been guarding the perimeter were dead. Hell, she'd be lucky to make it to the operations center.

It's our only chance, she thought.

She glanced around for Cale, Dione, or Bradford, whom she'd seen quietly plotting together. None of them were in sight. She realized that somehow they—and who knew how many others—had slipped away without her noticing.

Probably going for the Onager, she thought. *Bastards.* But she couldn't really hate them for it. If she hadn't been waiting for Demian… hoping…

"Damn it," she snapped, marching away. She turned to Andrews. "You coming?"

He nodded. "Go. I'll grab some food and water, and catch up."

When people started milling about, some tearing open crates of supplies, Lydecker held up his hands.

"Calm down, folks," he said. "I'm staying right here, but I'm not going to stop anyone who wants to leave."

As if you could, Anne thought.

"We're only opening this door once, though. After that—"

"Out of the way, Lydecker," Anne barked. "Tim, help Private Yousseff."

Yousseff and Tim started pulling the crates away from the door again, aided by a couple of other colonists. By the time the door was hauled open—the two marines darting out, weapons leveled along abandoned halls—there were perhaps twenty people with armloads of goods, ready to make a run for it.

They'd barely gotten into the corridor and had the door slammed behind them when gunshots echoed from down the hall.

"Go, go!" Lt. Paris shouted as she and Yousseff raised their rifles and sighted along the corridor, toward the sound of gunfire.

Another marine came around the corner, limping badly and firing the last few shots from his plasma rifle before he ran out of ammo. Anne recognized Pvt. Dunphy, and cringed at the sight of the blood on the man's left hand, realizing that his sleeve was soaked with it. He'd been one of the marines on the perimeter, so they weren't all dead, but Dunphy didn't look far from the grave.

"Izzo's down!" Dunphy shouted. "I've got three coming this way!"

Julisa Paris turned and grabbed Anne's arm, staring into her eyes. "Listen to me. Yousseff and I came from down there. That's where we killed one already. If they're coming from there, your path may be clear to the ops center. Go through the unwelded door, and we'll lock it behind us when we catch up.

"Go fast, and we'll take care of this," she added.

Anne nodded. "We'll give you five minutes before we seal the door to the ops center."

Paris touched Newt's blond locks and then gave them a small shove. "Go! Tim, take care of your mom!"

Tim gripped Anne's hand tighter, and then they were running down the corridor, praying that the stairs up to the next level would be clear. Two minutes or less to get to the ops center, that was all they needed.

Anne glanced back, just once, at the doors to the storage area, wondering how long they could hold out. Even if they welded those internal doors, there were too many aliens. She felt sure that somehow they would get in, but it was too late for the others to follow them now. She and her kids, Bill Andrews, Parvati, Gruenwald and the others who'd followed her… they would live or die together.

She hugged Newt closer. Gripped Tim's hand tightly.

Live, she thought, almost a prayer. *We'll live.*

26 JUNE, 2179
TIME: 1359

The thing moving in the darkness had a human shape.

Brackett stared at it, sighting along his rifle.

"Who goes there?"

"Captain?" the figure ventured as he emerged from the shadows.

"Pettigrew? Shit, I thought you were dead."

The corporal had his rifle at his side as he rushed toward the elevators, moving urgently now that he knew Brackett wouldn't shoot him.

"One of them came for me two minutes after you'd all gone," Pettigrew said, anxiously searching the shadows, alert and intense as the second elevator hummed and rattled on its way down. "I'd hit the hold button on the elevator and figured I didn't need to stand there waiting to die. It's not like the alien knew which buttons to push. I took off with the thing on my tail, managed to get into a maintenance closet just before it caught up."

"How'd you get away?" Brackett asked, glancing up through the cage at the descending elevator.

"Didn't have to," Pettigrew said.

Something shifted and scraped in the shadows above the nearest machinery. Pettigrew and Brackett both whipped around, taking aim. The lights flickered and Brackett saw the sleek gleam of something black, flowing like water in the darkness.

"The gunfire started—you guys were under attack—and it took off, more interested in the fight at hand," Pettigrew said. "I guess it figured it could come back for me later."

The elevator clanged as it descended, sliding into the cage right behind them and rattling to a stop.

"I think it has," Brackett muttered.

As the elevator doors opened, the alien leaped down from atop the groaning generator across the floor from them.

"Go, go!" Brackett said, firing at the alien as he backed into the elevator.

Pettigrew opened fire as well, but his rifle jammed and he swore, turning to slap the button for level one. The alien sprinted toward them, arms outstretched, tail wavering behind it, ready to strike. Brackett pulled the trigger again and stitched bullets across its chest.

The creature faltered and fell, blood melting into the floor only feet from the acid-ravaged body of Dr. Hidalgo. As the lift began to ascend, it hissed, whipped around to glare at them with that eyeless carapace of a head, and then lunged to its feet.

It struck the cage beneath them just as the elevator rose out of range. Before they were lifted out of view, Brackett saw others gliding from the darkness behind it.

"How do we live through this, Cap?" Pettigrew asked, slumping against the inside of the elevator.

Heart pounding, Brackett turned toward him.

"We get off this fucking rock."

Pettigrew narrowed his eyes in disbelief.

"How?"

"There's a way," Brackett replied, silently thanking Theresa Hidalgo. "We just have to get there before your buddy Draper."

26 JUNE, 2179
TIME: 1359

Dr. Reese carried the silver case and Dr. Mori carried the gun.

They moved quickly and as quietly as possible, hoping not to be overheard by anyone, alien or human. Between the med lab and the research lab stood a single narrow door to which only the three primary members of the science team had access. On its metal surface were the faded words AUTHORIZED PERSONNEL ONLY.

Dr. Mori wore his key on a chain around his neck and used it to unlock the door as both men glanced anxiously around the hallway.

"I haven't been down here since the day we arrived," Mori whispered. "I never thought we would need to open this door."

Reese stared at him grimly, pleased with the weight of the case in his right hand.

"It was always a possibility."

Mori pushed the door inward and then stood back, covering the corridor with the pistol—the gun feeling so insignificant to him—as

Dr. Reese entered. The key had activated the lights inside, and they flickered to life.

He frowned, glancing toward the research lab. Had he heard a sound there? The shuffle of footsteps? He listened for several seconds, and then convinced himself he'd imagined it. Stepping into the narrow passage, he pulled the door closed and flinched as it clanged shut.

"Idiot!" Reese groaned, the word rustling along the featureless gray walls of the claustrophobically narrow space. But there was nothing to be done about it now.

"Just move," Mori muttered. Technically, Dr. Reese was his superior, but just then Dr. Mori did not care. In the quest to survive, to escape Acheron with their lives and their research, the two men were equals. The silver case held all of their data, as well as a single dead facehugger, and samples of an egg from the derelict and of the resin that came from the Xenomorphs' mouths. If they'd had more time they would have tried to take a living facehugger, but as much as they wanted to bring their research back to the company and reap the rewards, they could not do that if they hesitated too long, and ended up dead.

"Faster," Reese hissed quietly.

Mori gritted his teeth. "I'm not as young as I used to be."

They shuffled along the narrow corridor, shoulders brushing the walls, until they came to a slight turn where the hall widened enough to give them some breathing room. A dozen steps brought them through a low doorway where they had to stoop to pass through. Then the hall began to curve off to the right, leading to a second set of steps that descended at a right angle. The colony's first architects had designed this passage to be locked off and forgotten.

"Please, my friend," Dr. Mori said as he reached the bottom of the steps. "Give me a moment." Dr. Reese turned to glare at him, but then his expression softened.

"Only a moment."

Mori nodded. He'd been carrying the pistol, but there no longer seemed to be a need, so he clicked on the safety and slipped it into his rear waistband. When he glanced at the silver case in Reese's hand, he smiled even as he struggled to catch his breath.

He waited, nervously fiddling with a key hanging by a chain around his neck. The key they would need to get through the last door.

"Thank you," he said, taking a deep breath. "I'm all right."

Dr. Reese clapped him on the arm.

"Good. I don't want to go alone. It's a long journey."

As they started off again, leaving the stairs behind, there came a scuffing sound from back along the way they had come. The scientists froze and glanced at each other in frightened silence.

No, Dr. Mori thought. *Not when we've come so close.*

He drew his pitiful little gun as they stared back toward the steps and waited.

27

READY TO FIGHT

26 JUNE, 2179
TIME: 1400

Jammed into the surveyors' ops center, the colonists who'd followed Anne moved quickly. At the back of the center there was a shop for repairing the equipment, and Bill Andrews located a hand-welder within minutes of their arrival.

Anne sat on a bench with her children and watched as Bill fired up the welder, the blue-white flame hissing as it scorched the air. She wetted her lips with her tongue, recognizing just how hard her heart had been pounding. They had made it here without anyone else dying, and now the sight of the welder and the box-like nature of the room made her feel immediately safer.

But others had felt safe before, and it hadn't helped them.

Across the room, Stefan Gruenwald and Neela Parvati were checking over the case of guns they'd carried from the storage area, handing them out.

"Tim," Anne said, "you and Newt stay here a minute."

Newt grabbed her hand, looking anxiously at the door as Bill tested the welder on the hinges on the left side of the double entry doors. Then she peered at her mother.

"It'll be all right," Anne promised her. "Protect Casey."

Newt glanced again at the welder in use, and then nodded and hugged the doll closer, kissing the top of its head.

Anne hurried across the room, weaving through the frightened people who were trying to settle themselves in some way that they might be comfortable, locked inside that room for however long they would be there. What supplies they'd brought were stacked on desks, and chairs were allotted to the oldest among them. Others made camp on the floor.

Anne glanced at the vents above the wall monitors, and though she felt sure the ducts were too narrow for the full-grown aliens, she wondered how many new ones might be bred. The one thing the colonists could not afford to do was cut off their own air supply.

When she marched up to the group with the guns, Parvati glanced at her.

"I want a gun," she said quietly.

Parvati arched an eyebrow.

Gruenwald cocked his head and looked at her worriedly.

"Don't you think we're all better off leaving the weapons with those who know how to use them?" he asked.

"The creatures got my husband," Anne said, then pointed across the room at her kids—at Tim, on the verge of tears, and Newt, clutching her Casey doll. "If things go bad, I need something to make sure *they* don't end up the same way."

Parvati opened her mouth in shock, perhaps thinking that Anne meant to kill her own children, rather than let the aliens have them. Anne wondered if that might really have been what she'd meant.

The question haunted her.

Gruenwald handed her the gun. She turned without another word and walked back to the bench.

The pounding on the doors began before she'd even sat down.

"Mom?" Newt asked.

Tim stood and came up beside her, ready to fight. A moment later, Newt did the same, and the sight of that six-year-old girl preparing to defend herself and her family broke whatever remained of Anne Jorden's heart. She tightened her grip on the pistol and watched as Bill stepped back, welder in hand.

Gruenwald rushed toward the door, Parvati just behind him, along with half a dozen others who were armed.

"Lieutenant Paris?" Bill called. "That you?"

"It's Draper!" boomed a voice. "Let us in, dammit. They're on our tail."

Gunfire erupted in the hallway.

"Open the damn door!" Draper shouted, and the banging resumed. "Where are Mori and Reese? They in there with you?"

"We've got to let them in!" Bill Andrews said, glancing around for support.

"No!" Gruenwald snapped. "We can't compromise our own security. They'll have to make it on their own."

Another burst of gunfire, and then Parvati surprised Anne by pushing past Gruenwald and going for the door.

"You aren't giving the orders here," she snapped at him. "We're not leaving anyone to those creatures!"

Two others rushed to help her.

"You morons!" Gruenwald barked, rushing to stop them. "Think about the children we've got in here!"

But Bill Andrews got in his way, pushing him back.

"We're thinking about the men and women out there."

Parvati and the others dragged the right-hand door open, its hinges not yet welded. Only then did Anne realize that the shooting in the corridor had ceased.

"We've got it open!" Parvati called.

"Oh no," Anne whispered, tears springing to her eyes as she pulled her children close with her left hand, and aimed the gun with her right. When she saw Sgt. Draper coming through the door—slumped, pale and bloody, but alive—she exhaled, all of her strength draining out of her.

Draper had bought them time.

But then the sergeant staggered and fell, and everyone could see the hole in his back…

…and the aliens barged in behind him, trampling the corpse and killing Neela Parvati before they were even through the door.

Newt and Tim screamed, and then Anne joined them.

They had nowhere left to run.

Nothing left to do but scream, and die.

26 JUNE, 2179
TIME: 1400

Lt. Paris and Pvt. Yousseff had killed two more aliens before they heard the worst of the screams, coming from the storage area.

Yousseff broke into a sprint back toward the main doors. Anne Jorden, Bill Andrews, and a couple of dozen other people had left shortly before the aliens had attacked, and Paris couldn't help but wish she had gone with them—that they both had. Now she ran after Yousseff, caught up to her at a turn in the corridor, and slammed her against the wall.

"Don't be stupid!" she shouted into the other woman's face, hating herself as she did it.

"But we've got to—" The private began to cry.

"What, die? 'Cause that's what we're going to do if we go that way!"

Then Yousseff laughed through her tears.

"Lieutenant, come on! We're dead anyway!"

Something moved behind them and they both spun around, fingers on the triggers. They nearly shot Brackett and Pettigrew.

"Shit!" Paris cried, heart crashing about in her chest.

"Anne Jorden and her kids?" Brackett yelled, rushing toward them. "They're in there with those things?"

Paris shook her head.

"No. A bunch of the colonists split off, went to the surveyors' ops center."

Brackett hung his head, breathing deeply.

"Thank God."

"We ran into Draper and a few others—they headed over there to defend that position," Yousseff reported.

"Of course they did," Brackett snarled. "Son of a bitch."

"What's going on, Cap?" Lt. Paris added.

Brackett studied her.

"Yousseff said we were all dead. Maybe not."

"Maybe not what?" Yousseff asked, moving away from the corner now, away from the screaming and toward Brackett and Pettigrew.

"Maybe there's a way for us to get out of here," Pettigrew explained.

"You better not be messing with us," Lt. Paris said.

"I'm not," Brackett said, and his expression turned dark. He raised his plasma rifle, stepped away from the others, and opened fire as an alien came around the corner almost precisely where Yousseff had been standing moments before.

"Take us there, now!" Brackett yelled. "Take us to the ops center!" And then the four marines were all running and firing, and Lt. Paris was leading the way.

26 JUNE, 2179
TIME: 1410

Dr. Reese took two steps back, putting Dr. Mori between himself and whatever shuffled through the corridor at the top of the stairs.

Behind him, the hallway narrowed again. If he remembered correctly, another fifty yards would bring him to a hatch through which there was a short set of steps, and then another hatch. Beyond that was the small hidden hangar where the six-passenger evac ship waited.

He took another step. Dr. Mori had the gun—Reese could do nothing to help defend them.

Run, he told himself, tightening his grip on the silver case. He had dedicated his life to scientific discovery—to the detriment of family, health, and any hope of real companionship. He had eschewed courtesy and personal grace for the quest for knowledge and advancement… for creation, regardless of consequence.

Reese knew that Weyland-Yutani put their greatest efforts into exploiting science, both developed and discovered. To find more effective ways to kill and conquer. He had never had a crisis of conscience.

But to abandon Dr. Mori…

Dr. Reese told himself that Mori was not his friend.

No, he thought, *but he's the closest thing I've got.*

Forcing all guilt away, he began to turn, just as a slender figure came around the corner and onto the landing at the top of those twelve steps.

Dr. Reese stared.

"Khati?" Dr. Mori said, and he started toward the bottom step.

Reese grabbed his shoulder.

"Stop, you fool."

The woman had been one of their researchers, but had vanished the previous evening. The science team had assumed that she had been dragged off by the aliens, but now here she was. The left side of her face had a huge purple bruise and multiple scrapes. Her hair was matted and wild and her torn clothes were in disarray.

Khati Fuqua looked down at them, eyes full of sorrow.

"Please…"

She shuffled toward the top of the steps, grunted in pain, and bent slightly as she reached for the railing. Her hand missed the rail and her foot missed the step, and she fell, tumbling end over end, reaching out to try to arrest her fall, but failing.

"Damn it!" Dr. Mori snapped, rushing to her side.

Dr. Reese approached warily, looking over Mori's shoulder.

"Is she all right?"

Groaning, Khati rolled over. She had one hand over her sternum and Dr. Reese wondered if she had slammed her chest on the edge of a step.

She bucked in pain.

"Oh no," she whispered.

"Oh no," Dr. Reese echoed.

Dr. Mori stood and stared at her.

"Khati, I'm so sorry."

Reese shifted the case to his left hand. With his right, he snatched the gun from Dr. Mori's grasp. Stepping over the researcher, he went halfway up the steps, back the way they'd come. He needed the vantage point.

"How did she follow us?" Dr. Reese demanded. "Didn't you shut the door?"

"I didn't lock it," Dr. Mori said. "I never thought—"

"Bullshit!" Dr. Reese swallowed hard, sweat beading on his forehead. "You couldn't have even shut it tightly, not and have her follow us. I don't want this, Mori, do you understand me?" His voice had turned shrill. He heard the edge of panic in it, but couldn't help himself.

"Do you think *she* wanted it?" Dr. Mori asked, staring down at Khati as she began to buck and cry out, hyperventilating as she tried to process her pain.

From halfway up those dozen steps, Dr. Reese pointed the gun at her and let out a long breath. He wanted desperately to pull the trigger, to just end her pain and any danger she might present.

"Do it," he whispered to himself.

But he couldn't pull the trigger, could not murder the young woman in cold blood, though to his mind it would have been a mercy.

Khati bucked again and he could see the skin of her chest push upward as the parasite burrowed its way out.

We don't have time for this, he thought.

But of course, it wouldn't be long.

28

MONSTER MAZE

26 JUNE, 2179
TIME: 1411

In the midst of the screaming and gunfire, a strange calm enveloped Anne. It was as if the ops center had shifted into some parallel dimension, and she had been left behind.

Bill Andrews and Stefan Gruenwald were in the front line, strafing the aliens with plasma rounds that blew two of them apart. Acid blood splashed Gruenwald in the eyes and the man screamed and fell to his knees. He reached up and covered his face with the palms of his hands—and then screamed louder, in a melody of anguish and surrender, as the acid on his eyes also burned through his hands.

One of the Xenomorphs grabbed Bill Andrews and smashed him against the wall, breaking him without killing him. Saving him for later.

Those who weren't shooting were cowering, or searching for something with which to fight back.

Anne raised her pistol, exhaled, and fired three times as she backed up. She glanced over her shoulder at her children. Newt hugged her Casey doll so tightly that it looked like she might squeeze its head off. Tim had picked up a monitor screen, the only weapon he had close to hand.

No, she thought, the single word engraved in her mind.

No.

Then she saw the dark square on the wall behind her children.

"Tim! Newt!" she cried, her voice breaking. "Monster Maze!"

She saw them spin around, watched them realize what she wanted them to do. Then she turned back toward the screams and the carnage. The smell of blood and fear came at her like a stormfront. One of the aliens crouched above Newt's friend, Luisa. The little girl screamed so loud the shrieking seemed like a kind of madness that tore at her throat, and then the alien vomited its sticky resin into her face. The girl choked on it, and went silent. Her whole body jerked and then went still, driven into unconsciousness by shock and terror.

Something broke inside Anne.

"Leave her be!" she screamed, firing twice at the alien, her heart full of more hate than she had ever imagined it could hold.

One bullet cracked its carapace at the temple while the other punched a hole in its lower jaw. The small blood spatter missed Luisa, but Anne's heart stopped when she realized what she'd almost done.

The alien turned, and took a step toward her.

"Newt! Tim!" she shouted.

As the other colonists died or were dragged away around her, Anne's children were screaming for her. She turned and saw that they'd pried the grating off of the vent, but they'd paused, calling out for her to come with them. The anguish in their faces carved deep into her heart.

"Inside!" she shouted, running toward them. "Get inside!"

Tim shoved Newt into the narrow duct—much too small for one of the creatures—and then began to climb in behind her.

Anne heard a low hiss. She could practically feel the alien as it reached for her.

Russ, she thought. *I'm sorry*.

She turned, took aim, and fired once before its jaws punched through her forehead.

* * *

Newt heard her brother scream for their mother. He scrambled, banging against the inside of the duct as he climbed out again.

"Timmy, no!"

She grabbed his t-shirt but he tore free and turned toward her, furious tears streaming down his face.

"Go, Rebecca!" he roared. "Don't wait!"

But she watched him turn, watched him run over and bend to pick up the gun their mother had dropped.

"I'll save you, Mom!" Tim yelled.

But he couldn't. It was too late for that. Too late for their mother. Too late for Tim.

Numb, Newt turned away, but still she heard the scream—the last sound her brother—her best friend—would ever make.

She felt the alien coming for her and hurled herself deeper into the duct, crawling away as fast as possible. *Monster Maze*, she thought. But now these ducts were the only place the monsters weren't. She knew them better than anyone, but she'd never crawled around inside them alone.

Alone. The word echoed in her head the way her movements echoed along the ducts.

All alone.

26 JUNE, 2179

TIME: 1411

Khati sucked air in through her teeth, breathing in the pattern taught to women who were about to give birth. Then she bucked again, blue eyes wide as she let out a scream that tore down the walls Dr. Reese had built inside himself to hide away his emotions. He'd known this woman, dined with her, enjoyed the sound of her laughter.

"Why are we still here?" Dr. Mori shouted from below him. "We should just go!"

Reese stood halfway up the steps, looking down on that small space and the entrance to the next segment of the evac corridor. Dr. Mori took another step into the corridor, hesitating and confused, and Reese knew he was right.

No delay, he thought.

What the hell was he waiting for? Khati was in agony and would be dead moments after the thing burst from her chest. His instinct had been to wait for the parasite to emerge, and to kill it before it could grow.

They ought to be running.

Khati's anguish kept him frozen there.

He remembered the way she had smiled at her first sip of coffee in the morning, the little hum of happiness she made when she tasted it.

He pulled the trigger, shooting her half a dozen times in the chest. Dr. Mori cried out and spun away. Khati slumped to the floor, falling still. The thing inside her body pulsed once, as if making one last attempt to break free, and then it, too, went still.

Dr. Reese exhaled, grieving for the woman as her blood and the parasite's pooled under her body, hissing as the acid ate at the floor beneath them.

"Son of a bitch!" Mori said, turning to look up at him again.

He'd been shot.

Dr. Reese frowned, not understanding for a moment, and then he realized that when Mori had spun away it hadn't been out of horror or disgust. A ricochet had struck him in the left shoulder, and now he clutched at that wound. He hissed up at Reese.

"Asshole!" Mori barked. "Let's go!"

Dr. Reese stared down at Khati and told himself that he saw relief in those dull, dead eyes. He lowered the gun and nodded, starting down the steps.

Mori whispered his name.

Frowning, Reese glanced up and saw the terror in his colleague's gaze. Then he heard the hiss behind him, the creak of weight on the stairs, and the dappling drip of liquid hitting metal.

He hung his head, not bothering to turn, knowing it was futile to try to run.

The alien's hands wrapped around his right shoulder and his throat, drawing him toward it like an insistent lover. Only when he felt its drool sluicing hotly down onto his neck did he begin to scream, thinking of the suffering he'd just witnessed in Khati.

He turned the gun upon himself, and pulled the trigger.

26 JUNE, 2179
TIME: 1412

Brackett was the first one through the door. They'd heard the screams and gunfire coming down the hall, but by the time they reached the surveyors' ops center, the room had gone silent—except for the hiss of the aliens.

He slid along the corridor wall, then saw that only one side of the double doors stood open. Holding up a hand to halt the others, he raised three fingers, counted down, and then spun through the open part of the doorway. His eyes widened as he tracked the five aliens in the room, all of them bent to the task of covering living colonists in the sticky resin that slid from their mouths.

Brackett opened fire as Yousseff slammed into the other half of the double door, only to find it had been welded at the hinges.

"Make way, Cap!" Lt. Paris shouted. "Let us in!"

Brackett's plasma rounds blew apart one alien and wounded a second as they turned to come for him. Advancing would have been idiotic—trapping him in that small room with the demons. Instead he backed out, barking at the other marines, and all four of them retreated back down the corridor the way they had come.

"They've got to come out one at a time," he snapped, heart racing, his body flush with adrenaline. "We've got them!"

Pettigrew whooped in triumph as he realized Brackett was right. The four of them lined up across the corridor and shot the hell out of the aliens as they barged through the opening one at a time. Acid blood splashed all over the floor, burning holes in scattered patterns.

When it was over, the gunshot echoes still hammered at Brackett's eardrums. He took a moment to stare numbly at the carnage of shattered ebon carapace and limbs and tails, and then he started forward again.

"Watch 'em, Cap!" Pettigrew called, but Brackett knew they were all dead, or they would've just kept coming, following what seemed a genetic need to destroy everything they encountered.

He stepped carefully around the acid-eaten floor and the remains of the aliens and slipped back into the ops center. He took a deep breath as he scanned the bodies there, and then he started moving among them, checking for pulses, taking note of which were obviously dead, and who might still be breathing, having been intended for breeding by the aliens.

Those still alive had been in the process of being cocooned, and were unconscious.

"What are we going to do with them, Cap?" Julisa Paris asked as she came into the room and began following his lead, searching for survivors. The stench of blood and death made Brackett knit his brows. It hurt his head. He did not answer, because he knew they weren't seeing these people the same way. Paris saw friends and acquaintances where Brackett saw people who were mostly strangers. He sought three faces only.

Anne. Newt. Tim.

"There are other aliens," Paris went on. "More will come. How are we supposed to get these people free before—"

"We don't," Yousseff said, coming into the room behind them. With her helmet on, she almost looked like a little girl playing make-believe. The grim glint in her eyes revealed the truth. "It's a noble thought, Lieutenant, but as far as we know, there's room for five or six passengers on the evac ship."

"We'll make room," Lt. Paris said.

"Who will you leave behind for them?" Yousseff asked. "Me? Corporal Pettigrew?"

Brackett stopped hearing them.

He stood above a familiar corpse. Recognized her clothes and her hair. Not enough of her face remained for him to identify her that way, but he knew, and he felt ice sliding through his veins as a hollow opened up deep inside him.

"I'm sorry," he whispered, lowering his head.

He kneeled beside her, putting down his weapon, and he covered his head with his hands as if he could trap the grief inside. In his mind he could still see the girl she'd been when they had first met. His body remembered her touch. His heart remembered the pain as he felt forced to break off the relationship when he shipped off to join the marines, and then the regret when he learned of her plan to marry Russ.

It would've been better if I'd never come, he thought. *Never seen you again.*

Pettigrew had remained out in the hallway, guarding their exit. Now he stuck his head into the room.

"Make it quick," he said. "I heard something out here. Back the way we came."

Yousseff came to stand beside him, staring down at Anne Jorden's corpse.

"I'm sorry, Captain," she said, "but we can't stay. If we don't make that evac ship, we're all dead."

Brackett nodded slowly. Blinking as if waking from sleep, he glanced around at the corpses and the cocooned, so many of them unrecognizable like Anne. Then he froze a moment, shook it off, and staggered to his feet. Six feet from his mother's corpse lay the body of Tim Jorden, a gun in his small hand.

"Newt?" Brackett said, glancing around. "Do any of you see Newt?"

"Holy shit, here!" Lt. Paris snapped as she ran toward a small, cocooned body.

Hope surged in Brackett, images of the little girl filling his head. He raced over and set to work beside Paris, the two of them tearing the hardened resin away from the little girl's body while Yousseff stood near the door and Pettigrew kept watch in the corridor.

When they broke away a piece of the material that had hidden her eyes, the hope withered inside Brackett.

"I'm sorry," Paris said quietly. "It's not her."

Brackett nodded. "Who is she, this little girl? You know her?"

"Her name's Luisa. One of Newt's friends."

Yousseff gestured to the far side of the room, where other bodies lay bloody and broken. "She must be one of those."

"Search," Brackett said. "Please, the two of you, see if you can confirm, one way or another." *Confirm that Newt is dead*, he meant, but they didn't need him to explain that, and he was glad. The words wouldn't come.

Brackett tore away more of the hardened cocoon, reached in and lifted Luisa out. Her red hair was matted with the stuff and she looked inhumanly pale, but as he stood with the little girl in his arms, she moaned softly and her eyes fluttered.

She would come around soon. She would live. He intended to make sure of that. There was nothing more he could do for Anne or Tim, but he could do this for Newt. He could save her friend.

Yousseff and Paris continued searching the rest of the room.

"Guys, we've gotta go!" Pettigrew called from the hallway. Gunfire rattled and echoed out in the corridor, and that was that.

They had run out of time for humanitarian acts. If they stayed and tried to defend those who were still alive, they would all surely die. There were simply too many aliens, too hard to kill, and the monsters were still breeding. Brackett glanced at the little girl in his arms.

You'll have to be enough, he thought. *If I can keep you alive...*

If he could keep Luisa alive, then he could live with the decision to run. To survive.

"You heard the sergeant! Move!" Brackett commanded.

Yousseff was the first to join Pettigrew in the corridor. Brackett followed, carrying Luisa, and Paris brought up the rear. As the lieutenant came through the door, Pettigrew shouted a warning and opened fire. Brackett turned to see two aliens rushing toward them from down the hall. Paris and Yousseff fired as well, tearing the aliens apart so that their blood sprayed and their carcasses crashed to the floor thirty feet away.

The little girl squirmed in Brackett's arms, whimpering but not regaining consciousness. He held her more tightly and shushed her as the gunfire echoes died away.

"Quickest way to the med lab?" Brackett asked.

Lt. Paris shot him a look.

"Why the hell would we—"

"Private passage to the evac ship is right next to it," Pettigrew said. "You know that door—"

"I know it," Paris interrupted, and then they were moving. The lieutenant took point this time, with Brackett carrying Luisa behind her and Pettigrew and Yousseff guarding their rear. The aliens had followed their trail, and they felt sure there would be more of them.

Brackett's legs felt as if they were made of lead and his heart thundered against his chest as he ran, the girl jostling in his arms. Paris swung her weapon in a sweeping arc as they ran past the elevator bay, its doors closed and quiet. They turned a corner, reached the stairwell door that would lead them up a level, to within spitting distance of the med lab, and Brackett turned to see Pettigrew and Yousseff hurrying up behind them.

"Anything?" Brackett asked.

Yousseff stayed at the corner, aiming her weapon back the way they'd come.

"Not a hint," Pettigrew replied. "Doesn't mean they aren't coming."

"Agreed," Yousseff said. "We're not safe until we dust off."

Paris ducked into the stairwell and motioned for them to follow. They raced down the stairs, Brackett flinching at the noise of their boots on each step, thinking of how far up and down the sound would carry. Luisa couldn't have weighed more than sixty-five pounds but his arms had grown tired. The temptation was strong to try to wake her, to get her to run for herself, but if the girl was very lucky she would sleep until they were well away from Acheron.

In the silence of space, they could all grieve together.

Paris left the stairwell at the next landing, sliding out into the corridor and scanning both directions.

"Clear!" she called, and they followed her out into the hall.

"Lieutenant, cover right. Yousseff, cover left," Brackett said.

"Pettigrew, check the door." There was no questioning which door he meant. Set into the wall between the med lab and the research lab they all saw the narrow black door that hung halfway open, the AUTHORIZED PERSONNEL ONLY sign partly in shadow.

Yousseff slid down the hall first, with Pettigrew behind her. Brackett saw the ruined elevator doors across from the med lab, and directed Yousseff toward them with a lift of his chin. She nodded and padded along the corridor, clicking on the guide-light on top of her pulse rifle and aiming the beam into the darkened elevator shaft.

Pettigrew pushed the evac passage door open with the barrel of his rifle.

An alien burst from the shadowed interior, drove him to the ground, and grabbed him by the face. Its extruding jaw punched down through his chest, smashing bone and tearing muscle. As he died, Pettigrew fired half a dozen rounds from the plasma rifle, three or four of which hit the alien and spilled its blood all over him. The acid burned into his flesh, but Pettigrew was already dead.

"Paris!" Brackett shouted, backing away with Luisa in his arms.

Yousseff shouted Pettigrew's name, along with a string of profanities that cut off halfway after "mother." Brackett spun and looked down the corridor just in time to see Yousseff's legs flailing as she was dragged through the twisted opening in the elevator doors.

Lt. Paris saw it, too.

"This isn't going to happen," she said coldly. "We've got a way home."

"Then let's go!" Brackett snapped.

The alien Pettigrew had shot lay on the floor, struggling to rise. Its tail whipped around, the deadly tip trembling, ready to strike. Julisa Paris shot it three times, blew its skull apart, and then they were running again.

They darted through the narrow evac door, Paris watching the corridor ahead as Brackett kicked the door closed. He threw Luisa over one shoulder in a fireman's carry and heard her grunt, mumbling as she skirted at the edge of consciousness. Brackett threw both of the locks, bolting the door shut. It wouldn't stop the aliens for long, but he hoped it would be long enough.

Then they were running along the corridor, Paris out in front with her gun, praying that no more surprises waited for them ahead.

29

ENOUGH DYING

26 JUNE, 2179
TIME: 1412

Dr. Mori ran, one hand clutching the bullet wound in his shoulder. The scraping behind him was close, but he couldn't afford to look.

The smell of his own blood made him want to vomit or faint or both. Tears ran down his face, his mind filled with images of Khati's hideous demise and of the alien killing Reese. Those memories were burned into his soul, and he knew he would see them every time he closed his eyes for as long as he lived.

For at least six or seven seconds, he fooled himself into thinking that *as long as he lived* would include more than just the next minute. But then he looked ahead, and saw that he had a hundred feet or so of corridor in front of him before he reached the door into the evac hangar.

A door that required a key.

And the time to use it.

A sob escaped from Dr. Mori. Regret washed through him—so many things he wished he had done, and so many more he wished he could take back. But he was all out of wishes.

He fell to his knees, weakened by blood loss and shock. One hand still pressed to his shoulder, where the wound began to sing with pain, he turned to watch the alien rushing toward him. He studied the smooth carapace of its enormous head and the nimble, darting predator's gait as it rushed after him. It saddened him that he would never have the chance to study it.

Beautiful, he thought. And it really was.

"Hey, ugly!" a woman's voice called.

The alien turned back toward the voice, its tail scraping the wall. It hissed.

"Get down, Dr. Mori!" a man shouted.

The bullets tore into the alien just as Dr. Mori threw himself to the floor. He scrambled away, staying down, as it juddered and then collapsed, twitching as it died. Dr. Mori stared at his shoes, one of which was steaming as several drops of acid burned through it. Shouting in panic he reached down and ripped the shoe off his foot.

Then he stared at his pitiful foot in its gray sock, the fabric thin at the toes, and he leaned against the wall, shaking.

Capt. Brackett stepped carefully around the dead alien, carrying a little girl in his arms. Lt. Paris followed behind him, gun still in her hands, ready to fight.

"Get up, Dr. Mori," Brackett said. "You're our ticket out of here."

Mori looked up at him, hollow and bereft.

"You'll take me with you?"

Brackett glanced at the little girl in his arms, but his eyes still seemed far away, as if he saw someone else there.

"I think there's been enough dying, don't you?"

Lt. Paris helped him to rise and he limped toward the door in his one remaining shoe, thankful for the key on the chain around his neck.

Dr. Mori opened the door to the hangar and cool air rushed around him.

He felt alive.

* * *

26 JUNE, 2179
TIME: 1433

The evac ship shuddered violently as it passed through the debris-filled atmosphere of Acheron. Brackett had laid Luisa down in a hypersleep chamber but the lid remained open. The girl deserved to know what had happened, deserved to be a part of whatever came next for them. She was only a child, but Brackett wasn't going to hide the horrors from her. He would let her grieve, comfort her if he could, and hope she would be strong enough not to be destroyed by all she had lost.

He hoped that he was strong enough, too.

"We're exiting the envelope," Lt. Paris called from the cockpit. "Anyone want to have a last look before we leave this rock behind?"

"I'm good," Brackett said.

He glanced over at Dr. Mori. The man looked pale and weak, but he would survive. In a few minutes, when they'd cleared the turbulence and were on course, Brackett would remove the bullet from his shoulder and stitch up the wound. It would be painful, and there would be something in the medical supplies on the evac ship to dull that pain, but Brackett would not offer it. Mori deserved all that pain he had coming to him.

"What about you, Doc?" he asked.

Mori shook his head. "There's nothing for me back there."

Brackett nodded, a tight fist of anguish forming in his stomach. He breathed evenly and forced it away. He would grieve for Newt and Tim, for Anne, and for lost opportunities, but he could not allow himself to be broken. The hollow place inside him where his heart had been felt cold and dark, and perhaps it would remain that way forever. But he had work to do, and he could not let sorrow get in the way.

Use it, he thought. *Turn it into fuel.*

"Lieutenant Paris," he called, facing the front of the ship, "I assume the ship's navigational computer has a preset course."

"It does. Gateway Station. We'll be in hypersleep most of the time."

Brackett stared at Dr. Mori, thinking about how insidious the science team's behavior had been. They had known all along that there could be an alien threat on Acheron. Known enough that they had established their own escape plan. When word had come down from Weyland-Yutani to send surveyors out to those specific coordinates, they had known that the Jordens would have been in terrible danger.

Even when the worst happened, they had been more interested in studying the aliens, fulfilling their mission for the company, than in trying to figure out how to kill them—how to keep the people alive.

The colonists had been expendable.

Even the children.

But that protocol hadn't begun with Dr. Reese or Dr. Mori. It had come down from on high, from their employers.

"Turn it off," he said quietly. "Turn off the nav system."

Dr. Mori glanced up, brows knitted with surprise and worry.

"What's that, Cap?" Lt. Paris called back.

Not Lieutenant, he thought. *Not anymore.*

"Disable the preset course, Julisa," he said. "And figure out a way to keep them from tracking us, if you can. We're not going to Gateway Station."

"What are you doing, Captain?" Dr. Mori asked.

"I kept thinking of your Xenomorphs as demons, Doctor," Brackett replied, loud enough for Julisa to hear. "But they're not demons. They're merciless killers, and they're as alien as I can imagine any sentient creature ever being… but they're following their own biological imperatives. They're not evil."

Brackett smiled darkly.

"Weyland-Yutani, though… if there's evil in the universe, a scourge that needs to be exposed to the light and then destroyed, it's the company. From now on, that's my fight. That's my war. And if you don't want to be stranded on the first planet we come to, Dr. Mori, it's going to be your war, too."

In the open sleep chamber, Luisa began to mutter quietly, blinking her eyes as she started to rustle and wake. Brackett took her hand,

and her small fingers gripped his larger, scarred ones.

"Now the real fight begins."

26 JUNE, 2179
TIME: 1618

Newt and Tim and the other kids who played Monster Maze had always called it "the clubhouse," but she knew that the boxy space in which she had taken refuge wasn't meant to be a house, or even a room.

The rectangle might have been ten feet long by six feet wide, and while Newt could stand up there, a grown-up would have had to stoop or crouch or kneel. There were things there already—a blanket and various sweatshirts and jackets and books and old snack boxes left behind, as well as a handful of toys. Half a dozen air ducts led away from the clubhouse, while one blower fan pushed air in from above. Sometimes it grew too warm in there, and sometimes too cold, but it was hers and it was safe.

The aliens could never find her in here, which would be perfect…

Until she needed something to eat or drink.

Newt wrapped herself in the blanket and leaned against the metal wall of the box. She clutched her Casey doll to her chest, careful with it because its head had begun to detach from the body.

"It'll be all right," she whispered to Casey, heart pounding. Eyes wide, she glanced around at the ducts, knowing they couldn't come after her, but still afraid. Images flashed across her mind, striking like lightning, but she shook her head and forced them away.

Her mother.

Her brother.

Better not to think about them, or about the blood and the screaming. Better not to think at all. Just survive. That was what her mother would have told her. The Jordens had always been survivors.

"I'm quick," she whispered to Casey. It was true. Tim had said she cheated, but Newt had always been best at Monster Maze. If she was careful, and she listened well, she could avoid them when she needed to get food or something to drink.

"I'll protect you," she promised, and kissed the top of Casey's head.

Newt fell quiet after that, listening. When the blowers cycled off for a few minutes, she heard echoes making their way through the ducts from distant rooms and other levels within the colony. The sounds were strange and soft and sad, at least to her, but she thought that if she followed them back to their origins, the noises she was hearing might turn out to be screams.

She stayed where she was, and she tried not to cry.

Sometimes she succeeded.

30

BUILDING BETTER WORLDS

5 JULY, 2179

On Gateway Station, every day blurred.

Every day of being no one, doing nothing, having little in her life. Every day of mourning her long-dead daughter—both the little girl she had left behind, and the woman who had grown, matured, loved, lived and died without Ripley ever getting to know her.

I told her I'd be home for her birthday, she kept thinking, always the last thing at night, and every day when she woke. That guilt was as rich and raw today as it was every day.

Every day blurred into one, into weeks, into months…

Sleeping. Waking. Working. Returning to her cabin. Eating, washing, drinking, smoking, watching the body of her cigarette turn to ash and flitter away like the years of her life, unknown and unmissed by anyone. A life without meaning was no life at all.

Today had been no different to any other day. Just one of many, all the same.

Until the door buzzer sounded.

It jarred Ripley out of her sad contemplations, and for a few seconds she couldn't place what it was. She hardly ever heard the noise. No one came to visit her, she had no friends. She was a woman out of time, and if people did speak to her—at the loading docks, in the mess—she always had the impression that she was seen not as a real person, but as a curiosity. An exhibit from the past.

She stood and went to the door, wondering who was there. When she opened the door and saw Burke, her heart sank.

He wasn't alone.

"Hi, Ripley," he said. "This is Lieutenant Gorman of the Colonial Marine Corps—"

She closed the door again. Burke, through all his efforts to ingratiate himself, had never come across as anything other than a slimeball working his own game. He pretended to care, and sometimes she thought he genuinely did. There were aspects to his personality that made him inscrutable, yet there was a vulnerability, too. Perhaps it should have made Ripley like him more, but he came across as weak.

As for the guy with him, he just looked like a grunt.

She turned away from the door, but Burke's voice came again from outside.

"Ripley, we have to talk. We've lost contact with the colony on LV-426."

She froze. Her heart stuttered. The heavy darkness within her seemed to pulse, and she turned slowly to the door. Opened it again.

On what? she wondered. *What am I letting back into my life?* She stared at Burke and the marine for a long time. Burke grew uncomfortable. The marine stared back. Then she let them both inside.

Jonesy grumbled and jumped from the stool. Ripley sat down slowly. She didn't ask Burke and Gorman to sit.

"So?" she asked.

"It's been a while," Burke said. "Last contact was pretty standard. A series of colonist messages and a request for equipment on the next resupply ship. Since then there's been no response to any Company requests or personal messages, no replies to scientific queries. Nada."

"Technical fault," she said, but her skin was cold, her insides colder.

"Distinct possibility," Gorman said.

Damn, Ripley thought, *he even talks like a grunt*.

Burke raised an eyebrow.

"What?" Ripley asked. She had a bad feeling about this. After everything they'd done to her, all that she'd told them and been ostracized for, why would Burke come all the way out here to the scummiest accommodation pod in Gateway?

With a soldier in tow.

"We're mounting a rescue mission," Burke said. "We want you to go."

Ripley's stomach dropped. A rush of memories flooded in—Kane's last supper, the *Nostromo*, the beast, the deaths she'd seen and those she had not. Dallas, her sometime lover.

She stood quickly from the stool, shoving it back so that it bounced from her cot and tumbled to the floor. Jonesy hissed and scampered away, hiding somewhere out of sight. She so wished she could do the same.

She went to the kitchen unit and poured coffee for the two men. Not because she wanted them to stay, but because without something to occupy her hands and her mind, she might lose it.

Did he really just ask me that?

"I don't believe this," she said. "You guys throw me to the wolves, and now you want me to go back out there? Forget it. It's not my problem." She handed Burke his coffee. She had to resist the temptation to fling it into the smug bastard's face.

"Can I finish?" he asked.

"No. There's no way."

She handed Gorman his drink, and he seemed to wake up.

"Ripley, you wouldn't be going in with the troops. I can guarantee your safety." At least it seemed he could say more than one word at a time.

"These Colonial Marines are very tough hombres," Burke said. She turned her back on him and poured herself a drink. Her heart was thudding as the memories grew more real. "They're packing state-of-the-art firepower; there's nothing they can't handle," Burke went on. "Lieutenant, am I right?"

"That's true. We've been trained to deal with situations like this."

"Then you don't need me," Ripley said. "I'm not a soldier." She hated the fact that her voice wavered, but the fear was rich and real.

She couldn't hide it. Maybe she shouldn't even try.

"Yeah, but we don't know exactly what's going on out there," Burke said. "It may just be a downed transmitter, okay, but if it's not, I'd like you there as an advisor. And that's all."

Ripley stood and approached Burke. He was a company man, Weyland-Yutani, so he'd told her many times.

"What's your interest in this? Why are you going?"

"The corporation co-financed that colony, along with colonial administration. We're getting into a lot of terraforming now, building better worlds—"

"Yeah, yeah, I saw the commercial," Ripley said. "Look, I don't have time for this. I've got to get to work."

"Yeah, I heard you're working in the cargo docks."

"That's right."

"Running loaders and forklifts, that sort of—"

"So?"

"I think it's great that you're keeping busy, that it's the only thing you could get. There's nothing wrong with it."

Son of a bitch, Ripley thought. She was letting him get to her, and that made her even angrier.

"What would you say if I told you I could get you reinstated as a flight officer?" he asked. "The company has already agreed to pick up your contract."

She looked sidelong at Gorman—inscrutable, silent—then back to Burke.

"If I go," she said.

He nodded. "Yeah, if you go. Come on, it's a second chance, kiddo! And personally I think it would be the best thing in the world for you to get out there and face this thing. Get back on the horse—"

"Spare me, Burke, I've had my psych evaluation this month."

"I know," he said, standing and invading her personal space. "I've read it. You wake up every night, your sheets are soaking wet—"

He was reminding her of the nightmares, the dark places where she was chased by the beast, and that darker place that still weighed heavy within her when she was awake.

"Damn it, Burke!" she shouted in his face, "I said no, and I mean it! Now please leave. I am not going back, and I am…" She swallowed, caught her breath. "I would not be any use to you if I did."

"Okay," Burke said softly, as if suddenly he was talking to a child. Ripley lit another cigarette, shaking, and heard Burke drop something on her table. A comms card, she guessed.

Screw him. Screw him for making me feel like this.

"Want you to do me a favor…" he said. "Just think about it."

"Thanks for the coffee," Gorman said. He smoothed his buzzcut, put his cap back on, and led the way from her cabin. Burke closed the door softly behind them.

Ripley was shaking, and it wasn't because she was drinking too much coffee. She knelt and stroked the cat, and wondered whether he had nightmares, too.

6 JULY, 2179

They were chasing her. No longer just one, now there were many beasts, and the corridors weren't just those of a dank spacecraft. She bounded from rough stone, slick with a viscous layer from which she shrank away. She tripped over coiled things that looked as though they belonged inside a body. She tried to scream.

I have to warn them. They're coming, they know we're here, and I have to warn the others!

She did not know what "others." Not Dallas and Lambert, not Kane—they were all dead and gone—but those other others who belonged somewhere else, somewhere deep in that dark, heavy memory that threatened so often to burst free and reveal itself fully.

So she ran. The beasts hunted her, and she knew without a shadow of a doubt that they would run her down and tear her to shreds before she found any friend ever again.

* * *

Ripley started awake, shouting, gasping, sweating, taking a few seconds to realize that she was no longer being chased and that, in fact, she was as safe as she'd ever been.

Almost.

Almost as safe, because the nightmares carried on. She was haunted by them, and as much as she hated to admit the psych evaluations—desired to prove them wrong—she knew that she was damaged. Her mind was not her own. The gravity of that dark potential within her was slowly, inexorably crushing her to its will.

She splashed water on her face and down her neck, washing away the sweat of the nightmares, but not their taste. Then she stared into the mirror and knew what she had to do.

Burke's comms card was where he'd left it. She plugged it into the unit and buzzed him. He responded, sleep-addled and confused. It took him a moment, then he spoke.

"Ripley?" He glanced at the clock behind him, saw how early it still was. "You okay?"

"Just tell me one thing, Burke," she said. "You're going out there to destroy them. Right? Not to study. Not to bring back. But to wipe them out."

"That's the plan. You have my word on it."

She paused for a moment, and her life rested on a ledge. Stay as she was and she would eventually fall off. Confront her fears—face those nightmares—and perhaps one day she could move on.

"All right," she said. "I'm in." Burke went to say something else, but she broke the connection and sat back in her chair.

She felt lighter. Different. The weight from inside, that dark star… it was gone. Whatever it had been, it was lifted from her, and though confused, she did not mourn its passing. Whatever memories she had been reliving in those deep, dark nightmares were gone forever, and she was glad.

She looked at Jonesy, still sitting at the bottom of the bed.

"And you, you little shithead. You're staying here."

Jonesy looked very fine with that.

31

THE CRUELEST TRICK

27 JULY, 2179
TIME: 0900

"We're on an express elevator to hell, going down!"

The ship dropped toward Acheron. Someone shouted *whoop*, but Ripley had her eyes squeezed shut, and she was concentrating hard to hold onto her dinner. The whole dropship rattled and shook, metal creaked, marines grunted, and she clasped onto her armrests so hard that her fingers cramped.

This was the most aggressive of atmosphere entries—an assault more than a landing—and Ripley had never trained for any of this.

But she'd been through worse. She opened her eyes, stared at the ceiling, and wondered what was to come.

27 JULY, 2179
TIME: 0958

They'd done a fly-by of the colony. It still had power, the outer structure looked undamaged, and the giant atmosphere processors remained operational. Other than being so quiet, it didn't look like a colony that had suffered any mishaps.

But there was still no contact. If the colonists had heard the dropship circling around, surely they'd have emerged by now to welcome it?

Ripley was nervous as hell. The silence and stillness troubled her.

"Man, it looks like a fuckin' ghost town," one of the marines whispered.

She felt a chill go through her.

If they are all dead, then it's far from a ghost town, she thought. *It's a monster town*.

The lieutenant issued the order to land. Ripley, Burke, and the marines were in the ground assault vehicle held in the dropship's belly, with the android Bishop at the controls.

"I prefer the term artificial person myself," he'd said to her, but screw him. Bishop, Ash—different names for the same bastard, as far as she was concerned.

Seconds after the dropship ramp touched the landing pad, Bishop hit the gas. The atmosphere had changed now, going from bullish bravado to steady and calm, loaded with a readiness that almost set Ripley at ease. Almost. She'd seen the firepower these guys packed, and the professionalism with which they had prepared. But she also knew what could be inside this complex.

I should never have come, she thought for the thousandth time. But once out of hypersleep on the *Sulaco*, she'd decided to join the away team on their journey down to the surface. The *Sulaco* remained in unmanned orbit, and she had no desire to be left up there all on her own. She'd been alone for too long.

"Ten seconds people, look sharp!" another grunt bellowed. "All right, I want a nice clean dispersal this time."

The ground assault vehicle skidded to a halt and the door slid open.

Ripley held her breath. The marines streamed out and the door slammed shut. Gorman remained, along with Burke and Bishop. All she knew was what appeared on the display screens of Gorman's control centre. She felt immediately cut off from the rest, as if they were somewhere far away.

It was raining heavily, the ground thick with muddy ash. There were several abandoned vehicles in the midst of the complex. One solitary sign, BAR, glowed a steady red, the only sight that wasn't a bland gray.

The team spread out around a wide vehicle doorway labeled "North Lock."

"First squad up online," Gorman said. "Hicks, get yours in the corridor, watch the rear."

Ripley watched on various head-cam monitors as the first squad approached the door. They moved with calm, economical movements, quickly and calmly. Hudson ran a bypass on the door's locking mechanism, and then the heavy metal barrier started to slide open.

"Second squad move up," Gorman said. "Flanking positions."

The doors opened.

Inside, all was shadow.

The marines entered the complex grouped in close formation, checking corners, using attached shoulder-torches to illuminate their way. The inner lock doors were jammed half closed, and two marines pulled them all the way open.

Vasquez moved forward, and then Ripley saw what was revealed.

The corridor beyond had been ripped apart. Ceilings were down, wall paneling shattered, spewing guts of tattered pipes and hanging wires. Water dribbled from a ruptured channel.

Oh shit, Ripley thought.

"Second team move inside," Gorman said. "Hicks, take the upper level."

As the second squad moved up a staircase just inside the opened doors, the first squad edged deeper into the complex. The damage to the corridor was even more apparent now, and there were a few scattered piles of furniture that might have been blockades of some sort.

If so, none of them had worked.

"Sir, you copying this?" Apone asked. "Looks like hits from small arms fire, with some explosive damages. Probably seismic survey charges. Are you reading this? Keep it tight, people."

Ripley checked Hicks's head-cam and saw that he'd just reached the head of the staircase. The corridor beyond was equally dark, and also showed signs of damage.

"Okay, Hicks, Hudson, use your motion trackers," Gorman said. As Ripley saw the two men look down at devices in their hands, a chill went through her. Ash had designed units very like these to help them hunt the beast aboard the *Nostromo*. These units looked sharper and more solid, but she guessed that the technology was much the same.

The teams advanced. Ripley felt sweat trickle down her back. Burke watched with her, and Bishop stood back a little, observing the operation. She was stuck here with an android and two men she didn't like, and she started to wish she'd gone with Hicks.

"Quarter and search by twos," Gorman said.

It was Hudson who saw movement on his tracker. He called it in, and he and Vasquez advanced slowly along the dark corridor, guns at the ready. Hudson's heart rate increased. Vasquez's barely changed.

Pull them out, Ripley thought. She almost said it, but realized how panicked it seemed. They'd come this far, over such a vast distance, to discover what had happened here and to help anyone that had survived. So they had to go on.

But that didn't prevent her from being terrified.

Hudson kicked a door in and… gerbils. They skittered away in a panic.

"Sir, we have a negative situation here," Hudson drawled. "Moving on, sir." Ripley couldn't tell whether or not he sounded sarcastic.

Something caught her eye on another screen. The view from Hicks's head-cam swept across a corridor and Ripley saw something amiss, a series of dark, uneven patches on the floor.

"Wait! Wait, tell him to…" She snatched up a headset. "Hicks. Back up. Pan right." He did as she said and revealed the acid burns across the floor. Metal grill flooring, melted away as if it were made of ice. "There."

Like ice, her blood chilled. She felt sick.

"You seeing this all right?" Hicks said, looking at them through

Drake's head-cam. "Looks melted. Somebody must have bagged one of Ripley's bad guys here."

Ripley glanced back at Burke. She didn't know why, wasn't even sure what she was expecting of him.

"Acid for blood," he said, apparently amazed at this confirmation of everything Ripley had told him.

"If you liked that, you're gonna love this," Hudson said. He and Vasquez had found a much larger burn site, a hole melted through several levels and wide enough for a man to fall through. *Maybe if one of them was blown apart*, Ripley thought. *Maybe then*.

"Sir, this place is dead," Apone said. "Whatever happened here I think we missed it."

Gorman scanned the screens and the bio readouts of his marines.

"All right, the area's secured, let's go in and see what their computer can tell us."

"Wait a minute," Ripley said, that familiar panic rising again, "the area's not—"

"The area is secured, Ripley," he said, dismissing her without a look. "First team, head for operations. Hudson, see if you can get their CPU online."

"Affirmative."

"Hicks, meet me at the South Lock," Gorman said. "We're coming in."

I bet they feel safer already, Ripley thought. She considered arguing with Gorman, telling him that there was no way the area could be declared secure until his teams had performed a full sweep. Though huge, vicious and violent, she also remembered how the beast had hidden itself away on board the *Narcissus*, remaining so still and quiet that she hadn't noticed it for some time.

Those corridors she'd seen on the head-cams—the warren of rooms, the stairwells—there could be a hundred Xenomorphs in there. But the assault vehicle was already moving, and soon they had skirted around the edge of the colony and pulled up at the South Lock.

I'm being drawn in, Ripley thought. *I should have stayed on the* Sulaco, *but I didn't want to be alone*. And now she should sit tight, right where she was… but she wouldn't. She would go with Gorman and Burke.

I can't not *go.*

She had to see what had happened to the colonists. Like it or not, she knew more about the Xenomorphs than anyone else on this mission.

It was still raining heavily as they exited the vehicle and approached the South Lock. Hicks and another marine was waiting for them there, and Gorman and Burke entered ahead of her.

Ripley slowed to a halt, still outside, a short distance from the open door.

I can still turn around, she thought. But in truth, she had come too far already.

"Are you all right?" Hicks asked. He'd turned, noticed her standing there, and come back for her. She liked him for that.

"Yes," Ripley said softly.

She stepped inside, and the doors slid shut behind her.

27 JULY, 2179
TIME: 1003

In the maze of ducts, out scavenging for food, Newt heard voices.

They frightened her, those voices, but they also gave her hope and that made her angry. She had learned the hardest way imaginable that hope was the cruelest trick she could play on herself.

Hope might get her killed.

Still, she slipped through the ducts, following the voices…

…and she hoped.

ACKNOWLEDGEMENTS

I saw *Aliens* when it first hit theaters, right around my birthday in July of 1986. I was nineteen years old and it was the first time a movie ever gave me nightmares. Thanks to James Cameron for those nightmares. Deep thanks to my editor, Steve Saffel, for watching my six, and to the entire team at Titan for their dedication to this new voyage into the Alien canon. Special thanks to Josh Izzo at Fox for his passion and for reminding me to stay frosty, and to James A. Moore and Tim Lebbon for friendship and brainstorming. Finally, my gratitude, as always, to my fantastic family for their support, and to my agent, Howard Morhaim, for navigating the universe with me.

ABOUT THE AUTHOR

CHRISTOPHER GOLDEN is the *New York Times* #1 bestselling, Bram Stoker Award-winning author of such novels as *Of Saints and Shadows, The Myth Hunters, The Boys Are Back in Town, Strangewood,* and *Snowblind*. He has co-written three illustrated novels with Mike Mignola, the first of which, *Baltimore, or, The Steadfast Tin Soldier and the Vampire*, was the launching pad for the Eisner Award-nominated comic book series *Baltimore*. As an editor, he has worked on the short story anthologies *The New Dead, The Monster's Corner,* and *Dark Duets*, among others, and has also written and co-written comic books, video games, screenplays, and a network television pilot. The author is also known for his many media tie-in works, including novels, comics, and video games, in the worlds of *Buffy the Vampire Slayer, Hellboy, Angel*, and *X-Men*, among others. Golden was born and raised in Massachusetts, where he still lives with his family. His original novels have been published in more than fourteen languages in countries around the world. Please visit him at www.christophergolden.com